JACOB JERLOW

TO THE FOUR CORNERS
OF THE EARTH

LANCE PELTIER

ISBN-10: 1483933873

ISBN-13: 9781483933870

Library of Congress Control Number: 2013906020

CreateSpace Independent Publishing Platform,

North Charleston, South Carolina

To my family, who makes me want to be a better man,

and my God, who gives me strength eternal.

I would like to thank my wonderful children, who were supportive and loving, even on the longest of days; and my beautiful wife, Robin, and my mother-in-law, Vicki, for their words of wisdom and encouragement. And last, but definitely not least, there are not any human words that could ever describe my heart filled gratitude to my God, who has brought me out of the deepest and darkest of destinies.

TABLE OF CONTENTS

LIST OF CHARACTERS

VERITAS

Don—an Elder at Heldago who teaches angelic powers

Esteban Enrique Eastes (Triple E)—an Elder who is caretaker at Heldago

Father Santiago Rivera—the spiritual Elder at Heldago

Frederick Albas (Fred)—a Bethal student from the US

Jacques Leroux (Jack)—a French-speaking Bethal student from Canada

Jezebel Flores—a Bethal student from Mexico

Luke Cartwright—a Bethal student from the US

Master Kang—an Elder at Heldago who teaches body control
and martial arts

Miguel Cruz—a Bethal student from Spain

Ramiro Vasquez—a Moldan student from Cuba

Sarge—an Elder at Heldago who teaches the sword

Shawn—an Elder who watches over Jacob

Shir—an Elder at Heldago who teaches the fine arts

TENEBRAS

Prince Muammar—the leader of the Tenebras

Bodach—Prince Muammar's personal bodyguard

Diablo Florentine—a Bethal student

Joan Braile—a Bethal student

Master Fu—an Elder at Muerte Palace who teaches martial arts

OTHER CHARACTERS

Bina Feldman—Jacob's best friend at Sulley Middle School

Buck Jensen—Jacob's granddad

Domenico Fontana—architect and engineer of the new St. Peter's Basilica in 1586

Felix Matthews—a student at Sulley Middle school who dislikes Jacob

Jacob Jerlow—a student at Sulley Middle school in search of the dalet

Michael—an unknown man seen at the funeral, sword trial, and the Certatim

Mr. Jonas Matthews—Felix's father, who is a science teacher at Sulley Middle School

Mr. Wolfe—a history and religion teacher at Sulley Middle School

Professor Tom Jerlow—Jacob's father

Rebecca Feldman—Bina's mother

Sarah Jerlow—Jacob's mother

CHAPTER 1

A FATHER LOST

It had been one week since the airplane crash, and cars were backed up for blocks in the procession to the town of Hickson's Catholic church. A small town located in eastern North Dakota, Hickson was a place where the residents knew each other by first name and weren't afraid to call upon each other at home in times of need. But on this day, not one person was to be found at home. They were all going to pay their respects to a warm and beloved man named Professor Tom Jerlow.

Tom's wife and teenage son walked hand in hand into the church that morning with all eyes on their every step. As others were seating themselves, Jacob heard one person whisper, "Sarah is all he has left now. Poor Jacob has no other relatives around." Jacob bit his lip and fought back the tears with all of his strength. He didn't want anyone to see him cry.

Jacob and his mom sat in the front pew of the church and stared forward at the casket as the priest began to speak: "On this day we remember a great friend..."

The 125-year-old Catholic church was beautifully adorned with statues and paintings, and the smell of oak and burning incense seemed to radiate from its walls. People would drive from miles around just to view its majesty, but no one was admiring its artwork on this day. The people in the small town of Hickson were not themselves, for their hearts grieved over a man who would be dearly missed.

Jacob tightly grasped the last thing his father had given him—a medallion on a necklace that he had received just the previous week. As Jacob stared into his hands at the medallion, he recalled the last time he saw his dad alive.

"I'll be back in two weeks," explained his dad as they walked toward the airport ticket counter. "I'm going to Australia to do some archaeology digging. You know, nothing too fun," he said with a smile.

"Why can't I go with you this time?" Jacob whined. "You haven't let me go on an archaeology find in almost a year. This is really hampering my growth and development as a future leader in archaeology!"

"I know, I know, but your mother would kill me if I let you miss two weeks of school right now," Tom said, laughing. "I'll tell you what: if you promise to help look out for your mom and keep up your grades— later this year I'm planning on going to Brazil, and you can come with me then. OK? I'll be back before you know it."

Jacob's dad reached into his jacket pocket, pulled out a small box, and handed it to Jacob saying, "Here, I've got something for you."

"What is it?" asked Jacob in anticipation.

"Well—there's only one way to know." Tom grinned.

Jacob opened the gift box, which was wrapped with care, and found a medallion connected to a long silver necklace inside. The back-side was inscribed with some type of hieroglyphic-like pictures that he could not understand. Jacob flipped the medallion over and admired the front, which was ordained with a beautiful carving of a sun and moon.

"My father gave this medallion to me when I was your age, and now—well, I want you to have it," explained Tom. "It has brought me nothing but good luck. As a matter of fact, don't think I'm crazy, but if I listen really closely, I can sometimes hear it speak to me. Now put it on...let's see how it looks on you."

Jacob slid the medallion over his head as he gleamed with pride. "I'll keep it safe, always," he said, puffing his chest out proudly.

Jacob broke away from his recollection as he heard his mom cry-ing next to him. He grabbed his mother's hand and whispered, "It's going to be OK, Mom. I'll be here for you."

"Thank you, sweetheart," Sarah said as she wiped a tear from her cheek.

As the funeral came to a close, people began standing in line to approach Tom's casket and say their last good-byes. Jacob's mom went first. She whispered some words toward Tom and walked away slowly to the back of the church.

Next, Jacob approached the open casket slowly with both hands firmly grasping his medallion. His knees were shaking, and tears were welling up in his eyes as he tried to muster up enough courage to talk to his dad. Mostly because of denial and anger, Jacob had not cried yet since hearing of his father's death. But now, as he looked at the casket, the recognition of his father's death touched his soul. He realized that he would never be able to share in anymore of the beloved memory-making trips overseas searching for lost artifacts, nor would he ever again be able to talk to his best friend. Jacob looked down at the medallion, and then stared at his dad's face and with tear-filled eyes said, "You are my hero, Dad, and I'll never do anything to let you down. I'll watch over Mom just like I promised, and I'll be the best I can be in all that I do. I love you."

Jacob walked toward the back of the church with his head hanging down, trying to cover up his tears so that his mom couldn't see. "Let's go to the car," she said gingerly. As they exited the church, the sun's rays touching their skin and their interlocked, sweat-filled hands seemed to dampen the cold effects of the funeral, even if for just a moment.

As his mom drove, Jacob closed his eyes and went back to the many happy times he had shared with his father. "I've got to stay strong," Jacob said to himself—still trying not to show any tears. "Mom needs me."

Jacob's mom pulled their car into the cemetery's parking lot with a loud screech. The car had seen far too many North Dakota winters, with more rust holding the metal together than paint. Everyone already standing in the cemetery snapped his or her head toward the awkward sound. Jacob's mom exited the car as if nothing had occurred, but Jacob felt just a tad bit lower than he already had been.

A few minutes later the priest began, "Ashes to ashes and dust to dust..." Just then, Jacob looked off through the nearby trees and saw a man he had never seen before looking in his direction. The middle-aged man had a look of maturity that Jacob could not explain. Not that the man looked old, just that he looked like he had seen and experienced enormity. His darker, longer than average beard also captured Jacob's curiosity, as the only time he had seen this type of beard was in one of his travels to Israel with his dad. The man's clothes were light in color, loose fitting, and swayed rhythmically in the light breeze, keeping time with the nearby branches and leaves. The stranger had a look of kindness and remorse in his eyes, and for some reason, Jacob felt at ease—like he had no worries when he looked at him.

When the priest was done speaking and others were walking back to their cars, Jacob went to the spot where he had seen the stranger, but he could not find him. Jacob looked over his shoulder and saw his mom approaching.

"What are you looking for?" she asked, looking around the trees.

"I thought I saw someone I knew," explained Jacob. "But I guess...I was wrong. Let's go home."

Upon returning home, Jacob entered his bedroom and saw a sealed envelope with his name written on it lying on his bed. "Your father wanted me to give this to you," his mother said from the end of the hallway. "He gave it to me shortly before his trip last week."

"Thank you," Jacob said, holding the envelope with care.

Jacob sat on his bed next to the envelope, took a deep breath, picked up the envelope, and opened it carefully. He nervously began to read:

MY DEAREST SON,

IF YOU ARE READING THIS, IT MEANS THAT SOMETHING HAS HAPPENED TO ME AND RIGHT NOW YOU ARE PROBABLY UPSET. JUST REMEMBER THAT SOMETIMES LIFE WILL DEAL YOU AN UNLUCKY HAND OF CARDS, BUT THAT'S OK, BECAUSE TOMORROW IS A NEW DAY AND YOU CAN GET A WHOLE NEW HAND OF CARDS. KNOW SOMETHING FOR CERTAIN, THOUGH: I LOVE YOU AND ALWAYS WILL. THROUGH OUR FAITH I KNOW THAT I AM NOW IN HEAVEN WITH GOD. BE ASSURED THAT I AM HAPPY AND WELL, AND THAT I WILL ALWAYS BE WITH YOU.

YOU AND I HAVE HAD SOME GREAT ADVENTURES TOGETHER TRAVELING THE WORLD. THERE ARE SOME THINGS I HAVEN'T SHARED WITH YOU THAT I NEED TO EXPLAIN. MY FATHER AND MY GRANDFATHER—AND HIS FATHER AND SO ON—HAVE BEEN SEARCHING FOR ARTIFACTS, WORLDLY SECRETS, AND LOST TREASURES OUR ENTIRE LIVES. WE HAVE KEPT THESE DIARIES OF WORLD FINDINGS AND SECRETS IN A CHEST CALLED THE "HOKMAH." THIS WORD COMES FROM THE HEBREW LANGUAGE AND REFERS TO A "SKILL IN LIVING." ALL OF MY, AND YOUR RELATIVES', MOST IMPORTANT ARCHAEOLOGY FINDINGS ARE CONTAINED IN THIS CHEST.

JACOB, YOU MUST HEAR ME IN THIS AND NEVER FORGET. THE HOKMAH CHEST AND ARTIFACTS ARE NEVER

TO BE SHARED WITH ANYONE YOU DON'T COMPLETELY TRUST. IF THIS INFORMATION WERE TO FALL INTO THE WRONG HANDS, THE IMPLICATIONS COULD BE DEVASTATING.

I DON'T KNOW HOW, BUT THERE ARE PEOPLE WHO KNOW OF THE EXISTENCE OF THE HOKMAH. THERE ARE WRITINGS CONTAINED IN THE HOKMAH ITSELF THAT SPEAK OF THESE PEOPLE AND TEACH OF THEIR UNDYING THIRST FOR POWER. THESE PEOPLE ARE MORE EVIL THAN CAN BE IMAGINED. THEY WILL KILL ANYONE OR DESTROY ANYTHING THAT GETS IN THEIR WAY. SO YOU MUST ALWAYS BE WATCHFUL.

I AM GOING ON A DANGEROUS, AND JOYOUS, JOURNEY TO AUSTRALIA THIS WEEK IN SEARCH OF A LOST ARTIFACT THAT OUR FAMILY HAS BEEN SEARCHING FOR SINCE THE BEGINNING TIMES OF THE HOKMAH. FOR SAFETY REASONS I WILL NOT DISCUSS THIS MATTER WITH YOU NOW BUT WILL DIRECT YOU TO THE HOKMAH'S CHEST.

THE CHEST IS IN A PLACE WE HAVE BOTH BEEN TO TOGETHER. IT IS WHERE YOU AND I DID YOUR FIRST ARCHAEOLOGICAL FIND TOGETHER. AT SUNSET, GO TO THE PLACE WHERE THE WATER ENTERS THE POND AND LOOK TOWARD THE SETTING SUN, AND THE SUN'S LIGHT WILL SHOW YOU THE WAY.

REMEMBER, NOW MORE THAN ANYTHING YOUR MOM NEEDS YOU. SHE NEEDS YOU TO BE STRONG FOR HER. I NEED YOU TO BE STRONG. I LOVE YOU ALWAYS.

DAD

Jacob carefully folded the letter into its original shape, placed it back in the envelope, and began to picture the place his dad was describing.

"I know where he's talking about," he said aloud. "It's at the mouth of the Sheyenne River and Old Man Johnson's pond. Dad and I went looking for Native American arrowheads there."

Jacob lay down on his bed, closed his eyes, and dreamed, like he did every night, of faraway lands.

CHAPTER 2

A NEW FRIENDSHIP

The next day Jacob got ready for school, just like any other school day, and went downstairs for breakfast. His mom was making breakfast with her back to him. He stood in the kitchen's doorway, staring at his mom in concern for her well-being. Sarah was a strikingly beautiful woman with long red hair and caring eyes who enjoyed every day of her job. She was, after all, the last of a dying culture—a stay-at-home mom.

"How did you sleep, Jacob?" she asked.

"Fine, Mom, and you?" asked Jacob, concerned. He slowly sat at the table.

"Oh, all right, I suppose," she answered. "I tossed and turned quite a bit. Are you sure you're ready to go back to school today?"

"I'm ready," answered Jacob confidently. "It's just the way Dad would have wanted. Do you suppose it's OK if I'm a little late coming home tonight, Mom? I wanted to do some extra studying at the library tonight."

"How could I ever say no to extra studying?" said Sarah with a grin.

Jacob finished his breakfast, gave his mom a hug and a kiss, and started walking to school.

Jacob, a thin, taller than average boy, was fourteen years old and nearing the end of his eighth-grade year at Sulley Middle School. He had golden brown skin—from many hours in the sun—and dark hair color that was becoming more blonde with each passing year. Unlike the outgoing, confident personality that he shared when with his parents, he was very quiet and shy at school, with no real friends to speak of. Jacob was an intelligent boy and excelled in school when he thought it necessary. He was athletic but lacked the confidence to play any organized sport.

Although his parents were a big part of their Catholic church, Sulley Middle School, and its organizations, Jacob never thought much of religion. "I like Sulley Middle School for its educational process. The religion they teach is just bearable," Jacob would say.

Sulley Middle School was a private Catholic school in Hickson—the same small North Dakota town where Jacob lived. Hickson was a ten-minute drive from the state's largest city, Fargo. With around 110,000 residents, to Jacob and other Hickson residents, Fargo was a metropolis in comparison to their small, quiet town.

Jacob entered his school that morning feeling a little awkward, as if everyone were staring at him. He was used to students looking at him peculiarly on a regular basis, but today was a little different. Students had more sadness and pity on their faces.

As Jacob approached his locker, he felt an unfriendly hand jolt his shoulder.

"Good to have you back, Jerlow," said a boy's familiar voice sarcastically. Jacob turned and saw Felix Matthews and a few other boys walking away.

Felix had moved to Jacob's school the previous year and had an uncanny knack for creating friends, soon becoming the most popular boy in the school. He was tall and muscular for his age, and had longer dark hair that he wore in a ponytail most of the time. Being a fair-skinned, handsome, and intelligent boy, he possessed something about him that both children and adults were drawn to for conversation. He was also the wealthiest boy in the school and had no qualms about telling, or showing, others that he was. For some unknown reason he had a dislike for Jacob that had been apparent since Felix's first day of school. It was unsettling to Jacob; Felix would go out of his way to make sure that Jacob felt insignificant and demoralized on a daily basis.

Just then, a girl Jacob had never seen before quickly stepped behind him. Jacob felt something lift from the back of his shirt as he spun quickly around to see what was happening.

"Here you go," the girl said as she handed the piece of paper to Jacob. "Have a nice day!"

Jacob looked, puzzled, at the unknown girl as she walked away toward the school office. He grabbed his books from his locker and was off to his first class. When seated, Jacob looked at the piece of paper that had been taped to his back. It read, "Only God could love a face like this."

"It doesn't matter what is going on in my life. I always have the security and stability of my peers at school," Jacob whispered to himself with a sneer.

Just then, Mr. Wolfe, Jacob's first period history and religion teacher, approached Jacob. "How are you today, Jacob?" he asked in his strong accent.

"Just fine," Jacob replied. "I'm happy to be back at school"

"It's positive people like you that make this world a better place," said Mr. Wolfe, placing his hand on Jacob's shoulder. "Even in times of trouble and challenge, good people rise to the top just like every morning sun," he said while looking at the crumpled piece of paper in Jacob's hand.

Mr. Wolfe was a newer teacher at Sulley Middle School, but taught his classes as though he had been teaching for many years. He walked with a slight limp and the aid of an old cane that was so weathered and twisted many students thought it was a tree's root. He had an uncanny wit and sense of humor that made history and religion classes enjoyable for most.

"Well, if there is anything that I can help with, let me know," Mr. Wolfe instructed.

"Thank you, Mr. Wolfe," replied Jacob gratefully.

"Let's stand for prayer," said Mr. Wolfe as he approached the front of the class.

All of the students rose to their feet and faced the crucifix on the wall.

"In the name of the Father, Son, and the Holy Spirit—amen," said Mr. Wolfe, while making the sign of the cross across his head, chest, and shoulders. "God our Father, you redeem us and make us your children in Christ. Look upon us, give us true freedom, and bring us to the inheritance you promised. Amen."

As the class took their seats, Mr. Wolfe announced, "Class, I know it's the end of the school year and we only have one month of school left, but we are blessed to have a new student with us today."

Just then, the girl who had taken the piece of paper from Jacob's shirt earlier entered the classroom. She had long black hair that she wore up in a bun, and a beautiful smile that showed off perfectly straight and white teeth. She wore glasses and had a look of maturity compared to many other eighth graders at Sulley Middle School.

"This is Bina Feldman," explained Mr. Wolfe. "She has just moved here from Israel and will need someone to help show her around the school. Do I have any volunteers?"

Jacob raised his hand. "I will," he said assertively.

"Great. It's settled then," said Mr. Wolfe. "Mr. Jerlow will be your guide for the next few days here at our school. Go ahead and take the open seat next to Mr. Jerlow."

"Thank you—Mr. Wolfe," replied Bina in her Middle Eastern accent. She took her seat.

Mr. Wolfe began to stroke his long, gray goatee with one hand, while using his other hand to point at a map of the Middle East on the wall. "Who can tell me, besides our new student, Ms. Feldman, what the name of this country is?" he asked.

Jacob raised his hand confidently and said, "Mr. Wolfe, that's Israel. I've been there twice."

"Very good, Mr. Jerlow," said Mr. Wolfe with a grin. "And, Ms. Feldman, can you tell us what language most Israelis speak?"

Bina replied in a language that none of the class had ever heard before, and to the class's surprise Mr. Wolfe replied back to her in the same language. The two exchanged words back and forth in what seemed to be questions and answers.

From the back of the room one of the students raised her hand. "Yes, Ms. Winslow?" asked Mr. Wolfe.

"What language are you two speaking to each other?" asked Molly Winslow in her high-pitched, squeaky voice.

"It's Hebrew. Ms. Feldman was explaining to me that she speaks four different languages—English, Hebrew, Arabic, and Spanish," explained Mr. Wolfe.

"And how does a Catholic school teacher in North Dakota know Hebrew?" asked Felix Matthews rather rudely.

"In my younger days I spent some time in Israel, and I picked up the language," said Mr. Wolfe. "Now, let's continue with our subject matter. Today we are going to be talking about..."

That morning Jacob showed Bina from class to class, introducing her to the teachers. Jacob, the students, and the teachers were amazed at the intellect that Bina showed—answering questions from the teachers in class as though she had already studied all of the material ahead of time.

During lunchtime Jacob walked Bina through the lunch line. For some time now he had been very intrigued by his new acquaintance.

"Why did you help me out earlier today by taking that sign off of my back?" Jacob asked. "I'm not complaining...I just appreciate the helping hand."

"I've seen people from my own country picked on and bullied," Bina replied. "No one deserves to be picked on like that. Besides—you looked like you needed a hand. Why does that boy pick on you? Who is he?"

"Who—err, you mean Felix Matthews? I wish I knew," murmured Jacob as he fidgeted with his food on his plate. "If you can figure that one out, please let me know."

"Well, if he is your enemy, then who are your friends?" Bina asked as she led Jacob toward a table full of students. Jacob quickly turned and nudged Bina in the other direction, toward an empty table, as to lead her away from the other students.

"Umm—well..." Jacob thought for a second. "I'm so busy with traveling and studying ancient artifacts that I don't have much time for friends." There was an odd silence with Jacob looking off at an empty wall.

The smell of freshly grilled chicken and a plethora of middle schoolers' colognes and perfumes clouded the cafeteria.

"Hmm—who would not want to be friends with a bright, intelligent boy such as yourself?" Bina said with a great smile. "It is settled then. You and I shall be friends."

Jacob was lost for words and with rosy cheeks looked around the lunchroom to break conversation for a moment, because—besides his mom and dad—he had never had a real friend before. "What should I say? How should I act? What if she begins to hate me after she really gets to know me?" were some of the thoughts that danced through Jacob's mind.

"I am so sorry about your father's death," Bina said gently.

"Oh—you heard about that, huh?"

"I read it in the newspaper. Your father was a professor of archaeology at North Dakota State University—right?

Jacob started to stare and fidget with his food on his plate again, and began to look sad—deservingly so. "Yes, that's right," he mumbled quietly.

Bina, being a caring and uplifting sort, could tell that Jacob was turning sad and wanted to uplift his spirit. "I love archaeology, and your dad is known throughout the world as being one of the best archaeologists. He was a genius!" she said.

Jacob's eyes grew big as he sat up a little straighter. "You knew my dad?" he asked.

"Knew him? I have read both of his books, and I met him once in his visit to Jerusalem. He was speaking at a convention at the Hebrew University of Jerusalem that my mother was speaking at as well. They were speaking on the history of the Catholic Church," instructed Bina.

"Your mom is a speaker as well? What type of work is she in?" Jacob asked curiously.

By now Bina and Jacob had forgotten the normal hustle and bustle of the middle school lunchroom as they grew deeper in conversation.

"My mother is an expert in linguistics, concentrating mainly on Catholicism and Christian history. She travels all over the world speaking on the history of the Church. Many times, if I am so fortunate, I get to travel with her."

"Wow—we have a lot in common!" exclaimed Jacob. "You and your mom have traveled around the world just like my dad and me."

Suddenly, the bell rang and startled them both. Bina and Jacob had enjoyed each other's company and conversation so much that they'd barely touched their food and had lost track of the time.

"Off to my favorite hour of the day," Jacob said sarcastically. "Our next class is science with Mr. Matthews."

Jacob and Bina walked side by side down the hallway, getting bumped and battered by all of the hastily moving children. Bina noticed that Jacob began walking more and more slowly as they approached their next class, stopping to get two drinks of water.

"I saw the name 'Jonas Matthews' on my class schedule," said Bina. "He wouldn't be Felix Matthews's father—would he?"

"The one and only. It's not every day that a boy can get a double dose—from a father and a son—at the same school," Jacob said jokingly.

Jacob and Bina approached the doorway to Mr. Matthews's room and noticed Mr. Matthews and Felix having a conversation, making sure no one could hear them—and looking out of the corner of their eyes at Jacob.

Mr. Matthews was a heavyset, shorter man who was balding and obviously, by his hairpiece, did not want others to know. He was not someone the students took lightly, because—even though he was a newer teacher—he already had the reputation of being someone not to cross.

Mr. Matthews spoke with a raspy, growly voice that was hard to interpret many times. After going on and on about some "scientific jumble"—as many students called it—students sometimes would look at each other and whisper, "What did he just say?" Of course, they would say this very quietly and always watch their behavior while in Mr. Matthews's class for fear of their own early demise.

"Good afternoon, Jacob," Mr. Matthews said with an unkindly growl. "I would gather by the looks of things that we will be needing to make room for one more person at your lab station today."

"I am so sorry to inconvenience you in any way," Bina said with a snicker.

"Inconvenience?" grumbled Mr. Matthews. "A fire hazard is what it is. Can't believe they're sending me another student when my room is already far too full!"

Mr. Matthews grabbed an unclaimed chair and cleared room at the lab station next to Jacob. "Will this do?" he snapped.

"Oh—just fine, Mr. Matthews. Thank you very much!" said Bina.

Bina always tried to live by the motto "Smother unkindness with kindness."

Mr. Matthews rolled his eyes in disgust as he moved toward the front of the class. "Open your books to page 299, follow the instructions—as I hope by now you know well how to do—and begin your dissection of the frog."

Bina and Jacob looked at each other, bit their lips, and tried whole-heartedly not to laugh.

"Well, on to the frog's disembowelment," said Bina as she began to read the instructions.

Bina began to dissect the frog as Jacob looked on. "You OK with this?" asked Jacob.

"Oh—yes, fine, intriguing, isn't it?" she replied with a slice of the scalpel.

"I—uh—I don't think I feel so good." Jacob's skin had turned whiter than the walls that surrounded him, and the more he viewed the opened amphibian, the more he felt himself sway from side to side.

Felix Matthews walked up to Jacob's lab table. "Jacob, buddy, you don't look so good," he said. "How about I get you a cold drink of water?"

Felix left for a moment and returned with a plastic water bottle. "Here you go, bud," he said, passing the drink over to Jacob.

Without thinking, Jacob took the lid off of the drink and took a quick sip. While slowly taking the drink away from his mouth, he noticed a pair of bloody frog's eyes staring at him from the water bottle's bottom. It was uncontrollable—everything that he eaten that day was now all over Bina in one large regurgitated explosion.

The class roared with laughter.

"Is that a proper way to treat a new friend?" said Felix with an unfriendly laugh.

"Oh—great Darwin!" shouted Mr. Matthews. "Don't think that I am going to clean up that mess, Jacob Jerlow! People with weak constitutions are weak themselves. I guess, unfortunately, you inherited your father's characteristics. Now go straightaway to the janitor and retrieve the proper cleaning supplies to clean up my room, and take your new friend with you as well."

Jacob was so embarrassed that every muscle in his body was frozen in time. He resembled one of the hairy stuffed creatures that lined Mr. Matthews's walls.

Bina grabbed his hand and pulled him out of the room. "It's OK," she said. "Now go get the cleaning supplies, and I will clean up in the locker rooms."

When Jacob and Bina returned to the science room, the class bell rang. Mr. Matthews, still very irritated by the mess that was left in his precious science room, held both of the newfound friends to clean the entire room until the end of the school day.

"You can catch up on your other classes tomorrow," he growled. "As for now your most important priority is cleaning up your mess."

By the last bell, Bina and Jacob were done cleaning not only Jacob's vomit but also every beaker, flask, crack, and corner of the science room. Still weak in the knees, Jacob walked Bina to her locker.

"Thank you," he said humbly to Bina. "Thank you for everything today. No one has ever stuck by me like you did today—no one."

"I'm sure if the tables were turned, you would have done the same for me," she replied. "I will see you tomorrow morning."

"OK!" Jacob said happily.

With all of the excitement of the day, Jacob had forgotten his plans for after school. "The Hokmah," he said aloud, suddenly remembering.

Jacob opened his backpack, took out all of the books, and started to confirm all of his equipment to his checklist for the night's journey:

✓ FOLDING SHOVEL

✓ FLASHLIGHT

✓ COMPASS

✓ POCKETKNIFE

✓ ROPE

✓ GLOVES

✓ BINOCULARS

✓ GRANOLA BAR

✓ BOTTLE OF WATER

"Looks like I have everything," thought Jacob.

Even as horrible as the day had gone, it became a mere forgotten memory as Jacob threw his backpack on and scurried out of the school. Jacob began his long walk toward his destination. While walking, he pulled out the letter from his pocket to remind himself of his dad's instructions. He read aloud, "'This place is where you and I did your first archaeological find together. At sunset, go to the place where the water enters the pond and look toward the setting sun, and the sun's light will show you the way.'"

"It will be nearly dark when I arrive. Just what I'll need—a setting sun," he thought.

Jacob approached a heavily wooded area that in some parts was nearly impassable with thick brush and fallen timber. With each step he took into the forest he became more and more aware of an awakening army. Mosquitoes, which some North Dakotans had claimed to be the state bird, were just starting to come out from their frozen winter sleep. Jacob looked like a kung fu master with hands swinging at the biting creatures.

After struggling through evergreens, oak trees, and gooseberry bushes for what seemed like hours, he neared the Sheyenne River. Before even seeing the river through the thick woods, Jacob knew he had reached its edges because of the changes in smells from just blooming flowers and bushes into that of murky, stagnant water with muddy, decaying fish.

Coming upon the river, he noticed a deer path worn into the ground along its side that was much easier to walk upon. He continued to follow the river's edge by way of the path, toward Old Man Johnson's farm.

When he reached the farm, it was nearly dark, and the temperature was dropping quickly. Jacob had forgotten a warm hat, and his ears and face were turning pink and blue from the cool night air. His heavy breathing from the strenuous walk was making a noticeable cloud of vapor come from his mouth with each breath, and with only sounds of slow moving water in the surroundings Jacob could not only feel his heart beating faster, he could hear it.

Jacob arrived at the river's entrance into the pond and began looking toward the setting sun as his dad had instructed. He stared at the sunset for a few minutes in anticipation; and then, a flash of light like the light from a marina's lighthouse came shining through the thick tree branches toward the side of a nearby small hill. The light pointed at the hill for no more than a few seconds, and quicker than the light had appeared, it was gone.

Jacob could not believe what he had just seen. He was nervous and excited all at the same time. He started to approach the hill where the light had directed him.

Just then, over his shoulder, he heard a snap, as though a branch had just been broken behind him. Jacob quickly turned to the sound and saw a group of bushes and leaves, obviously disturbed, swaying back and forth. His heart rate increased, and he felt a great anxiety overwhelm him.

Jacob recalled his dad's warning of the evil people in the world and their undying pursuit of the Hokmah, and with no thought, he dropped his backpack and ran through the trees as fast as he could. Bushes and branches were scraping and cutting his arms as he ran, but it did not slow his pace. Jacob was more frightened than he had ever been, and all he could think about was getting to the safety of his home.

Upon returning to his home, Jacob stormed through his front door.

"How was your day?" asked his mom. "I was waiting for your phone call to come and pick you up, but I guess you decided to run home, huh?"

"Uhh—it was—it was great, Mom. How was yours?" Jacob asked, still trying to catch his breath.

"It was good. I was just going through your dad's suitcase. By the way, I found some kind of an artifact in your father's satchel that I thought you might want. So I placed it on your dresser."

"Thank you. G'night, Mom," Jacob said. He rushed up the stairs toward his bedroom.

It took a few minutes, but Jacob calmed himself down from the excitement. He picked up the artifact his mom had described from his dresser and looked at it in amazement.

"I've never seen anything like this before," Jacob thought.

The object appeared to be a carved piece of wood but felt lighter than a feather. It was no larger than the palm of his hand and was in the shape of the letter L. "Kinda looks like the corner of a table," he thought, while holding and turning the artifact around and around in his hands.

After further studying the artifact, Jacob noticed small flowers on the sides of the piece. Curious, he smelled the piece and found that it had an aroma that was so sweet it made his mouth water in hunger.

"Very odd—I've never smelled anything so sweet and aromatic," Jacob thought.

Jacob put the object in his father's satchel and placed it on his dresser.

"Oh no—I left my backpack by the river," he moaned. "I'll have to go back tomorrow."

* * *

At this time, in a distant land, where no words of beauty can describe, a gathering was occurring. There had not been a meeting such as this in centuries. The assembly was that of neither the dead nor the living, but of heaven's angels.

"The boy has begun his journey," said Archangel Aaron. "He just may be the one that is to fulfill the prophecy."

"And what of our doorway?" asked Archangel Samuel. "What of the Dalet?"

"It is hidden—for now. You know the rules as well as I. We are not to interfere with humans. We can give guidance and God's blessings, but we may not have direct contact with them," Archangel Aaron instructed.

"What if the Tenebras were to get control of the Dalet?" Archangel Samuel shouted. "They could have unstoppable power over the Earth and the humans."

"Pray that this does not happen, my friend—we must pray!" said Archangel Aaron gently.

"And what of Michael? Has anyone seen him?" asked Archangel Samuel.

"No, Samuel. His whereabouts are unknown, and God still has a turned cheek from him."

CHAPTER 3

THE HOKMAH

The next day Jacob arrived at school and gladly went about his assign-
ment in showing Bina around from class to class.

At lunch Jacob and Bina sat together again and very much enjoyed
one another's company. Next to their empty table was a full table of
fellow students, the "popular kids," others would say.

"Want me to get you some more water today?" asked Felix from
the next table over. "Perfectly good water I gave you yesterday, and you
had to go throwing it up all over our new classmate. You're hopeless,
Jerlow!"

Felix's table erupted in laughter.

"I would say that I'm more hopeful than hopeless," said Jacob
sarcastically.

"Yeah, whatever," said Felix, laughing.

All morning Jacob struggled to find a way to ask Bina an important question but could not find a way. He couldn't wait any longer. "Do you want to go on a short archaeology find with me tonight?" asked Jacob so quickly and nervously that Bina could barely understand.

"I'm sorry… what was that?" she asked.

"I'm sorry," Jacob apologized. "I just asked if you want to go on a short archaeology find with me tonight."

"Sounds like fun," Bina replied. "Where are we going?"

"It's close by. You can tell your mom that you will be home before ten p.m.," Jacob instructed.

"OK. I'm excited," Bina said eagerly.

The next hour, in Mr. Matthews's science class, Jacob was taking a test when he heard a voice speaking in his head. Like most others, Jacob had always had inner conversations with himself—like speaking to his conscience—but never anything like this. The voice was as clear as though the person was seated next to him. "Jacob—Jacob Jerlow," the voice called to gain Jacob's attention. "Your hands will open the way." And then the voice was gone.

Jacob looked around the classroom, bewildered and frightened by the voice that had just spoken to him. Bina and Jacob made eye contact, and Jacob whispered, "Did you hear that?"

"Hear what?" Bina's mouth motioned with little sound.

"The man who was just talking to me," Jacob insisted.

Bina looked at Jacob with a puzzled face, shrugged her shoulders, and went back to her test.

"If two individuals, and you know who I am talking about, would like to have their tests thrown into the garbage, then by all means keep talking," said Mr. Matthews, glaring piercingly at Jacob and Bina.

Jacob swallowed whatever saliva was left in his mouth, and with sweaty hands he returned to his test.

After school was out, Jacob and Bina began their walk through the thick woods toward Old Man Johnson's farm and the place where Jacob had dropped his backpack the previous night.

"So—you still have not told me what we are looking for," said Bina.

"Oh yeah," Jacob replied, looking for the right words. "It's a family heirloom that my dad described in a letter before his death. I don't know a whole lot about it yet, but my dad said that it contains many secrets and archaeology finds from throughout the world."

"I knew there was more to you than meets the eye," Bina said.

The evening was colder than average, and a fog was settling into the river's edges, giving it an eerie and unsettling appearance. As each leaf crackled and each branch snapped with every footstep, they grew nearer to their destination—and that much more nervous. Coming upon Old Man Johnson's farm, Jacob saw his backpack where he had so hastily dropped it the previous evening.

"Accidentally dropped this last night," Jacob said, calmly pulling the backpack over his shoulder. "OK—you have to see this, Bina! Watch the light shine through these trees braches. It's amazing!"

Just as on the previous night, the light showed itself through the thick tree branches and pointed to a spot on a nearby hill. Jacob and Bina walked to the hill, and the light was gone. The sun was setting on the horizon, and the light was nearly gone. Jacob reached into his backpack and pulled out a flashlight. They began to search back and forth in the area that the light had shown but could not find any apparent opening or passage.

"Your father gave no other clue as to where this artifact is hidden?" Bina asked.

"No, just the light shining the way—wait..." Jacob paused to think a moment. "Don't think I'm crazy, Bina—but do you remember today in Mr. Matthew's class when I asked you if you heard a voice?"

"Yes—I thought you were joking. Why?"

"Uhh, because I really did hear a voice. A man was speaking to me, but obviously no one else could hear him but me," said Jacob.

"OK. What did the voice say, then?" asked Bina.

"It said, 'your hands will open the way,'" explained Jacob, looking down at his outstretched hands.

"OK, I am not one for magic or hocus-pocus stuff, because everything should be able to be explained through logic and good old-fashioned science," said Bina. "But for amusement, there is a stone next to your feet; place your hands on it and see if anything happens."

Jacob knelt down and placed his hands upon the rock, and to their surprise, a piece of the hillside seemed to sink into the ground. It looked as if a doorway had been opened into a cave.

Jacob and Bina looked at each other in complete disbelief and approached the entrance. They entered slowly and cautiously down a series of short steps that brought them slightly underground. Upon entering the cavern they both were amazed at the artifacts hanging on the wall and neatly organized upon tables and shelves. What should have been a dark cave was illuminated by strange stones emitting a deep glow that lit up the cavern like an oil lantern in an old log cabin. Jacob looked for a way to close the doorway and saw another rock similar to the one outside the cavern resting on a stone table. He placed his hands on the rock, and the door closed. It was obvious that a door had closed over the opening because of a movement that could be seen across the entrance, but from the inside the door was transparent so he could still see outside.

"I cannot believe what I am seeing!" Bina said in amazement. "There are artifacts and treasures in here that look hundreds and thousands of years old. How can it be that your dad had such a collection?"

"I can't really answer that yet, Bina," Jacob said. "All that I know so far is what my dad wrote to me in his final letter. He mentioned something about my family handing down artifacts and secrets from generation to generation for thousands of years. That's about it."

Bina didn't say anything, but her body language said enough. Jacob could sense she was beginning to doubt Jacob's story and she did not know whom or what to believe.

"I don't have all of the answers. All I know is what I've told you," Jacob said as he sat on the floor in frustration. "This is a lot to take in all at once. I don't know what to believe."

Bina could tell that she had added to the already confusing and stressful situation.

"OK—so where is this chest that we are looking for?" Bina said, as she started to look around the room. "Jacob—*look*! Is this it?"

Jacob hustled to his feet in a rush and ran over to Bina, who was standing next to a wooden box that was covered in brown rough leather and many inscriptions.

"This is it—this is the Hokmah my dad told me about. This will explain everything," said Jacob, opening the lid to the chest. The

Hokmah contained many books and scrolls—many weathered and showing their age—and it smelled of an old, mildew-ridden basement.

"Jacob, look here," Bina pointed out. "There is an envelope with your name on it."

Jacob opened the letter and began to read aloud:

JACOB, MY DEAREST SON,

IF YOU ARE READING THIS, SOMETHING HAS HAPPENED TO ME AND YOU HAVE BEEN DIRECTED TO COME HERE. FOR MANY YEARS I HAVE DREAMT ABOUT TAKING YOU TO THIS SECRET PLACE TO TELL YOU ALL ABOUT OUR FAMILY'S HISTORY AND THE HOKMAH. IT HAS BEEN OUR FAMILY'S TRADITION FOR HUNDREDS AND HUNDREDS OF YEARS TO TAKE THE FIRST-BORN SON TO THE HOKMAH ON HIS SIXTEENTH BIRTHDAY, BUT SINCE SOMETHING HAS HAPPENED TO ME, I WILL DO MY BEST IN WRITTEN WORDS TO TELL YOU ALL THAT I CAN.

THIS CAVE WAS CHOSEN BY MY GRANDFATHER IN 1912 TO BE THE HOKMAH'S NEW RESIDENCE AFTER HE AND HIS FAMILY MIGRATED TO NORTH DAKOTA FROM GERMANY. THE STONES THAT YOU HAVE PLACED YOUR HANDS UPON TO OPEN AND CLOSE THE HIDDEN DOOR ARE THOUSANDS OF YEARS OLD. THESE STONES, CALLED ABELS STONES, WERE SAID TO BE MADE WITH THE HELP OF ONE OF GOD'S ARCHANGELS, AND ONLY OUR FAMILY IS ABLE TO OPEN AND CLOSE THE DOOR WAY.

THE CAVE YOU NOW STAND IN CONTAINS ARTIFACTS AND RELICS FROM HUNDREDS AND THOUSANDS OF YEARS AGO, MOST OF WHICH ARE EXPLAINED IN THE BOOKS AND SCROLLS OF THE HOKMAH. THE SECRETS OF THIS CAVE AND THE HOKMAH MUST NEVER BE RELINQUISHED TO ANYONE THAT YOU DO NOT WHOLEHEARTEDLY TRUST WITH YOUR LIFE.

OUR FAMILY STARTED THE HOKMAH AND ITS CONTENTS IN THE EARLIEST OF TIMES. IT WAS STARTED TO BE A SAFE HAVEN FOR WORLDLY SECRETS, AND TO KEEP ITS KNOWLEDGE OUT OF THE HANDS OF THOSE WHO WISH TO USE ITS CONTENTS FOR EVIL. THERE ARE MANY MYSTERIES THAT ARE STILL UNEXPLAINED, BUT THE HOKMAH DOES CONTAIN CLUES THAT CAN HELP LEAD US TO THE ANSWERS. MY GRANDFATHER, FATHER, AND I HAVE BEEN WORKING ON A COUPLE OF UNEXPLAINED MYSTERIES THAT I PRAY YOU WILL BE ABLE TO FINISH. PIECING TOGETHER CLUES AND PUZZLE PIECES HAS BEEN OUR FAMILY'S MISSION FOR HUNDREDS OF YEARS. I WILL UNDOUBTEDLY HAVE A JOURNAL IN MY SATCHEL THAT YOU WILL WANT TO KEEP SAFE AS SOON AS YOU CAN. IT WILL CONTAIN NOTES AND OUTLINES AS TO WHAT I HAVE BEEN WORKING ON AS OF LATE. THIS JOURNAL WILL HELP YOU GET ON THE RIGHT TRACK IN STEPPING INTO MY SHOES AND FULFILLING OUR FAMILY'S OATH TO KEEP THE HOKMAH SAFE AND TO UNCOVER MANY OF THE WORLD'S MYSTERIES THAT HAVE BEEN LOST.

I KNOW THIS MAY BE DIFFICULT TO TAKE IN, BUT THERE IS NO EASY WAY TO BRING THIS NEXT THING OUT INTO THE OPEN. SO...ARE YOU READY? THERE ARE DESCENDANTS OF ANGELS AND HUMANS IN THE WORLD. IN THE BEGINNING OF MANKIND, GOD LET ANGELS ROAM THE EARTH, BUT WITHOUT GOD'S APPROVAL MANY OF THESE ANGELS FELL IN LOVE, MARRIED, AND HAD CHILDREN WITH HUMANS. THIS CAN BE SEEN AND PROVEN BY THE BIBLE IN GENESIS 6:2; THE NEW INTERNATIONAL VERSION STATES THAT "THE SONS OF GOD SAW THAT THE DAUGHTERS OF MEN WERE BEAU-TIFUL, AND THEY MARRIED ANY OF THEM THEY CHOSE." GOD FOUND OUT ABOUT HIS ANGELS' MARRIAGES AND THE CHILDREN THEY HAD WITH HUMANS. HE ALSO SAW HOW THEIR CHILDREN WERE DIFFERENT THAN OTHER HUMAN CHILDREN IN THAT THEY RETAINED SOME OF THEIR ANGEL PARENT'S GIFTS AND POWERS. GOD WAS FURIOUS. HE MADE A LAW THAT FORBADE ANGELS TO HAVE DIRECT CONTACT WITH HUMANS ANY LONGER WITHOUT PERMISSION, AND THE ANGELS WHO DID NOT REPENT OF THEIR SINS WERE SENT INTO HELL. THIS IS PROVEN AGAIN IN THE BIBLE BY 2 PETER 2:4, "FOR IF GOD DID NOT SPARE ANGELS WHEN THEY SINNED..." FROM THIS POINT ONWARD, GOD'S ANGELS WERE ABLE TO WATCH OVER AND BESTOW GOD'S BLESSINGS, BUT THEY COULD NO LONGER FREELY ROAM THE EARTH.

BUT WHAT WAS STARTED COULD NOT BE UNDONE; THE ANGELIC CHILDREN HAD CHILDREN THEMSELVES, AND

THROUGH THE AGES ALL OF THE ANGEL-BORN CHILDREN HAVE SHOWN TO PASS ON THEIR GIFTS AND POWERS TO SOME OF THEIR DESCENDANTS. MANY OF THESE DESCENDANTS LIVE FOR HUNDREDS OF YEARS AND GAIN MORE AND MORE POWER AS THEY AGE.

WHY HAVE I TOLD YOU THIS? BECAUSE THERE ARE DANGERS YOU MUST BE AWARE OF. YOUR GREAT GRANDFATHER FOUND ARTIFACTS IN SUDAN AND NIGERIA THAT HELPED PROVE THAT THERE IS A GROUP THAT HAS A DIRECT LINEAGE FROM WICKED LOST ANGELS AND HUMANS IN OUR WORLD THAT ARE VERY EVIL. THEY ARE KNOWN AS THE TENEBRAS, WHICH COMES FROM A LATIN WORD THAT MEANS "DARKNESS." THEIR THIRST FOR BLOOD AND CONTROL OVER HUMANS WILL NEVER DIE—UNTIL THEY CONTROL EARTH. THEY WILL KILL ANYONE OR DESTROY ANYTHING THAT COMES IN THEIR WAY. YOU MUST NEVER TRUST THEM! AGAIN, WHY HAVE I TOLD YOU THIS AND HOW DOES THIS APPLY TO US? BECAUSE I HAVE HAD DREAMS OF THEM FOLLOWING ME AND WHAT EVILS THEY MAY DO TO OUR FAMILY.

BUT FOR EVERY EVIL THERE IS GOOD. YOUR GREAT GRANDFATHER ALSO LEARNED OF ANGELIC DESCENDANTS THAT ARE FROM GOOD AND HOLY ANGELS THAT BATTLE THE TENEBRAS AND OTHER EVIL OF THE WORLD. KNOWN AS THE VERITAS, WHICH COMES FROM THE LATIN WORD THAT MEANS "TRUTHFULLNESS," THEY HAVE SWORN AN

ALLEGIANCE TO PROTECT ALL THAT IS HOLY AND RIGH-
TEOUS IN THE WORLD.

I WISH I WERE THERE TO TEACH YOU MORE, BUT KNOW
THAT I WILL BE WITH YOU IN SPIRIT ALWAYS. GO TO MY
SATCHEL AND FIND MY PERSONAL JOURNAL TO SEE WHERE
I HAVE LEFT OFF, AND KEEP IT AND YOURSELF SAFE.

I LOVE YOU ALWAYS,
DAD

Jacob carefully folded the pages of the letter and placed them into the envelope. Bina looked at Jacob and said, "I am very sorry I doubted you and your father, Jacob. It was a lot to take in all at once."

"It's nothing," replied Jacob. "Let's get going home now so I can get my dad's satchel safe."

Upon returning to Jacob's house, Jacob introduced Bina to his mom. "It is very nice to meet you, Mrs. Jerlow," Bina said with an outstretched hand. "Jacob has told me so much about you and your family."

"Oh, it's a pleasure to meet you as well. I see now the reason that Jacob has had a little more a hop in his step as of late," said Sarah.

Jacob's face turned red as he pulled Bina's hand as to leave the living room and go to Jacob's bedroom. "Come on...my mom is such a jokester. Let's go grab that satchel in my room," he said.

In Jacob's room he opened the satchel and pulled out the unknown artifact. "This was the last piece of history my dad got to find," Jacob said as he handed the L-shaped object over to Bina.

"It is so light," said Bina in amazement. "It's like it weighs nothing!"

Jacob was busy digging into the satchel. He hardly noticed anything Bina had said. "Here it is. Here's my dad's journal!" Jacob shrieked embarrassingly with a pre-pubescent squeal. He quickly shrugged at the pitch problem and excitedly pulled the journal from a hidden flap inside the satchel.

"Oh my—is that the time?" Bina said when she saw the clock on the wall. "As much as I would love to see what's contained in that journal, I must be returning home. My mother is probably worried sick about me by now."

Jacob threw the satchel over his shoulder and began walking Bina home.

"Thanks a ton for coming with me tonight, Bina," Jacob said with another embarrassing crack in his voice.

By Jacob's nervousness and random fidgeting, it was becoming more apparent to Bina that Jacob had never had a real friend before. "Good night, Jacob," said Bina. "If our second day of friendship was this much fun, I can't wait to see what tomorrow will bring."

The next morning Jacob arrived at school, and while walking the hallway he heard a singing voice coming from the music room that he had not heard before. Intrigued, he began to walk slowly closer to the sound. "This voice is like an angel. Who could this be with such a voice?" Jacob thought to himself. Jacob peeked through the partially opened door and saw that it was Bina singing. She was apparently practicing a solo with the music teacher, Mrs. Roberta Rubis, who was playing the piano. Jacob stared and listened to the beautiful music, making sure to not be seen.

When the song was completed, Jacob rushed down the hallway so that Bina would not see him. When he saw her leave the room, he walked casually toward her. "What ya doing?" he asked.

"I was trying out for next year's honor choir with Mrs. Rubis," she said. "I hope I made it."

"I'm sure you did. You are pretty much brilliant at everything," Jacob said, confidently.

"I wish that were true, but thank you, Jacob."

"I love music as well," said Jacob. "I've played the trumpet for as long as I can remember."

"Really! I never knew you were a musician," said Bina as her face lit up.

"I have enough challenges at school. I guess I never told anyone here that I play the trumpet because I thought that kids would make fun of me," Jacob said gingerly. "I have been taking private lessons for many years now, and I really enjoy playing. It's somewhat of a release for me."

"Well, I would very much like to hear you play," said Bina.

"OK then," Jacob said, closing his locker.

Jacob and Bina grabbed their books and went to first-hour history and religion with Mr. Wolfe. They were the first ones to enter the room and saw Mr. Wolfe kneeling by the cross on the wall and quietly saying a prayer. Mr. Wolfe slowly stood with a loud crack from one of his knee joints, wiped a tear from his face, and walked to the front of the class as though no one were watching.

"Good morning, you two," he said with a grin. "Off to an early start, are we?"

"Yes sir," they replied as other students began to filter in through the doorway.

As with every morning, Mr. Wolfe started the class with a prayer and began teaching, "Who can tell the class a miracle that we have learned about this year that Jesus performed?"

Molly raised her hand and was called upon. "He changed water into wine," she squeaked.

"Very good—and another?" asked Mr. Wolfe. "What about you, Mr. Matthews? What is a miracle that you can recall?"

"Uh—it may be a miracle that I am passing your class!" Felix said to the tune of an uproar in the class.

"You may be partially right on that one, Mr. Matthews, but I was looking for more of a miracle by Jesus instead of yourself. Ahh yes—Mr. Fellows," said Mr. Wolfe, pointing at Gregory Fellows's uplifted hand.

Gregory Fellows was a nervous boy who would stutter and shake at the sound of a student's pencil hitting the floor. "Jesus fed the five thousand and their families with just a little fish and bread," he said nervously.

"Very good—very well said indeed," Mr. Wolfe said, opening his Bible. "Can anyone tell me where we can read the miracle of Jesus raising a loved one from the dead?"

Bina raised her hand. "I can!" she unexpectedly shouted. "It is in the book of John—specifically John chapters eleven and twelve."

"Impressive, Ms. Feldman, and your enthusiasm is uplifting," Mr. Wolfe said. "Let us all turn to John chapter eleven verse one."

The class turned to the proper page, and Mr. Wolfe called upon Jeffrey Johnson, a slightly obese teenager who was notorious for sneaking candy into classes, to read aloud the Scripture from the Holy Bible.

"Mary and Martha, the sisters of Lazarus of Bethany, sent Jesus a message that His friend Lazarus was ill. Jesus stayed two days longer in the place He was, before setting out for Bethany. When Jesus arrived, He found that Lazarus had already been in the tomb four days. Martha told Jesus that if He had been here, her brother would not have died, but Jesus said to her, 'Your brother will rise again.' Jesus asked where Lazarus was laid out. Jesus began to weep as they walked to the tomb. The tomb was a cave with a stone lying against it. He asked to have the stone removed. Martha said to Him, 'Lord, already there is a stench because he has been dead four days.' Jesus answered, 'Did I not tell you that if you believed, you would see the Glory of God?' When the stone was removed, Jesus looked upward and prayed to the Father. He then cried out in a loud voice, 'Lazarus, come out.' The dead man came out with his hands, feet, and face wrapped in a cloth. Jesus said to them 'Unbind him, and let him go.'"

Mr. Wolfe instructed the class to close their Bibles and place their heads upon their desks. "I want you all to imagine this miracle in its entirety. Now, I will walk you through my depiction of this historical event and you can see, in your mind, if you agree...The year was 27 AD. There wasn't any electricity, there were no TV or video games, no heaters for winter, and no air-conditioners for summer, nor were there many of the home luxuries that we take for granted every day in our society today.

"The story takes us to a small town. The town was called Bethany, and it was only about two miles away from the large city of Jerusalem in Israel. It had been extremely rainy for that time of year. Many of the crops had been destroyed by flooding, and countless farmers were worried that they would not be able to pay their taxes to the Romans because of their financial losses."

Mr. Wolfe played an audio recording of people talking in Hebrew, as a background noise, while he continued his story. "In a smaller-than-average, two-bedroom home in Bethany lived two sisters and one brother. Their parents were both deceased, leaving the two older sisters to manage the household and its small farmland. The eldest sister, Mary, was twenty-three years old; the middle child, Martha, was nineteen years old; and the youngest boy, Lazarus, was eleven years old. Although they longed to have families of their own, neither of the sisters was married yet.

"Since his toddler years, Lazarus had loved to spend time with his very best friend. Even though his friend was very much older than himself, he very much looked up to and aspired to be like him. His friend was Yeshua, or in today's English language, Jesus. Whenever Jesus was in the area of Bethany, he was sure to visit Lazarus, help him learn Scriptures of old, and play games with him.

"Since Lazarus's father had died when he was an infant, he looked at Jesus as a second father and loved him dearly. He would count the days until Jesus's next trip to Bethany so that he could spend time with his very best friend.

"After many days of tending to the farmland in the rainy weather, Lazarus began to have a high temperature and lacked the strength to lift himself from his bed. He could not eat anything, and he began to sleep for very long periods of time. His sisters grew more and more worried that their beloved younger brother would not be able to defeat the illness, so they sent word to the one man that they felt could save him—Jesus. After all, they had heard of Jesus healing others who had been sick and even blind, so surely he could heal their brother—whom Jesus loved.

"After Jesus received the message of Lazarus's illness, he immediately knew what needed to take place. It was for God's glory that he would need to wait, and then go to Lazarus.

"When traveling to see Lazarus, he knew that his very close friend had died, and as much as he knew Lazarus would be in a well-kept place, he felt sadness for Lazarus's sisters and the loss of the boy.

"Upon arriving in Bethany, Jesus met Martha and Mary and was overwhelmed with grief and sorrow when he saw their sadness. He now knew that he would raise the boy Lazarus from the dead for God's glory, and to show once again that he was the Son of God and the answer to the Jewish prophecies.

"Upon awaking from his sleep, it took the boy Lazarus a full day to be able to eat and to regain complete consciousness. After feeling better, Lazarus ran to Jesus and greeted him with a hug and kiss on his cheek. He kept telling Jesus, 'I knew you would come...I knew you would come.'

"Jesus was very happy to see his young friend once again, and even in the midst of multitudes of followers, he would find time alone with Lazarus to play with him and tell him stories.

"Soon after these happenings, Lazarus was given word from Jesus that he must move far away to live with his uncle, because the Jews were planning to kill Lazarus to cover-up Jesus's miracle. With much sadness, Lazarus left his sisters and his very best friend to live with his uncle in a faraway land.

"Three years after his move, Lazarus received word that Jesus was killed on a cross. Lazarus held much anger toward the Jewish people for what they had done for many years. It wasn't until he was visited by the resurrected Jesus and given instructions to forgive that he replaced his energy in anger and spite with doing good toward others."

By the end of Mr. Wolfe's interpretation of Lazarus's resurrection, the class was buried in thought about the historical event. In their eyes, Mr. Wolfe had told the story like no one had ever told it before—mostly because the story of Lazarus was usually told with the image of Lazarus being a man, not a child.

"This is just my depiction of the event," said Mr. Wolfe calmly. "You may raise your heads up off of your desks and come to your own conclusions."

Just then the bell rang, and the students began filing out toward their next class.

Bina and Jacob walked down the busy hallway.

"Wow! I have never heard Mr. Wolfe get into a story like that," said Jacob.

"He has a vivid imagination and is a great storyteller," Bina replied. "Are we going to meet after school today?"

"Most definitely—let's meet in the library and take a look at my dad's satchel."

CHAPTER 4

THE SATCHEL

After school Jacob and Bina met in the school library. "Do you have the satchel?" asked Bina curiously in a whisper.

"Roger," Jacob said, looking around the library as if someone were watching him. He pulled the unknown L-shaped artifact from the satchel and placed it on the table.

Bina looked rather peculiarly at Jacob. "'Roger,'" she thought. "What does that mean?" She shrugged her shoulders and labeled it as "nerves."

"I still have no idea what this could be," Jacob said, shaking his head. He pulled the journal from the satchel and began to turn through the pages. In a moment or two, Jacob realized that he was holding his breath and released the trapped air from his lungs.

"It's OK—breathe," Bina said as they both looked at each other and laughed quietly.

While reading through the beginning of the journal, they learned of the many great adventures Jacob's dad had been on and the dangers he'd encountered along the way.

"Each one of these adventures was a mystery that the world had not yet known," Bina said. "Your father took pieces of the Hokmah and put them together to lead him to solving many mysteries."

Bina pointed out one particular adventure as they read quietly.

"Jacob, it says here that your father found the spear that stabbed Jesus's side while he was on the cross," Bina said, pointing at a drawn picture of the spear. "It also says that he has hidden the spear in a secret location for fear of the Tenebras finding it. The spear is said to hold supernatural powers because of Jesus's blood that was spilled upon it. Furthermore, it says here that your father was nearly killed by an unknown sea creature while recovering the spear from waters near Italy."

The time began completely slipping by while Bina and Jacob read countless stories of adventure, near-death experiences, and mysteries solved—and unsolved. As they approached the journal's midpoint, they started to see a pattern that was leading all of the adventures to one main conclusion. Jacob's dad was searching for one thing in particular, all with one main goal. He was searching for something that had been hidden since the beginning of humankind.

The artifact Jacob's dad was in search of was the Dalet. Legend told of a door that could be opened and would give passage to almost any destination in the blink of an eye. Also, when using this doorway time almost stood still in the person's place of origin.

The Dalet was said to be made by angels from heaven that used the doorway to travel from place to place while on Earth during their time of intermarriage with humans. When God forbade angels from having physical contact with humans, the angels hid the four pieces of the Dalet in separate locations so as to protect humans from its power. Also, legend said that the human who held all four corners of the Dalet would become one with the doorway, meaning that until this person's death, no other could gain control of its power.

"Look at this sketch of one of the corners," Jacob said, holding the picture closer to their faces. "This looks just like..." He reached for the L-shaped object that was resting on the table in front of him. "This is what my dad went looking for in Australia! This is one of the corners of the Dalet! My dad gave his life for this piece."

"Needless to say, we'd better find a safe place for this piece, because I am sure there are others after it as well," Bina said.

"Right you are, Bina. I think the safest place would be in the hill-side cave—in the Hokmah."

Jacob and Bina continued reading into the journal and learned more and more about the clues that had been compiled by Jacob's dad. The clues were pointing to four distinct regions of the world where they were hidden.

"Look here, Bina," Jacob pointed out. "My dad gives reference to the origins of the phrase 'To the four corners of the Earth' as the first clue given in allusion to the Dalet and its whereabouts. The 'four corners of the Earth' were representing the four corners of the doorway and also referring to four distinct, hidden places on Earth."

Other than the Australia site, the journal plotted three other locations as to where the door pieces were hidden. Jacob's dad had done most of the groundwork and found the general vicinity of each piece, but as to their exact whereabouts, there were pieces of the puzzle that needed to be found and placed together. The three remaining locations were in Brazil, Alaska, and Italy.

"How will we ever get to these three sites?" asked Jacob in frustration.

"I'm sure a way will be given," said Bina confidently. "God always grants a means and a path to those who believe."

Jacob rolled his eyes. "'Believe'—believe in what?" he thought.

Just then Bina received a text message from her mother, who was waiting outside the school. She was wondering if Bina was done. "Do you want a ride home?" asked Bina.

"That would be great," Jacob said as he packed away the Dalet corner, journal, and satchel into his backpack.

Jacob and Bina walked outside, and Bina introduced him to her mother. "This is my mother, Rebecca Feldman." Bina's mother was short and slender with a somewhat crooked nose and a heavy Middle Eastern accent that was difficult to understand.

"It's a pleasure to meet you, Mrs. Feldman," Jacob said with a firm handshake. He was trying his best to make a good first impression.

"The pleasure is all mine," Rebecca replied. "Bina has told me so much about you. I was sorry to hear about your father. He was an amazing man."

"Thank you," said Jacob.

"Mother, is it OK that we give Jacob a ride home with us?" asked Bina.

"Why certainly it is OK," said Rebecca.

Upon arrival at Jacob's home Bina's mother, Rebecca, and Jacob's mom, Sarah, were introduced, and they became familiar with one another over a cup of coffee. They were both amused at each other's heavy accents—Rebecca with her Middle Eastern accent and Sarah with her strong-voweled North Dakota inflection. Soon the amusement of their spoken intonations wore off, and they got familiar with their lives—as women will do.

Meanwhile, with their mothers' permission, Jacob and Bina walked hurriedly to the hidden hillside cavern to store their corner of the Dalet and to view more of the hidden clues in the Hokmah.

"Your father has some gathered clues here pertaining to the Dalet corner in Brazil," Bina said, holding up some loose-leaf notepaper from the Hokmah. "He has notes here from architectural digs around the world that give reference to the 'eyes showing direction.' You see, here," she pointed, "he found inscriptions in an Egyptian pyramid that referred to the eyes pointing the way to an endless doorway. Your father theorized that one of the Dalet corners was hidden in a hillside tomb that the Egyptian Sphinx's eyes were directed toward, but later was moved for security.

"He continues on and explains how he was led from Egypt to Brazil—for the hiding place of the Dalet corner. It says here there were 'writings found in the secret Vatican library, in Rome, that spoke of a mysterious artifact that was found by the Holy Catholic Church in Egypt and brought to Brazil.' The clues seem to stop there."

"So how the heck are we going to get to Brazil to investigate?'" Jacob complained.

"My mother has speaking engagements in Brazil, usually twice a year. We should check with her first."

Jacob held up a sketch on a parchment that was very weathered from age. The drawing was of the four corner pieces of the Dalet in their position, two suspended in air and the other two on the ground. A man was pictured stepping into the Dalet with an outstretched hand. The man's hand held an object that was difficult to make sense of. Jacob and Bina studied the hard-to-see drawing for some time, trying to decipher what it meant, before making their way back to Jacob's house.

Upon returning to Jacob's home, Bina, out of the blue, asked her mother, "I have noticed that you have not been to South America in some time for a speaking engagement, so I was wondering if you have any travels to Brazil coming in the near future?"

"It is funny you should ask, because the week after school is out I need to travel to Rio de Janeiro, in Brazil, for a seminar, and I was going to ask you if you would like to come," said Bina's mother. "Why do you ask?"

"Uhh—err—Jacob and I were doing some studies for history class on Brazil, and we had some questions about the country's historical background in relationship to the Catholic Church," Bina said, saving the moment. "You know, Mother, it would be very educational for both Jacob and me to learn more of Brazil by going on this trip with you."

"This would be fine with me if it is OK with Jacob's mother," said Rebecca, turning toward Jacob's mom. "I have plenty of airline miles accumulated on my credit card for numerous free flights. Plus my hotel is completely prepaid by the hosting seminar in Rio. So all Jacob would need is a little money for food and that is all."

Sarah paused for a moment to process everything. With the recent passing of her son's father she thought it to be the natural thing for Jacob to go on an adventure. He after all, was accustomed to traveling often in school breaks with his father, and this would be more of a natural summer time if he traveled. Sarah thought if Jacob was just kept home all summer he would probably hurt worse with the loss of his father.

"Oh—absolutely," said Sarah. "It will be summer vacation, so no school will be missed, and it will be an educational trip for the both of them to boot."

Jacob's mom and Bina's mother both exchanged necessary information for the Brazil trip while Jacob and Bina quietly discussed their plans in Brazil.

The next day at school, Jacob and Bina had a great difficulty staying focused on their studies with the upcoming Brazil trip being the center of their thoughts. After lunch Bina walked to her locker to get her science homework that was due, and noticed that her lock was covered in gooey, sticky gum.

"Oh, fabulous!" she exclaimed. "And this has to occur directly before Mr. Matthew's class. I have to have my science homework from my locker or I'll get a zero!" she shouted toward Jacob.

Jacob ran over to Bina's locker and began picking at the gum and sticking it to a piece of paper from his folder—he had experience in dealing with such atrocities before. "There—you can at least see your numbers so that you can open the locker," Jacob said, trying to remove gum from under his fingernails.

Bina opened her locker and grabbed her books, and they both hurried off to science class. Looking down the hallway, they could see Mr. Matthews, as he did every day, waiting at the doorway to his classroom. The students of the school were sure to never be tardy to his science class for fear of his cruel detention duties. Mr. Matthews took pure enjoyment in seeing students squirm and shudder with fear of his detentions.

Jacob and Bina both felt themselves shrink in size, and their heads tilt toward the floor, as the tardy bell rang while they were ten feet from the science room's doorway.

"It will be nice to have you both after school in detention today," Mr. Matthews said with a tilted smile and an outstretched hand. "I have some chores that I have saved just for such an occasion."

Forgetting about the gum still adhering to his fingers, Jacob respectfully shook Mr. Matthew's hand. Mr. Matthews felt something foreign gluing their hands together. He jerked his hand forcefully downward from Jacob's grasp and looked slowly at his gum-filled hand. Mr. Matthews did not utter one syllable, but his anger boiling from within forced his face into shades of color that matched the steaming Bunsen burners on his lab tables. Jacob felt as if his height had immediately shrunk six inches as he sensed that his after-school-detention duties were going to be that much more unimaginable.

As the two friends took their seats, they kept their eyes fixed on the chalkboard in front of them as if nothing had happened. Every second or two, Jacob would catch out of the corner of his eye the look of pity from his staring class.

Felix Matthews caught Bina's attention with a thrown wadded-up paper ball to her back. "Did you find yourself in a sticky situation—or what?" he said, laughing. Bina then knew that it was Felix who had put the chewing gum on her lock, and from that moment on she had one thing on her mind—payback.

Following science class was physical education with Mr. Colby. Derived from students, Mr. Colby had the nickname "Four-by-Four," and for good reason; he was, after all, not much more than four feet in height, and his width—shoulder to shoulder—about the same. He was a power lifter, one of the best in the United States—with the trophies to prove it. He showed an energy and enthusiasm toward exercise and fitness that students were almost frightened of.

"Let's get those bodies moving today," he said with a shout and a whistle, getting the class through their warm-up exercises.

As the class started playing volleyball, Bina went to Mr. Colby and asked permission to use the restroom. "Of course," he replied. "Hurry back for some volleyball action." Bina approached the locker rooms and looked to make sure no one saw her enter the boy's locker room. A few minutes later, she secretly exited the locker room and entered the volleyball game.

After class was completed, the boys entered their locker room to get changed back into their school clothes. Felix Matthews was bragging to his entourage, as usual, about what a great game he had in physical education class. While pulling his school shirt over his head, he saw a giant, hairy spider looking at him eye-to-eye—no more than one inch from his face. Felix let out an ear-piercing high-pitched scream, which many in the locker room thought came from a girl, and threw his shirt toward the lockers. The entire boy's locker room erupted in laughter at the popular boy and his unmanly behavior. Felix checked his shirt for the hairy creature, making sure it was gone, and pulled his shirt over his head as he hurriedly bolted out of the locker room.

Upon leaving the locker room, Jacob caught up to Bina in the hallway. "Was that your doing?" he asked.

"Jacob, what on earth are you talking about?" Bina asked, inconspicuously.

"Yeah, right—you know exactly what I am talking about," Jacob said. "You just pulled the best prank ever, and on the most deserving kid ever!"

After school Jacob and Bina entered Mr. Matthew's class room for detention. "You two would not know how my wolf spider somehow got out of its cage, out of my classroom, and into the boy's locker room, would you?" Mr. Matthews growled.

"Oh no, Mr. Matthews, not a clue how that occurred," they said, looking ever so innocent.

"I should hope not. For I pity the person found for such an act of thievery. It would be better that this person had not been born when I am through with him or her," Mr. Matthews said, grumbling as he walked toward his classroom's bathroom. "Come with me."

"This latrine has not been cleaned in ages," he said. "You will find all of your cleaning supplies on the counter. When you are finished, I expect to see my reflection on the floor."

"Mr. Matthews, I think you forgot to leave us gloves," Bina said.

"'Forgot?' My dear, I did no such thing. I—do—not—forget. A couple of young healthy kids such as yourselves will do just fine without gloves. There is plenty of soap and water there in the sink so you may wash up when you are done."

Jacob and Bina looked over at the faucet and saw a small sliver of bar soap resting on the sink's edge. Mr. Matthews started walking toward the exit. "I will be back in a short while. I had better see results when I return."

The toilet looked as if it had not been cleaned since the construction of the school twenty-five years earlier. With feces, urine, and who knows what animal dissection parts decorating it, the toilet smelled worse than it looked.

After cleaning the bathroom for an hour, Jacob needed a drink. "I'll be back in a few minutes," he said.

As Jacob passed Mr. Matthew's desk on his way to the water fountain, he saw a drawer left slightly open with some strange piece of metal from within reflecting the setting sun's rays, which were breaking through the nearby window. This sparked Jacob's curiosity. He opened the drawer to the desk a little farther to remove a small book that was decorated with a strange emblem he had never seen before. The emblem was of two snakes twisted into an eight-shaped infinity symbol. The snakes gave off an eerie sensation to Jacob that was heightened further when he thought he saw one of the snakes turn and look at him.

Jacob rushed to place the book back into the drawer as he heard footsteps approaching the doorway.

"What are you doing away from your chores, Jerlow?" asked Mr. Matthews, looking toward his desk.

"I was just going to the water fountain," replied Jacob.

"Well then, don't just stand there looking confused," Mr. Matthews snapped.

Jacob rushed out the door to get a drink as Mr. Matthews went to his desk to check on his secret book, which Jacob had discovered.

* * *

The last couple weeks of school were a little less stressful for Jacob and Bina as Felix Matthews was, to their enjoyment, staying a safe distance from them both. They found themselves in conversation and study of Brazil, and the Hokmah, every chance they had, and they grew more anxious as the days came and went.

On the last day of school, Jacob and Bina entered the classroom of their beloved teacher, Mr. Wolfe, with their heads hanging low and looking gloomy.

"All of the other students are happy and excited for the summer break, but the two of you look as if the school year were just starting," said Mr. Wolfe, slowly walking toward the two with a limp and the aid of his old weathered cane.

"I guess we're excited about the summer but disappointed that we won't see you for a quite a while," Jacob said with a frown.

"Who says you won't see me this summer?"

"Really? Can we really see you?" asked Jacob with brightened eyes.

"I cannot see why not. Now—off you go to your seat."

After a quick prayer Mr. Matthews started his last day of the school year. "On our last day of school, I wanted to talk to you all about faith and what it means exactly. 'Faith' is a word that is commonly thrown around without thought in religious conversation, but what does it mean to you?"

Molly stretched her hand to the sky and spoke before being called upon. "It means that I believe in something," she squeaked.

The classroom lit up with a small giggle from the students.

"All right then—a good thought. Anyone else?" asked Mr. Wolfe, looking around the classroom. "Ms. Feldman, by chance do you have anything more to add?"

"Molly is correct in saying that faith is something that we believe in, but there is more to it than just this," Bina said. "Faith is believing in something that you have never heard, smelled, touched, or seen with your own eyes. This is true faith."

"Ah yes—very good, Ms. Feldman," said Mr. Wolfe. "Faith is following our hearts and spirits, not just our minds and bodies. Our minds and bodies are of this world; their sinful desires are separated from our heart and soul. For what the mind and body want many times is not what the soul desires. It is our hearts and souls that long to have a direct relationship with our Father in heaven. So, class, I ask you: Where is your heart? Where does your 'faith' live?"

As Mr. Wolfe came to a close on his lecture, Jacob heard the voice that he'd heard once before speak in his head: "Follow your heart, Jacob. Follow your faith always."

Jacob looked around the room, knowing that no one else could hear the voice, and felt a goodness overwhelm his heart. He looked over at Bina and smiled, for he knew that their adventures were just about to begin.

CHAPTER 5

THE EYES OF RIO

The morning of the flight to Rio de Janeiro, Brazil, Jacob hugged and kissed his mother good-bye before jumping in the car with Bina and Bina's mother, Rebecca.

"I love you. Be careful!" Jacob heard his mother shout.

"I will. I love you, too," he yelled out the window of the car.

While they drove to the airport, Jacob kept looking over his shoulder at other cars, as he had the unnerving feeling that someone was following him.

"Are you OK?" asked Bina. "You keep looking all over and fidgeting."

"Yes—I'm quite all right. I think I'm just nervous for the airplane ride."

The flight went quickly with only one stop to change planes in Orlando, Florida. As the airplane began to descend over Rio de Janeiro,

Bina and Jacob were amazed at the beautiful scenery that was beneath them. The ocean, trees, hills, and small islands decorated the landscape.

"There it is—our first adventure awaits us," Jacob said to Bina.

Upon exiting the airport, the three were bombarded by taxicab drivers, each looking for a cab fare. "I have many children to feed. I will take you anywhere you need to go," many of them said in broken English.

Just when Rebecca was going to choose a taxicab randomly, Jacob saw a man quietly standing next to his taxicab, looking at the three of them. Jacob was curious.

"Rebecca—is it OK if we use that taxicab?" asked Jacob.

"I don't see why not," she said, looking over at the taxicab driver. The three walked over to the driver and handed him their luggage before jumping into the car. "The Sheraton Hotel at Avenida Niemeyer 121 please," Rebecca instructed.

The driver smiled and nodded his head in agreement as they left the airport. The driver was a younger man with reddish hair and a bright smile. By his light complexion, it was obvious he was not a Brazilian native. He had a partially visible tattoo, or birthmark, on the side of his neck that caught Jacob's attention, but as much as Jacob tried to view what the marking was he could not. The entire drive to the hotel, the driver, to the surprise of the three, did not say a word.

"I don't think he knows English," Bina and Jacob thought.

Upon arrival at their hotel, Rebecca paid the driver, who was quickly on his way, and the three excitedly went through the massive glass doors. There was some remodeling occurring in the lobby, which was embellished with fresh indigenous flowers, that made the air smell of sweet, fresh paint. They checked in at the front desk and were off to their room.

"Mother, Jacob, look out the window! You can see the ocean," Bina said excitedly.

"Whoa—that is beautiful," Rebecca and Jacob said in unison.

"Tomorrow I don't have to work...so I was thinking that we could go and see some sights. What do you two think?" Rebecca asked, holding up a guide to the city.

"Most definitely," Jacob and Bina said, looking at each other.

The next morning the three left the hotel and, to their surprise, saw the taxi cab driver from the previous day standing next to his car, waiting to transport them.

"Wow—now that's service," said Rebecca to the driver. "I must know your name."

The driver opened the door and looked at Jacob. "It be Shawn, ma'am," he said in a strong Irish brogue.

"He sounds like a pirate," thought Jacob.

"I detect an Irish accent there, Shawn," Rebecca said while stepping into the car. "How is it that you are here in Brazil, if I may ask?"

Shawn started the car and began to drive down the busy street.

"I be here only fer a short while fer work, ma'am," he said. "Would you be likin' to see the crown jewel of Rio then—the statue of Christ the Redeemer?"

"That is exactly where we wanted to go," Bina said, looking over to her mother and Jacob with surprise.

The drive went very quickly for the eager travelers; when they arrived at the statue, Rebecca asked, "Would you like to join us on our tour of the statue?"

"It would be me pleasure, ma'am," Shawn said.

The four started the climb up the mountain's steps to gain a better look at the beautiful statue of Jesus Christ with his arms open wide.

"Where are we going to find more clues for the hidden Dalet piece?" Jacob quietly asked Bina. "Right now we know we are in the right country, and we know that eyes will show us the way, but we don't have much more than that to go on."

"Something will give us a heading. I just know it," she whispered confidently. "God has blessed us in getting us to Brazil, so I know he will guide us more."

Near the base of the statue of Jesus, the four signed themselves up for a guide to give them a tour and history of the sculpture.

"You are all on the Corcovado Mountain, and I welcome you to our Christ the Redeemer statue in beautiful Rio de Janeiro," the tour guide started. The guide began walking the tour group around the statue while speaking on facts of the statue. "A local engineer named Heitor da Silva Costa designed this statue, and it was sculpted by French sculptor Paul Landowski. Completed in 1931, the statue is almost forty meters in height and is thirty meters wide, measuring from one outstretched hand to the other."

At the end of the tour, Rebecca walked with Shawn out to the walkway that overlooked the city. Bina grabbed Jacob's hand and pulled him away from the group, as she obviously had something strong on her mind.

"Where have I heard the name—'Paul Landowski'—the sculptor of this statute?" she asked. "Let me see your satchel for a moment."

Bina started hastily looking through her notes and Jacob's dad's notes to find the name.

"Here it is," she said, pointing to the journal. "It says here that Paul Landowski was known to be a curator at the Vatican secret library in the early nineteen hundreds. Your father had printed a reminder to himself here of Paul Landowski's name and vocation and the words, 'the eyes will show direction,' but had no other notes written related to his name."

"OK, so we have the name Paul Landowski and the clue the eyes will show direction," Jacob said. "How are these two related?"

Both Bina and Jacob looked at each other as if they had both come to the same conclusion at the same moment. "The statue's eyes," they thought. Their heads turned, slowly, toward the statue of Jesus. They looked at the statue and how his eyes gazed out at the city and the small islands off in the near distance.

"It's difficult to say exactly where the statue is looking," said Jacob.

"Do you have your binoculars in your bag?" asked Bina while unzipping the backpack.

"Yeah, they're in there."

Bina grabbed the binoculars from the bag and started looking closely at the statue's eyes, which were nearly forty meters away.

"I can see something engraved on the eyes, but it is difficult to read," she said, struggling to see the tiny print. "I think that it reads something in French. Jacob—write this down... Île de mort.'"

"'Île de mort'—what does that mean?" asked Jacob, sighing. "Don't you speak like ten languages, Bina? Can't you translate it?"

"No—I speak four languages, and French is not one of them," Bina said, giggling.

Jacob and Bina went to Rebecca, asked for her pocket translator, and found that the French words meant "Island of Death."

Shawn saw the translation on the translator and asked, "Why do you two be lookin' fer the Island of Death?"

"Uhh..." Jacob searched for words. "We saw it written on a sign and wondered what it meant. What do you know of this island?"

"I be hearin' the Brazilian people talk of this island, but very few have ever made the journey out to it," Shawn said, pointing out to one of the many islands. "There be stories told about this island fer decades, and all natives be terrified of it."

"Stories? What kind of stories?" asked Rebecca.

"The native people believe there be a creature that be protectin' the island and will kill anyone that dares a settin' foot upon it. They call it the 'besta,' or beast."

"That is just silly superstition," Rebecca said. She began to laugh. "'Besta,' how silly."

Jacob recalled the information from the Hokmah and stories of beasts that helped protect holy artifacts, and he began to become nervous, but excited. He felt hair on his neck, which he never knew he had, standing taller and more concrete than the statue next to him.

The next morning Rebecca was to be performing lectures all day and did not want Jacob and Bina to travel alone around the city for fear of their safety. She gave Bina and Jacob strict instructions to not leave the hotel; then she turned to Bina and spoke the same words of instruction in Hebrew, as if Bina had not heard them the first time, as she exited the hotel room. Bina always knew her mother meant business when she gave instructions in Hebrew.

Jacob and Bina paused to think a moment while looking at each other.

"We are near a shipyard, you know," whispered Jacob. "We could get a ride out to the island."

"Why are you whispering?" whispered Bina in return. "My mother is gone."

"Err—I don't know."

They both began to laugh and look out their window at the ocean.

After gathering up some snacks and belongings into Jacob's backpack, they started their walk to the shipyard. Upon arrival, they found themselves getting turned down by every able-bodied sailor. All the sailors tried not to act scared of the island, so they made up some sad excuse as to the reason that they could not make the short journey out to the Island of Death.

When Jacob and Bina were about to lose all hope, they saw a small boat at the end of the shipyard with a man sitting inside. The boat was so small that they had missed it the entire morning.

"That looks like our last chance," Jacob said.

When they got to the boat, the man inside was facing the other way. He was wearing a long, black, hooded robe that made it difficult to see his face.

"I hear you be a lookin' fer a boat ride?" the stranger asked.

Jacob and Bina paused for a moment thinking about the man's accent. "Where have I heard that voice before?" they thought.

"Yes, sir, that's right," Jacob said.

"And you be a needin' this boat ride to take you to the Island of Death?" the stranger asked again. "And I suppose you are not goin' to be a-tellin' me the purpose of yer journey to said island—now are ya?"

"Yes, sir...that's correct. We're curious about the island," Jacob said, anticipating another negative response.

"Well then...climb aboard," the stranger instructed.

Jacob and Bina stepped aboard the boat, and the stranger turned to face them. The stranger was Shawn, their taxicab driver from the previous day. Jacob stumbled reaching his seat, and the medallion that was hung around his neck came out from underneath his shirt. Shawn saw the medallion and looked at Jacob curiously.

Shawn started up the boat and began the journey out to the island. As they grew closer to the island, the sun-filled day began to slowly get hazy. There was a disturbing fog and an increasing smell of decaying fish that infiltrated the salty sea air, and it became difficult to see the island.

Crack! The boat rubbed against a rock.

"We're almost there," Shawn said, while standing and struggling to see through the now-impenetrable fog.

The boat came to an abrupt stop as small pebbles from the beach rolled across its floor causing a horrific scratching sound.

"Well, if there really be a creature here, I be pretty sure he be knowin' that we've arrived," Shawn said with a grin.

The three stepped out of the boat and started slowly walking. The air had a chill to it that was increased by thoughts of the unknown. The fog was thick and difficult to see through, but they could make out that the island was desolate with close to no vegetation. "There are no animals visible, not even a bird flying overhead," thought Jacob.

"Can you tell me now what we be looking fer?" asked Shawn. "Because if we are goin' to be eaten by some hideous creature, at least I will be knowin' what I died fer." Shawn gave a contagious smile that helped to lighten the mood.

Jacob and Bina looked at each other.

"It's a lost artifact, "Jacob said, hesitantly. "It's something that my family has been in search of for centuries."

"Aye—and how will we be knowin' when we have found said artifact?"

"We will know. Definitely—we will know."

They continued to walk for close to an hour when on the side of the hill Bina spotted a hole in the earth. "*There—look there—there is a hole!*" she screeched.

With Bina leading the ascent, the three made their way up the steep mountainside. The shale rocks were very slippery on their climb up to the hole, but it was not too long before they reached the entrance to the cave.

The hole was so light deprived that nothing could be seen inside. It was no larger than four feet in diameter, so to enter they would have to crawl. Jacob pulled a flashlight from his backpack and shone it into the dark hole.

"Who's going first?" he asked.

The three looked at each other in hopes that someone would come forth to accept the responsibility.

"Oh, all right—give me the flashlight then," Shawn said, rolling his eyes. "I'm sure there be nothin' to be scared of."

Shawn led the way into the dark cavern with Jacob and Bina crawling closely behind.

"What is that ghastly stench?" Bina asked, covering her nose with her shirt. "It smells like rotten fish and sewage."

The three came upon a trench in the ground that was impassible on either side. Shawn stepped into the hole first and then helped Jacob and Bina enter. The trench was just deep enough for the three to walk instead of crawl.

Jacob tripped while walking, and his hands fell into what felt like honey in between his fingers.

"Yuck—disgusting," he said. "What is this stuff?"

Shawn pointed the flashlight to the ground and inspected the sticky goo.

"I don't know what it be," he said. "It sort of be a cross between paste and fish guts."

Bina picked up something from the ground that her foot had run across and brought it into the light to view. It looked like a shiny fish scale, but it was larger than Bina's hands.

"Hmm—that looks like a scale, but I don't know of any animal that would have one that big," Jacob said.

"Shh!" whispered Shawn. "Der ya hear that?"

Jacob and Bina held their breath to listen, trying not to look frightened.

"It sounds like running water," Shawn said while pointing down the cavern.

With Shawn leading the way again, the three climbed out of the crevice and continued toward the water's sound. They came to a sharp corner of the cave's wall and cautiously poked their heads around to see a beautiful waterfall. It seemed to flow directly from solid rock, and it spilled into a large pool of water that was as clear as glass. There was a small opening in the rock toward the ceiling that let in a small amount of light.

"Bina, Shawn, look down in the water," Jacob said. "I see something."

Jacob began to take off his shirt and shoes but then remembered that Bina was there.

"Uhh—will you look that way?" he said to Bina bashfully.

Making sure to leave his underwear on, Jacob removed the rest of his clothes. With a deep breath inward, he jumped into the water to retrieve the unknown object. When he resurfaced he could see that the object was a small chest. Jacob set the chest on the side of the pool and pulled himself from the water.

The chest was no larger than one foot in length, and it was sculpted from some kind of lightweight, colorful stone. "The stone statue of Jesus that pointed the way to the island was carved by the sculptor Paul Landowski," Jacob thought.

Jacob put his clothes back on and brought the chest to Bina and Shawn.

"Can you open it?" asked Bina.

Jacob lifted the lid of the chest with all of his strength. "No—there seems to be a triangular key hole here on its front that will open it," he said.

Just then, the three looked at each other and said in unison, "Eww—what's that smell?"

Shawn looked up to the cave's ceiling and saw a creature that was silently watching the three while hanging upside down. It had four legs and a long, thick tail that had tiny fins running along its length. Its claws were long and so strong that they penetrated the rock that it was hanging from. The beast had large scales running down its side and looked as if it would be as comfortable on land as it would be in the water.

Without a sound Shawn pointed a finger toward the creature to gain Jacob and Bina's attention. Jacob and Bina looked at the creature and were frozen in shock.

"The—the—the besta…" Bina gasped.

Shawn pulled on Jacob's and Bina's shoulder and started walking them backward. As the three slowly backed out of the cavern, the creature jumped to the ground to follow. From the besta's hiss and grinding of its teeth, it was obviously disturbed by the presence of the three trespassers.

The besta leaped at Bina and cut her leg with its razor-sharp claws. Bina screamed in pain and kicked at the beast with all of her strength. The besta lost its balance and fell down a nearby deep crevice as the three scurried out of the cave.

When they got out of the cave, they could hear the scratching of the besta's claws against the rock as it climbed the steep wall and knew that it would only be a few more moments and the beast would be free.

Shawn looked up above the entrance to the cave and saw a large boulder.

"Bina, Jacob and I be goin' up to that boulder," Shawn said while pointing to the rock. "I need ya to stay here in clear sight of the besta so when he be gettin' near the cave's openin', he will see ya and want to run after ya. When you see' em through the entrance, run away, givin' us a signal it be about to leave the cave. Can you do that?"

"Uhh, yeah, I guess," she said, hesitantly.

Shawn and Jacob ran to the boulder at the top of the hill.

"When Bina be startin' to run, the besta should just be exiting the cave," Shawn explained to Jacob. "At this point we will push this here boulder with all of our might toward the creature."

Bina could hear the hissing besta as it pulled itself from the crevice and ran toward the cave's entrance. She gained sight of the fast-moving creature and started to run down the hill as fast as she could.

Shawn and Jacob saw Bina start to run and pushed the boulder as hard as they could toward the cave opening below. The rock fell just as the besta exited the cave and landed directly on its neck, killing it instantly.

Bina turned around to see the dead beast and walked toward it slowly. Jacob and Shawn walked down from the steep hill, trying to catch their breath from the strenuous ordeal.

Shawn poked at the creature with his foot to confirm its death, and then turned to Bina. "Let me see that leg of yers, Bina," he said. He ripped a piece of his shirt and began tying it around Bina's leg wound.

Jacob knelt down by the besta's mouth and saw its large teeth. Its rear teeth were triangular in shape, and one was missing from its left side.

"The shape of this creature's teeth is triangular, just like the key opening to the stone box I discovered," Jacob thought. "There is one missing tooth from the creature. I bet this tooth was used by Paul Landowski to sculpt the key lock to the stone chest."

Jacob picked up a nearby rock and threw the rock at the beast's mouth, dislodging a tooth from its jaw.

Bina looked over at him and said, "I'm pretty sure it's already dead, Jacob."

Jacob lifted up the dislodged tooth and held it up for Bina and Shawn to see. "This is what I was after," he replied.

Jacob placed the tooth inside the keyhole of the stone box and turned it. The lid popped open so fast that it startled Jacob. He looked inside and pulled the L-shaped corner piece from the box. "I've got it! We've found the second piece to the door!"

Upon closer view, Jacob noticed the piece had a set of eyes on the corner that seemed to follow him with any given directional view. He could feel that the piece wanted to almost float out of his hand, so he let it go in midair, and it floated. The three looked at the floating artifact in bewilderment.

Jacob placed the corner piece inside his backpack, and they began walking toward their boat. The sun was starting to break through the fog, and as they neared their destination they could see what looked like a man sitting in their boat.

"Wait here fer me," said Shawn.

Shawn approached the boat while Jacob and Bina waited a safe distance away.

"Thanks for doing all the work for me," the stranger said to Shawn in a Russian accent. "I would've never found this island and defeated that creature all by my lonesome."

The stranger stood up and stepped out of the boat toward Shawn and removed his hood from his head, so as to be seen more clearly.

The man was wearing a long, dark, hooded robe that was very similar to Shawn's. He had very pale skin and teeth that were more black than white.

"Vladimir—I thought it be you," Shawn said. "It has been many years, me brother."

"*You are no brother of mine!*" Vladmir shouted. "I have been waiting for this day for a long, long time. My prince will surely lift my name up high for all to see and hear."

Vladimir began to move ever closer to Shawn until he was almost touching him face-to-face, saying, "Once we have all of the doorway pieces, every one of you filthy Verita will be done for. Yes—we know much more than you think, Shawn."

Vladimir looked over toward Jacob and asked, "Does the boy have the piece? Does he have a corner of the Dalet?

"This be not fer you to be a knowin'."

"*Says you, not me!*" Vladimir commanded. "I will give you the chance to get in your boat and float away, and no harm will come to you. Just leave the boy and girl with me, and leave now."

"This I will not do."

"*Have it your way then!*" Vladimir shouted. He pulled a sword from his long robe. The sword seemed to have just a handle one moment, and then a connected blade the next. It was as if the blade had magically appeared on the sword's handle. Vladimir cut through the air at Shawn's neck. Shawn ducked under the blade and quickly pulled his sword from his robe. In the same manner that Vladimir's sword had instantly appeared from the blade, Shawn's sword did the same. Shawn retaliated with a jab of his blade toward Vladimir's chest.

Vladimir swung his sword into Shawn's blade, blocking the deadly blow with a loud scrape of steel against steel.

Jacob and Bina looked onward in disbelief at the swordsmen's battle. Up until this point, they had no clue that Shawn was anyone but a taxicab driver trying to make some extra money. So to see him fighting as well as he was with a sword caught them by surprise. They stepped closer to the two fighting, trying to gain a better perspective.

Shawn and Vladimir were very skilled in their swordsmanship as they traded blows from their swords. They sliced through the air with such precision and accuracy that neither could find the other's weakness.

Vladimir pulled slightly away from Shawn, put his hand up, and made a fist. Suddenly, a nearby bush's thorns were hurled toward Shawn at a tremendous velocity. Shawn pulled his robe over his body and knelt down. The thorns penetrated his coat and pierced his protecting arms. He stood up and looked toward the water. Pieces of the water rose up from the ocean, formed spears, and shot violently toward Vladimir.

Vladimir raised his hand and forced a dust storm into the attacking water, encompassing the spears and making them fall to the ground. He lunged at Shawn, who could not see Vladimir through the dust storm, and struck him down with the blunt of his blade. Shawn was knocked unconscious from the blow and fell to the ground.

Vladimir looked over at Jacob and Bina and approached them in growing anger. Jacob and Bina began running, and Vladimir followed.

"Do not make this harder on yourselves," he yelled.

Vladimir raised his hand and made old, withered branches and roots lying nearby ensnare the two. Jacob and Bina struggled to release themselves but could not move.

"What is your name, boy?" Vladimir asked assertively.

"J-J-Jacob Jerlow," Jacob said, shaking in fear.

"Ah yes—Jerlow," Vladmir said. "I had a run-in with your father recently. He was quite uncooperative in Australia. After escaping me with the help of filthy do-gooder Veritas, he boarded a plane and I had no choice but to bring the plane down. It was very disturbing that I could not get to the plane crash to retrieve your father's satchel before the Veritas."

Jacob became furious and struggled to rid himself of the entrapment. *"You killed my dad!"* he cried. *"I'm going to kill you!"*

Vladimir laughed. "Such anger—you would make a good Tenebra. It's a pity that I must kill you."

Just then, an awakened Shawn tackled Vladimir from behind. The two wrestled on the ground, fighting for their lives.

Vladimir's teeth protruded from his violent mouth as he lunged toward Shawn's neck to take a bite. Shawn shoved his hand into Vladimir's neck and pushed with all of his might to keep him from biting him. Vladimir threw Shawn into the air and reached for his fallen sword. Shawn pulled his sword from his coat and in one unfailing cut beheaded Vladimir.

Shawn moved his hand through the air, and the entrapment fell from Jacob and Bina, releasing them both. He stabbed his sword into the ground near Vladimir's body, made the sign of the cross, and knelt down. Shawn had tears running down his cheek as he began to pray. "Lord, forgive me for what I have done, and forgive me brother Vladimir for his iniquities."

"You pray for the man who just tried to kill you and us?" Jacob said in anger.

Shawn stood and pulled his sword from the ground. "You be speakin' in anger," he said softly. "It be sad that someone can be filled with such anger and hatred. To take another person's life is nothin' to rejoice about."

Jacob looked at the handle of Vladimir's sword and saw an emblem with two snakes twisting, making a figure-8 infinity sign. "That's the same emblem that I saw on Mr. Matthew's book in his desk," he thought.

Bina noticed large teeth protruding from Vladimir's mouth and called Jacob over to see. As they both stared at the sharp teeth, a cold cloud of orange and red mist advanced from the ocean and came over Vladimir's body and head. In an instant his flesh became ash.

"What was he?" they thought.

"I know what you be thinkin' right now," Shawn said as he began to walk toward the boat. "You be thinkin' about vampires and the worst horror films imaginable—right?"

"Uhh—yeah," Bina said sarcastically, following close behind. "That's about right."

The three entered the boat and started their journey back to the mainland with Shawn ready to explain. "What has yer father taught you thus far?" Shawn asked Jacob.

"We know of a group called the Veritas that do good in the world," Jacob said. "And then there are the bad guys—the Tenebras. Both of these groups are descendants of angels and humans. Uh—that's about it..."

"Huh," Shawn shrugged. "Well—we've a lot to cover then. It be true that there be descendants of angels and humans. It also be true that these descendants be part of a family—either the Veritas or the Tenebras. However, what you have been taught about Tenebras, or vampires, through books and movies be havin' some truth, and some be just Hollywood. To start, the Tenebras are not burned up in the presence of light. Well—not literally anyways. They prefer darkness because this be what their hearts are filled with."

"And you don't need to stab them in the heart?" asked Jacob.

"Nay—ya don't be needin' to stab them in the heart. Actually, the only way their spirit be leavin' their body is by a-beheadin' them. For centuries, people have been seein' some of the horrific things that Tenebras be capable of and have made myth and legend accordingly; in fact, starting thousands of years ago, many Tenebras and Veritas be looked upon as gods by unsuspectin' humans. These people saw some of the powers that we be possessin' in battle and the like, which made them be comin' to the conclusion that we be gods."

"Interesting...so you are saying that many myths of Greek gods and the sort came from people viewing Tenebras and Veritas in action— showing their powers," Bina said.

"Aye—rumors, legends, and myths become factual in some eyes throughout the years."

"So...no changing into bats?" Bina asked, smirking.

Shawn laughed. "Nay—no bats—but don't be gettin' me wrong, though, 'cause some Tenebras be havin' powers to change shape into animals. It's just not like the movies where they be changin' into bats so they can fly into yer bedroom at night.

"You see... Veritas and Tenebras came to be possessin' their powers through their angel ancestors. As we age, we come into more control of these powers, or we be learnin' how to use them if you will. Many of me brothers and sisters who have been livin' fer centuries have become very powerful. But beyond havin' powers, we be just as mortal as humans. We be gettin' sick, we break bones, and we die just like non-angelic folk."

"So vampires—I mean Tenebras—don't have supernatural speed and strength like in the movies?" Bina asked, still smirking and trying to lighten the mood.

"Nay, no lightning speed and super strength," replied Shawn. "But it does be makin' the movie more excitin' though, don't ya think?" He smiled.

"I saw Vladimir controlling the dirt and the bushes," Jacob said.

"Aye, Jacob," Shawn said. "He be havin' a great control of the earth and its elements."

"So when he was trying to bite your neck, was he trying to suck your blood?" Jacob asked.

"Aye!" Shawn exclaimed. "This legend be unfortunately true. They can eat food just like you and me, but the Tenebras gain power and strength from drinkin' another's blood. This be especially true if they be drinkin' the blood of a member of me Verita's family. Any power that the Veritas be havin' would then be passed from his or her blood to the Tenebras—makin' him or her that much stronger."

"And you and your family cannot drink another's blood?" asked Bina.

"I would not be sayin' 'cannot,'" Shawn replied. "I would be sayin' 'will not.' If we were to do such an evil act, it could destroy us."

"So how long do the Veritas and the Tenebras live?" asked Jacob. "How old are you?"

"Some be livin' very long lives. I've heard of some livin' fer more than two thousand years. I meself am quite young at 326 years. But not all angelic descendants be livin' this long, nor do they all gain power as they age. The Veritas call these people 'Deacons,' and the Tenebras be callin' them 'Slugas.'

"So—these Deacons and Slugas are descendants of angels as well, but they don't show any of the powers?" Jacob asked curiously.

"Aye, for some unknown reason, the powers be skippin' some angelic descendants. Sometimes families will be goin' hundreds of years with Deacons or Slugas bein' born, with no Veritas or Tenebras. In this, some families have forgotten their ancestry."

The boat came up to dock, and the three exited to the shore. A sailor, who seemed to be surprised at the three travelers' safe return, approached Shawn and asked for money and the boat's keys. Shawn, unknown to Jacob and Bina, had rented the boat to help bring them to the island.

"Thank you, Shawn," Jacob said. "Thank you for everything."

"It be me pleasure. Let us be gettin' you two to yer hotel so that we can get Bina's wound cleaned."

After returning to the hotel, Shawn knelt by Bina as he cleaned and bandaged her leg. With every turn of his head, as he worked, he could sense that Jacob was trying to look at his neck. Ever since seeing a portion of the tattoo or birthmark in the taxicab, Jacob was dying to get a better glimpse of it, but Shawn's shirt covered his neck just enough to make it difficult to make out.

"If you would be likin' to see it," Shawn said, "all ya gotta be doin' is ask."

Shawn stood up and pulled his collar down so that Jacob and Bina could see the marking on his neck. The birthmark was a heart with a blade cutting it in two.

"What does it mean?" asked Jacob.

"Dunno—I'm still waitin' fer me vision," Shawn said, getting back to bandaging Bina's leg.

"'Vision?'" Jacob asked, looking ever more curious.

"Aye. Somewhere in our fourteenth year, a birthmark appears someplace on our body. This be a sure telltale sign that we be a Verita or a Tenebra. And then someday, you'll be a havin' a vision, or dream, to explain it."

"So some don't know if they are angel descendants because their families have forgotten?" asked Jacob.

"Aye. Through the years some families have been Deacons or Slugas for so long, with no powers, they be forgettin' their way."

Jacob saw the handle of Shawn's sword resting on the inside of his robe and asked, "How does your sword have just a handle one second, and then the next it has a blade attached to it?"

"When a Verita or Tenebra be born, there be a secret place where mysterious creatures build the sword," said Shawn, pulling his sword handle out of his jacket to be seen. "No one be knowin' quite fer sure how these creatures be knowin' when a Verita or Tenebra be born, but the sword becomes attached with an angelic born—so the sword and the owner can speak to one another. They be like brothers or sisters, if you will.

"The owner of the sword can control his or her sword and make the blade appear or disappear. It be a makin' it a little easier to carry around in today's society when ya can make the blade disappear... 'cause people look at ya a little off if you be carryin' a sword. A couple hundred years ago, not too big of a deal—but today...to jail ya be goin'.'"

Shawn looked at his sword for a moment, and the blade appeared. The blade was flawless and sharper than a razor. Bina and Jacob both took turns holding the sword for a moment and admired how beautifully constructed it was, with some type of unknown hieroglyphics on its blade.

Shawn finished bandaging Bina's wound and left for the night. When leaving the hotel, he met Bina's mother entering while he was exiting.

"Oh hi—Shawn, right?" she said.

"Aye, ma'am," he replied. "Will you be needin' a ride to the airport tomorrow?

"Why yes."

"I will be here when ya need me," he said, walking away.

Bina did a great job of disguising her wound and anything else that had transpired that day when Rebecca returned to the hotel room.

"Did you guys have a good day?" Rebecca asked. "What did you do all day?"

"Umm, we just hung out," replied Bina, smiling while looking over at Jacob.

The next morning Rebecca, Jacob, and Bina finalized packing their belongings and left the hotel for the airport, with Shawn driving.

"Will we see you again, Shawn?" Jacob asked quietly, away from Rebecca.

"God willing, you will be seein' me tomorrow," Shawn replied. "I'll be on the first flight to America tomorrow mornin'. Not without some regret, I suppose—fer I hate a-flyin'."

"Really?" Jacob said in disbelief.

"Aye, Jacob. You'll be a needin' to keep yourself and your artifact safe until I see ya."

Jacob gave Shawn a hug, to the surprise of Rebecca, and said good-bye. The three boarded the plane and flew home to North Dakota with no surprises—to the delight of Jacob and Bina.

CHAPTER 6

EVIL IN HICKSON

The next day, after a well-deserved night of sleep, Jacob enjoyed telling his mom about many of the things that he'd learned and experienced on his trip. Well, most of the trip anyway. He showed a great deal of enthusiasm in his description and made very sure to tell his mom how much he missed her and loved her, because he knew very well that he had two more journeys to take. He was going to need to be "most deserving" in his mom's eyes to gain permission to travel.

Later in the day, Jacob went up to his room and found a note on his bed: *I'm over by the big oak tree*, it said. Jacob looked out his window and saw Shawn standing in the backyard. "How in the world did he get into my room to leave me this note?" thought Jacob.

Jacob waved to Shawn and ran down the stairs. "I'll be back in a few hours, Mom," he said, running out the door.

"Did ya miss me?" Shawn asked with a smile.

"Definitely. Now that the Tenebras know about me," Jacob said, "I've been a little freaked out."

"Don't you be a fretting one bit," Shawn replied. "With God on yer side, ain't no harm gonna be comin' to ya. Now, let me be seein' that medallion around yer neck."

Jacob pulled out his medallion from underneath his shirt and handed it over to Shawn.

"My dad gave this to me. Is there something wrong?"

"Nay, Jacob," Shawn said, looking even more closely at the carvings on the front of the medallion. "I was thinkin' this be the Oracle when I caught a glimpse of it in Rio."

"Oracle, what be that?" Jacob asked, shaking his head because of the contagious misused verb he had just said. "I mean—what is that?"

"Legend be told that in the beginnin'—when angels and humans be together—the Archangel Michael was in love with a fair maiden. So much in love he was that he couldn't bear to be away from her. So he made this Oracle medallion fer her so she could not be seen by others when they be gettin' together."

"You mean this Oracle can make a person disappear?" asked Jacob.

"Aye, Jacob," Shawn said, "that's what I be sayin'. What be lost is the words to be said. Ya gotta be sayin' the magic words to make it work."

"Well, how on earth are we going to find that out?" Jacob said, slipping the Oracle back over his neck.

"I'm not sure, but I do be knowin' that the words gotta come from yer heart—with love to be makin' it work. Now, Jacob, let's be gettin' that Dalet piece in hiding."

"I have just the place for it—come with me," Jacob said, leading Shawn toward the Sheyenne River. "My family has a secret hiding place for old treasures that no one else knows about. Let's stop by Bina's house and pick her up on the way."

Shawn and Jacob picked up Bina and started their walk to the Hokmah. Upon arrival, Jacob opened the door to the secret cave by Old Man Johnson's farm and began showing Shawn some of the secret treasures the Hokmah contained.

"My dad said to only show someone I really trust these artifacts and journals," Jacob said. "Since you have saved my life, I'm pretty sure that I can trust you."

"I remember bein' told about this Hokmah when I be just a little lad," Shawn said. "Some said it to be a legend; others be sayin' it is lost. I guess we be knowin' fer sure now."

Bina was so engaged in reading scrolls from the Hokmah that she had all but forgotten that Shawn and Jacob were there.

Jacob had wondered for some time now just how Shawn had known of his whereabouts in Rio. "Shawn, I was curious about how you knew who I was and what I was searching for in Brazil," he said.

"Well—long story bein' short," Shawn said, "me family of Veritas has been watchin' yer family fer many years. Can't go tellin' ya exactly why just yet, but I will soon. As fer the Dalet—we've known of this since the beginnin', but not where it be hidden. We be learnin' of yer family's quest fer the Dalet in Australia while watching yer fader—that's a whole other story in itself, but needless to go sayin', we in no way can go lettin' the Tenebras gain control of the Dalet. That would be disastrous for us and the world!"

"Then how did the Tenebras know of me? How did Vladimir find me?"

"That I not be sure of," Shawn replied, shaking his head. "But ya can be sure that I will be a-gettin' to the bottom of it. Tomorrow I be a-havin' a meetin' with me elder friend. I will be a discussin' t'is with them."

"If this Dalet is so powerful and dangerous in the wrong hands, then why didn't the angels just destroy it?" Jacob asked, beginning to look through scrolls with Bina.

"Ah—nobody be knowin' fer sure. Some say that they be wantin' to leave the Dalet on Earth so that it could be used at a later time by the Chosen One. Others be sayin' that once it was made, it was too powerful to be unmade. Maybe it be a combination of the two reasons."

"'Chosen One'?"

"Aye, Jacob—the 'Electus' or 'Chosen One' be a Verita that will help bring God's goodness back to Earth. To be helpin' rid the Earth of evil. Also, he be foretold to be born of an angelic mother and father. This bein' very rare because most angelic born be marryin' regular humans—well, non-angelic humans anyway. Now, what clues do you be a havin' for the next Dalet piece?"

"Jacob's father had notes in his journal that the Dalet pieces were hidden in 'the four corners of the Earth,'" Bina interrupted, continuing to search the Hokmah. "He specifically told of four locations that archaeology clues throughout the world had pointed to; they are Australia, Brazil, Alaska, and Italy."

"Aye—and be there any more clues yet as to the exact locations in Alaska and Italy?" Shawn asked.

"Nay, err—I mean, no," Bina said, blushing, "at least not that I could find yet. I have read Jacob's father's journal three times and have found no other clues as to where exactly the Dalet pieces may be hidden in Alaska and Italy. Currently, I have narrowed my search to just Alaska—for now—and I am reading through the Hokmah's scrolls to find some clues."

Shawn noticed an old sword on the wall as Bina finished talking. He took the sword down and looked to Jacob. "While Bina be a searchin', let's you and I go outside fer a bit, Jacob."

They exited the cavern, and Shawn handed the sword from the wall to Jacob with one hand and pulled his sword from his robe with his other. Shawn began teaching Jacob how to stand and hold a sword with proper balance.

"Let the sword be one with ya, Jacob. Don't ever be lettin' it leave yer hands—till you see fit."

After practicing swordsman skills for almost two hours, which seemed like just minutes to Jacob, Bina ran outside to Jacob and Shawn. "I've found something!" she yelled. "It says here that there was a letter found years ago that was written from a Prince Hakim to a Prince Amir in the Middle East that spoke of 'music leading to an open door.' Furthermore, one of the princes talked of a 'land that is covered in massive mountains, barren tundra, and large unknown animals.'"

"That sounds like a pretty good description of Alaska to me," Jacob said with anticipation.

"I know, right?" Bina said excitedly. "'Music leading to an open door' is not a huge clue, but at least it's a start. The only problem is how we are going to get there. I don't think that our mothers are going to just say it is OK to fly to Alaska for no reason.'"

"Yeah, I've been thinking about the same thing," Jacob mumbled. "I've been struggling with this for a while now, especially since we found out that one of the Dalet corners is in Alaska...but it looks as if we have no other choice. You see, my granddad lives in Alaska and we could visit him."

"I didn't know you had a grandfather still alive," Bina said. "You have never spoken of him."

"Yeah," Jacob said, looking disappointed, "our family has tried for years to be a part of my granddad's life, but he has secluded himself from us. He didn't even care enough to come to my dad's funeral."

"No offense, Jacob, but if your mother doesn't have any communications with your grandfather then why is she going to let you go see him?" Bina said.

"If I may be interruptin'," Shawn interjected, "if it be love that is a separatin' you, then it must be love that will bring you back together. You may be havin' two reasons fer visitin' Alaska, eh?"

"Right—you're right, Shawn," Jacob said, smiling.

Shawn walked Jacob and Bina home and reminded them that he would not be seeing them for a couple of days. "I will be havin' a meetin' with me elder," he said, dropping them off at their houses.

The next day Jacob went out of his way to show his mom how much he loved her...along with a little sucking up. He started the day with breakfast in bed, followed by laundry duty, mowing the lawn, and pulling weeds from the garden. By the end of the day Sarah could sense that something was weighing on Jacob's mind. "I really appreciate all of your hard work today, Jacob," she said. "So what's going on? Do you have something that you want to talk to me about?"

"Uhh—nu-uh," Jacob replied, trying not to look in his mom's eyes.

Jacob's mom took his hand and sat with him on the couch. "It's OK, Jacob. We're a team, you and me. You can tell me anything."

"Well—it's about Granddad. I've been thinking more and more about him since Dad's death, and I'm worried that I will never be able to meet him."

"Oh—that's what this is about." Jacob's mother sighed. "You know, we've been down this road before. Ever since he left your grandma and me when I was a teenager, I've struggled to understand why he left us. He was so happy and such a loving father; for him to leave us like he did baffles me to this day. I have tried to invite him to birthdays, Christmas, Thanksgiving...nothing has worked. He just won't return my calls."

"I know—I know," Jacob confirmed, "but what if *I* called? Maybe he will talk to me. Maybe he needs to be reminded that he has a daughter *and* a grandson."

"You know what? I'm going to have to agree with you," Sarah said, proudly looking at her maturing son. "Let me get his phone number for you right now."

Jacob's mom retrieved the dusty old address book from the bottom of her bedroom's nightstand, which was only pulled out maybe once a year for Christmas, and handed it to Jacob. "Here you are. His number is under 'Dad,'" she said softly.

Jacob's heart sank as he noticed his mom wiping a tear from her cheek as she walked slowly away. He felt sad until he remembered the words that Shawn had told him earlier about love being the thing that could bring them back together.

Jacob took a deep breath in and dialed the phone number. There was no answer from his granddad but an answering machine saying, "Hello, you have reached the house of Buck Jensen. If you are anyone but a stinking telemarketer, leave a message."

"Beep," went the machine.

"Hello, Granddad," Jacob said into the recorder, "it's me, Jacob. Are you there?...I have been thinking a lot about you lately, and I wanted to come visit you if possible." Jacob paused. "I love you."

Jacob hung up the phone and started walking up to his room when the phone rang. For a brief moment he was in shock and froze where he stood. "Could it be my granddad?" he thought.

Jacob slowly picked up the phone. "Hello," he said gently, "Jerlow residence."

There was a brief, awkward silence.

"Is this my grandson?" asked the voice, sharply.

"Granddad—is that you?" Jacob asked, becoming ever more nervous. "This—this is—Jacob."

"Yes, it is me," Jacob's granddad said assertively. "What's this I hear of you coming to visit me?"

"If that's OK—yes, I would love to come visit you. In fact, I have a friend from school who would like to come as well...if that's OK with you."

"Why—that would be great! Why don't you work out the details with your mother and call me back with the flight times."

Jacob and his granddad said their good-byes and hung up the phone.

"He seems to be very coarse, kinda like he holds no love," Jacob thought.

Jacob's mom had overheard the phone conversation from the other room and began crying once more. Jacob could hear his mom crying so he hugged her and gave her comfort. After discussing some of the fond childhood memories she had with her father, Sarah did not think twice about a second trip so soon into the summer and gave her blessings for Jacob to go on the trip to Alaska for two weeks.

"I will go on the Internet tonight and see about booking the flight for you and Bina for next week sometime," she said. "I will call Bina's mother and confirm that the trip will be OK with her. Your father had built up many free miles on his credit card so we will take care of the flights this time. Jacob, your father would be so proud of you."

The next day Jacob and Bina met and went for a walk to discuss their trip.

"So, it was OK with your mom to go on the trip to Alaska?" asked Jacob.

"Oh yes," she replied, "quite all right. For some strange reason, she trusts you. You see, I told you God would help us." Bina grabbed her notebook from her bag and started rustling through her notes.

"OK, so let's review…We know there is a Dalet corner in Alaska, and we have the clue of 'music leading to an open door.' Do you think this is enough to go on?"

"Like you have said in the past, 'something more will come to us,'" said Jacob.

Jacob noticed that his shoelace was untied and bent over to tie it. His medallion came out from underneath his shirt, and he remembered the words that Shawn had told him about love being the clue to making the medallion turn the owner invisible.

"I sure would like to figure out how this medallion works," he said, holding the medallion up for Bina to see.

"Yes, it is most intriguing," Bina said, pausing to think a moment. "Jacob, who is the one person we know who knows the most about history?" she asked, as if she already knew the answer.

"Mr. Wolfe!" Jacob exclaimed.

Jacob and Bina grabbed their bags and rushed toward Mr. Wolfe's house. Although Jacob had never been in Mr. Wolfe's house before, he was familiar with the address. Upon arriving at his house, Jacob knocked on the door.

"Come in," a voice said from within the house.

Jacob and Bina slowly entered the house. They could see no one.

"Hello," said Jacob, looking down the hallway. "Mr. Wolfe, it's Jacob and Bina from school."

"Hi there, you two," Mr. Wolfe said, standing behind Jacob and Bina.

Jacob and Bina jumped, and Bina let out a high-pitched "screech" from being startled.

"Sorry to scare you like that," said Mr. Wolfe. "To what do I owe the pleasure of your company today?"

"Well, we came about an artifact that talks of everlasting love, and we were wondering if you knew of any stories about love that could help us?" asked Jacob, trying his best not to give too much away in his description.

"Hmm—this is quite vague what you are asking, but let me see if I have this correct; you have found an artifact that can be used or defined by love, correct?"

"Yes, sir," said Jacob and Bina in unison.

Mr. Wolfe began stroking his long gray goatee, as he always did when thinking hard, and slowly paced back and forth with the aid of his cane. "I will be back in just a moment," he said, opening a door in the hallway and walking down some stairs to his basement.

Jacob and Bina sat down on the couch in the living room and began looking at some of the magazines on the table.

"Jacob, do you know what Mr. Wolfe's first name is?" asked Bina, holding up several magazines.

"No, I don't think I've ever heard teachers or anyone call him by any other name but Mr. Wolfe. Why?"

"Oh, I was just curious what the letter L represented before his last name on these magazine addresses."

Jacob shrugged his shoulders as the hallway door opened.

"I think I have an idea," said Mr. Wolfe, trying to catch his breath from climbing the stairs. "I was just reviewing a book that I have stored in the basement that gives reference to an undying love that never ends. Specifically, I found reference in the early third century to Pope Saint Marcellinus talking of a 'love that conquers all.' He had written once that he had a dream of an unknown artifact that could be controlled by love. In Pope St. Marcellinus's words, *'amor vincit omnia,'* which is translated as 'the love that conquers all.'"

Bina grabbed Jacob's hand in excitement. Jacob tried to hide his blushing.

"Maybe that is exactly what we needed, Mr. Wolfe," said Bina. "Thank you very much for your time. We hope you have a great summer."

Jacob, who was still blushing, was still too embarrassed to talk. He could not muster the word "good-bye," so he felt obliged to just wave his hand in farewell to Mr. Wolfe.

"You two stop by anytime," said Mr. Wolfe, walking them to the front door.

Jacob and Bina walked to the Sheyenne River and hid themselves in the trees.

"Well, what are you waiting for?" said Bina. "Say the words."

"OK, here I go," said Jacob, holding the medallion in his hands. "*Amor vincit omnia.*"

Jacob closed both of his eyes.

"Can you see me?" he asked.

"Ah—yes, Jacob, I can still see you."

"Why didn't it work?" he asked, opening his eyes.

"Hmm—what were you thinking of when you said it?"

"I was thinking about disappearing, I suppose," Jacob grumbled.

"Well, that does not sound much like love to me," Bina described. "If you are going to say something about love, don't you think you should be thinking about love as well? Now—try it again. This time try thinking about something that is a great love to you and your heart."

Jacob closed his eyes and paused.

"*Amor vincit omnia,*" he said gently.

In a blink of an eye, Jacob disappeared from Bina's view.

"Jacob, you did it. You are invisible."

"No kidding...I can still see you and I can still see my hands. Are you pulling my leg?"

Bina scrambled through her bag and pulled out a small mirror. "Here—look in this mirror," she said, handing the mirror over to Jacob.

"Whoa—you're right! I can't see myself in the mirror," said Jacob, looking side to side in the mirror, trying to catch a glimpse of himself.

"Jacob, when you grabbed the mirror, it disappeared as well," said Bina in amazement.

Jacob looked over at Bina, who was still searching to find him, and reached out for her hand. When he grabbed her hand, Bina, unknowingly, disappeared and could now see Jacob.

"There you are," she said, looking down at her hand in Jacob's. "It seems to be that whenever you grab something in your hand, it disappears along with you."

They both became intrigued, staring into the mirror that gave no reflection of themselves. Then, Jacob looked over to Bina with a sudden idea. "Let's go visit someone while we are invisible," he said.

Jacob kept holding Bina's hand as he led her to an address that was unfamiliar to her.

"Whose house is this?" asked Bina quietly as they approached the window of the large home.

"It's the Matthews's house," Jacob whispered.

Even though it was a hot and humid night, with very little breeze, Bina had goose bumps popping up all over her body like on a fall frigid day. Jacob saw Felix Matthews walking through the living room. He could feel his heart rate begin to race. For a moment, Jacob became a little uneasy and almost felt like passing out from the flashback of frog's eyes staring at him from his drinking water.

Jacob waited until he could see no one near the front door, and then led Bina into the house as quietly as possible. The house was quite dark and seemed cold and uninhabited. It had a strange, overpowering odor in the air that smelled like rotting cheese.

"What are we doing here?" Bina whispered.

"I'm not sure." Jacob said quietly, trying to silence Bina. "I just had this feeling to come here."

Jacob led Bina down a hallway toward the sound of muffled voices.

"We have been waiting for centuries for this day!" shouted an unfamiliar lady's voice.

Jacob and Bina slowly and carefully peeked into the room the voices were coming from, as if someone could maybe see them, and saw four people standing in a circle around each other. Jacob only recognized one of the four people who stood in the circle. It was Felix's father, Mr. Matthews. All four adults were wearing long black robes with the same snake emblem printed on their hoods that Jacob had seen on Mr. Matthews's book and Vladimir's sword.

They inched a little closer through the doorway to see that the person in the middle was Felix Matthews.

"O glorious day!" said the unknown lady. "My nephew, Felix Matthews, has broken our family's curse."

"This woman is even scarier than Mr. Matthews," thought Jacob.

"Enough, Bamilda," snapped Mr. Matthews. "Let's get on with the ceremony."

"No little brother of mine will take such a tone with me," snarled Bamilda. The short, plump woman was slightly balding, and seemed to have a control over Mr. Matthews that Jacob somewhat enjoyed.

"Now—let's begin," said Bamilda, opening the book that Jacob had seen in Mr. Matthews's desk. "After generations of Slugas in our family, we at last have broken our curse with Felix Matthews, who will bring honor to our family name once again. Under the witness of myself, Bamilda Mathews; Felix's father, Jonas Matthews; and these two Tenebras Elders, Fu Chi and Mohammad Akbar, we begin our ritual..."

As the ceremony developed further, it became more and more apparent to Jacob and Bina that Felix Matthews was none other than a Tenebra. Bina pulled on Jacob's hand to tell him to leave. Just then, they were almost run over from behind by a large man, who smelled like sweaty socks, carrying a lamb. The man stood at the room's doorway, blocking the exit.

When the ceremony was nearing completion, Bamilda motioned for the large man to carry the lamb to Felix. "Now, Felix Matthews," she started, "take the purity and goodness from this white, untainted lamb and fulfill your destiny in strength and power."

The air in the house became cold—not cold like a North Dakota winter, but cold as if there was no happiness in the world. The few candles that were lit hanging on the walls began to flicker in and out as if they were starving for oxygen.

Felix aggressively grabbed the lamb and bit into its neck, sucking every drop of blood from its living body.

Bina couldn't bear another moment. She jerked Jacob's hand and rushed him out of the house. She was sobbing as they ran toward her home. When they neared the home, she let go of Jacob's hand and became visible once again, not even worrying if someone saw them or not.

"*Amor vincit omnia*," said Jacob, releasing the invisibility charm. "Are you OK?"

"I can't believe someone could be so cruel and heartless," she said, trying to stop herself from crying. "And—why—why of all places on God's Earth would Tenebras be in a small town in North Dakota? It doesn't make any sense. What could their family possibly want here?"

"You don't think they know of the Hokmah, do you?" asked Jacob nervously.

"I don't know," she replied, "but I guess we had better be even that much more careful."

The two friends said their good-byes for the evening and went home.

CHAPTER 7

A NEW BEGINNING

The next few days passed quickly with Jacob and Bina excitedly preparing for their trip to Alaska, each searching deeper and deeper into the Hokmah to find some hidden clue to the whereabouts of the hidden Dalet corner. Because of the scare that they'd received in the Matthews's house a few days earlier, they decided to use the medallion's powers to hide themselves when traveling to the secret Hokmah.

One night while walking home from Bina's house, Jacob was grabbed unexpectedly and pulled into thick brush.

"Shh—you are bein' followed," the stranger said, covering Jacob's mouth with his hand.

Jacob and the stranger looked through a crack in the bushes as a person in a long robe walked closely by.

"Sorry I had to startle ya like that, Jacob," the stranger apologized. He pulled his hood down and uncovered Jacob's mouth. Jacob turned to see that it was Shawn.

"Oh—it's you, Shawn," Jacob grumbled. "You almost scared me to death. I thought you were...eh—never mind. Who was following me?"

"Not sure. I was comin' to visit ya, and I had a bad feelin'. A feelin' like somethin' bad was goin' to happen to ya."

"Oh—fantastic," said Jacob sarcastically.

He walked with Shawn toward his home as he told him about the medallion and the Tenebras he'd discovered in the Matthews's house.

"Hmm—there be a great reason that this Matthews family be here, and we need to be findin' out why," said Shawn.

"I was thinking maybe they knew of the Hokmah and wanted it for themselves," said Jacob.

"Aye, could be. We will have to be findin' out fer sure though."

While sleeping that night, Jacob woke up to an extreme pain shooting throughout his back. The pain was so excruciating, it felt as if his skin was on fire. Jacob got out of bed, wiped the sweat from his brow, and stood in front of his mirror, trying to see what was on his back. Jacob's back looked a little red, but there seemed to be nothing that could be causing the pain. He jumped into the shower to cool the burn and returned to bed.

In the morning, after breakfast, Jacob walked to Bina's house to do some last-minute planning for their trip to Alaska. "Bina, something weird happened to me last night," he said.

"What do you mean?"

"I was awakened by an extreme burning pain throughout my back. It was extremely painful, kinda like someone was holding a lit match to my back. I don't know, maybe I have a rash," Jacob explained.

"Maybe you have picked up some poison ivy in our walks to the Hokmah. Lift your shirt up, and I will take a look at it for you," Bina said while walking to her bathroom to retrieve skin ointment.

Bina returned a minute later with some skin-care product and looked at Jacob's back.

"Jacob, I don't see any rash present, and your skin looks just fine. Although I did not know you had a birthmark."

"Birthmark?" replied Jacob. "I don't have a birthmark on my back."

"Well, of course you do, Jacob. Don't tell me you have never seen your own back before." Bina giggled. She grabbed two mirrors, one for Jacob to hold and the other for her to hold behind him. "You see? Right there." She pointed. "Kind of looks like a trumpet. That's funny...since you play the trumpet and all."

"Whoa! Bina, I never had that birthmark before last night!" Jacob exclaimed, looking at his back's reflection. "In fact, I looked at my back just last night when it was burning, and that mark was not there!"

"You don't think that you are a...well—you know—what Shawn told us about birthmarks and all," Bina said, looking for the correct words.

Jacob and Bina looked at each other, shook their heads no in agreement, and started laughing.

"That kind of thing would be impossible. Even if it were true, my parents would have told me that I was angelic born," said Jacob.

Later that day Jacob began walking home and stopped at the local store to grab a drink.

"Hey—Jacob," a familiar voice said from the other side of the candy wall.

Jacob stuck his head around the wall and saw Felix looking at him with a devilish stare. Felix's face had changed, looking more pale and lifeless.

"You having a good summer?" asked Felix without any real concern.

Jacob thought for a moment, "What could he be wanting?"

"Just great—and yours?" Jacob mumbled.

"Oh—this is the best summer I've ever had. In fact, it's the best summer my whole family has ever had."

"I'm very happy for you," Jacob said, trying to end the conversation.

Jacob quickly grabbed a drink, bought it, and exited the store. He could sense that he was being followed and kept looking over his shoulder as he walked toward his house. Jacob hurried behind an abandoned house to see if he could see anyone, but no one was present.

"Must just be nerves," he thought.

After dinner that night, Jacob found a note on his bathroom mirror that said, "Use your medallion and go to the Hokmah tonight." Upon approval from his mom, Jacob did as the note instructed and went to the Hokmah invisibly.

When Jacob reached the Hokmah, he could see Shawn standing by a tree near the cavern.

"*Amor vincit omnia,*" he said, making himself seen.

"Hey, Jacob," Shawn said. "I thought I heard yer footsteps."

"What's this all about? Is something the matter?" asked Jacob.

"Let us be goin' into the cave and talk a bit."

Jacob placed his hands on Abels Stones and opened the hidden door.

"Jacob, have you any news fer me?" Shawn asked, sitting down by the Hokmah chest.

"News? I don't think so. I told you all about the medallion and the Matthews family secret. Is there more?"

"Aye, Jacob," Shawn said, smiling. "There be glorious news."

Shawn stood up and walked to Jacob and said, "Let me be seein' yer back."

"Oh—the birthmark I never knew I had. That's what you want to see," asked Jacob, lifting his shirt to expose his back.

"*I knew it!*" Shawn shouted. "I felt a presence today in yer town, and I knew it be you, Jacob. You are angel born! You are a Verita!"

"That be impossible... I mean, that's impossible! I don't have angel-born parents! Err...they would have told me!"

"I could not be tellin' you before, when you asked me how I found you, until I was absolutely certain that you be a Verita, but now that I know...Me family and I have been watchin' yer family for centuries, Jacob. There be a vision more than eight hundred years ago by our elders that led me family to watch over yers."

"But...but why me? Why my family? What is so special about my family?

Shawn placed his hands upon Jacob's shoulders and looked him in the eyes. "Jacob, the elders who had the vision said that yer family will do great things for goodness in the world," he said softly.

"My family? 'Great things?' But we're not special. We're just—Jerlows." Jacob was still in a state of shock.

"Nay, Jacob, your family be destined fer great things. Yer family be settin' these great things in motion many, many years ago; yer father and now you be carryin' on righteous work. Ya be havin' much more potential than ya know. So...we have been watchin' yer family for years to help protect ya. Being guardian angels, if you'd like."

"Did my dad know?" asked Jacob. "Did my dad know he was angelic born?"

"Aye, Jacob. He knew he be a Deacon. I'm sure he was goin' to be a-tellin' ya soon."

"And my mother? Does she know that she's angelic born?"

"Nay, Jacob. She does not, but I will be lettin' yer granddad tell ya why."

"This is so overwhelming. It's almost difficult to believe."

"I understand," Shawn comforted Jacob. "This be much to take in...but there be more, me friend. Tonight while you sleep, you will be taken away in what be seemin' like a dream. Don't ya be frettin' one bit though. I'll be right there with ya, just as soon as I can."

"Taken away?"

"Aye, it be the way that Veritas come together—in yer sleep. Now, let's be gettin' ya home."

That night Jacob found it very difficult to fall asleep with fear of the unknown. He was so worried that his body shook terribly. With every violent tremor coming from Jacob's body, his bed would make an annoying screeching sound that Jacob thought was sure to keep the neighbors up all night.

After what seemed like most of the night, Jacob finally fell asleep. His eyes opened, and he found himself in a land that he had never seen, or dreamed about. There was a river that twisted through the hills making a loud sound of water battering against unmoving rocks, and trees as far as the eyes could see. The air was so fresh and clean that it smelled like freshly cut grass and blooming roses. The sky was a bright blue with no clouds in sight.

Standing before Jacob stood a white-as-snow castle that was carved into the mountainside. The stairs in the front of the massive structure, which led to the entrance, were made of some kind of semi-transparent stone.

As Jacob cautiously walked toward the stairs, he saw another boy, about his age, walking in his direction. The boy was taller than Jacob with a large nose and a slim build.

"Hey there—first time?" the boy asked in a German accent. "I could tell right away when I saw you in your pajamas. You learn to go to bed in regular clothes, because whatever you're wearing or holding in your hands will come with you here. My name is Frederick Albas. People call me Fred for short. What's yours?"

"Jacob—Jacob Jerlow," Jacob said, in somewhat of a shock. He stood at the base of the stairway in amazement at the beauty and majesty of the castle. For a moment he was at a loss for words.

"Great to meet ya," said Fred, walking up the stairs and looking back at Jacob. "Well—aren't you coming?"

Jacob walked up the stairs with Fred to the castle's entrance. At the entrance stood two guards; they had human bodies but their heads were those of lions. Their armor was heavy, and their spears were long and sharp as razors. From the bottom of the stairs, Jacob had thought they were statues, but as he came closer to the two creatures, he knew they were nothing but real.

"The guard on the left is Laborc, and the one on the right is Raman," Fred whispered, arriving almost to the door. "For thousands of years they have never let an intruder in these walls, and they're just proud enough to let you know it."

"State your name," both guards said together.

"Frederick Albas," said Fred.

"Jacob Jerlow," said Jacob.

"We do not have 'Jacob Jerlow' in our archives," said Laborc.

"It's my first day here," Jacob explained.

"I see—wait here then," Raman ordered.

Raman placed his hand on the door as Laborc stepped in front to block any entrance. The door had a large crest carved into it that was the emblem of the Veritas. The emblem was that of two doves in a pair that formed what looked like a drop of water. A beam of light seemed to emanate from Raman's hand as he touched the door. The door opened and Raman entered. Within a short while, he returned with a short, robust man.

"Señor Jacob Jerlow, I presume," the man said in a strong Hispanic accent. He grabbed Jacob's hand and shook it before Jacob could say a word. "Shawn told me to be expecting you. My name is Esteban Enrique Eastes, and I am your host and the caretaker of our castle, Heldago. Follow me please."

Esteban began giving Jacob a tour of the castle grounds. Jacob quickly noticed many creatures roaming around the castle that he never knew existed—not in his wildest dreams. The one that really caught his eyes, and he could do nothing but stare, was a six -legged horse with a head on its front and its rear— that made it difficult to figure out if it was walking backward or forward. "That is a horsorian," Esteban explained. "They are one of the oldest and wisest living creatures on the planet. You will come to know many creatures in Heldago that are unfamiliar to you now."

"Bzzzzz" went a tiny fairy flying past Jacob's head that hummed a little tune.

"Was that a fairy?" asked Jacob.

"Ah ya...be careful of them," replied Esteban. "Their sight is not the best in the west, or Heldago." He began laughing with a snort.

Three small men—not much above Jacob's knees—with long beards and large noses approached Jacob, saying in unison, "Welcome, Jacob Jerlow. If there is anything that we can help you with, say the word you must." The three small men shook Jacob's hand and disappeared as quickly as they had appeared.

"Who were those three, and how did they know my name?" asked Jacob.

"Those three were wilderness gnomes, and they come and go from Heldago as they please," explained Esteban. "They have been friends to Veritas for centuries, and they will always be welcome here. The goblins that live with the Tenebras have almost killed all of the gnomes in the world. There are only a few dozen remaining now. They are a powerful little people with magic and powers that most Veritas don't possess, but for some reason their magic has little effect on goblins. This makes them very susceptible to goblins and their insatiable appetite for them.

"As for your name, most everyone here knows of you and your quest for the Dalet. You are a bit of a celebrity, I would suppose. You have many people who are praying for your success to keep this powerful tool out of the hands of the Tenebras."

Esteban walked out to the edge of a hallway and looked toward the forest that surrounded the castle. He paused for a moment, as if he wanted to say something that was on his mind, but instead turned away. "Moving onward then," he said, acting as if to keep on schedule. "This castle was constructed by angels and angelic descendants at the beginning of Earth's time," Esteban instructed. "Its very foundation is protected by powers that are not of this world. Any worldly concerns or evil that may dwell in your mind easily fade away inside these walls.

"This location has taught and kept countless Veritas. Some you may know from your history books, and some probably are not familiar. But know this—Veritas have been saving the world, as humans know it, for thousands of years."

The large inner foyer was open with tall green grass that resembled a meadow. A light breeze made the grass sway in rhythm like the waves of the ocean. Jacob noticed there were young Veritas fighting and practicing with their wooden swords.

In front of the fighters stood an instructor giving reinforcement. "That's it—that's it—well done, soldier!" he barked. The instructor turned and noticed Jacob looking at the boys and girls he was training. He walked toward Jacob.

With his burn scar that ran across the entire left side of his body, he personified the look of a warrior who had seen many battles. His muscles in his arms and shoulders looked as though they were chiseled from stone through his tight-fitting shirt.

"And whom do you have today, Triple E?" the man asked, sternly looking into Jacob's eyes.

"Sarge, this is our newest family member, Jacob Jerlow," Triple E replied.

"Fan-tastic. I will be seeing you after your tour then, Jacob," said Sarge in anticipation. "We could use some fresh spirit on the training field."

"Thank you, sir," Jacob said hesitantly.

Triple E began walking up a nearby stairway. "Right this way then, Jacob—follow me."

"Sir, Sarge called you 'Triple E.' Is that your nickname?"

"Yes, maybe I should have told you that when I introduced myself—sorry about that. It's a little easier to remember than Esteban Enrique Eastes, eh?"

"Yes, sir," said Jacob.

Triple E continued to lead Jacob throughout the castle Heldago. It was full of classrooms, living quarters, a medical facility, a dining area, libraries, and much more. It seemed to Jacob to be a small town and a school more than just a castle. There were many teachers and staff who worked in the castle, but Triple E saw fit to not introduce them all at this time.

Triple E and Jacob stood at a balcony that overlooked much of Heldago's inner walls.

"We don't have enough time to see everything today, Jacob, but as the days and months progress you will learn where everything is and who all of your brothers and sisters are. Heldago is a training facility and living quarters for you for the rest of your life. You will be going through much training the next several years. Our Elder staff will help bring the best out of your abilities so that you may help the world with the gifts you have been given by God."

"Is Heldago a school?" Jacob asked.

"I guess you could say that, Jacob. We teach and train Veritas all that we have learned throughout the years to help them learn their way. There are four levels we place you in to better categorize your abilities. The first level is Bethal, which you are in now. The second level is Clevan, the third is Moldan, and the final level is Elder.

"In order to go to the next level, you will be tested by Heldago's Elders through a series of trials. At the end of your journey at Heldago, you will be an Elder and able to teach other young Veritas—such as you are now. It will be at this time that you can choose your life's calling. Much of this will become clearer through your training."

"I understand," Jacob recognized.

"Now follow me; there is one more person I wanted you to meet before you get started."

Triple E led Jacob through a series of corridors until they reached an inner sanctuary that resembled a church. He opened the large doors to the sanctuary and bowed to Jacob without making a sound—in reverence. The sanctuary was dimly lit with only a few candles lighting the way.

Jacob saw two men kneeling and talking by a cross as he slowly approached. He heard the word "Dalet" come from one of the men, so he approached as quietly as possible to hear what they were talking about. He stood behind a huge pillar to listen.

"Jacob be havin' two of the Dalet pieces hidden safely, Father Santiago, just as we discussed," said the one man, whom Jacob realized was Shawn.

Father Santiago had a small black mustache and large ears. "And the other two corners' whereabouts—have they been discovered as well?" he asked.

"The children have narrowed the search to Alaska and Italy," Shawn said.

"I think that it is wise for you to continue this journey with the children," Father Santiago instructed. "They need your guidance, experience, and protection."

"Aye, Father."

"As for how the Tenebras found you in Brazil, I haven't any inclination...but you can be certain that I will pray for your and the children's safety in your future endeavors," said Father Santiago.

Father Santiago and Shawn stood up and hugged.

"You keep me informed, my boy," Father Santiago instructed.

Shawn nodded in agreement as Father Santiago left the room.

"What ya think of Heldago?" Shawn asked, looking over toward Jacob.

"It's amazing! I can't believe I'm here —really," Jacob said, surprised that Shawn knew he was present. "I didn't mean to spy on you... err, I mean...How did you know I was here?"

"I can sense when people are near; it be a gift of sorts," Shawn said, walking toward the exit.

"Who was that man you were talking to?" Jacob asked, following Shawn.

"That be Father Santiago Rivera. He be the Elder priest for Heldago and a man that I be a lookin' up to fer many a years. Ya should be a meetin' him soon, I'd think..."

"Does he teach religion at Heldago?"

"Well—he used to...err, I mean we used to be havin' religion class at Heldago, but over the years religion class was slowly taken away," Shawn explained. "People, even angelic folk, be not as faithful as they once were."

"Hmm, you'd think that being descendants from angels, Veritas would be the most faithful and the strongest believers in God."

"You be exactly right, Jacob. You'd be thinkin' that, now wouldn't ya?" Shawn paused for a moment. There was an awkward silence, as if he wanted to say more. He turned his head and changed the subject, asking, "Ya meet Sarge yet?"

"Oh yeah—the drill instructor teaching sword skills?" Jacob answered.

"Scary beyond all comprehension, eh?"

"Yes, that about sums him up." Jacob laughed. "He taught you as well?"

"Aye, Jacob," Shawn confirmed. "Sarge be moldin' young Veritas into fightin' machines fer years before me. Ya nervous?"

"Does a pig love mud?" Jacob asked, trying to lighten the stressful situation.

"Ha-ha-ha—aye, a pig be lovin' mud. I guess that about sums it up. Ya know, one of me Elders once told me that 'you should trust what you can't see more than what you can see.' He be meanin' to trust your heart and spirit more than what your eyes and mind comprehend."

Shawn and Jacob further talked about Heldago and what was going to be expected of Jacob's training. Shawn led Jacob to a changing room so that Jacob could get out of his pajamas and into training clothes. "Here is your robe," said Shawn. Jacob felt a great pride as he held the hooded dark robe in his hands. It was just like Shawn's. Jacob felt like a real part of the Verita family now. Then, Shawn brought Jacob out to Sarge in the training field to begin his training.

"Ah, Jacob, it's good to have you back," said Sarge with a nod toward Shawn. "Grab a wooden sword over there and let's begin."

Jacob entered a group of four others who were training, including the boy he had met earlier, Fred Albas.

"OK—stances, everyone," Sarge directed. "You follow along, Jacob. Bethals, always remember, never forget—your sword is a part of your body. You lose it from your hands in battle, and you may have just lost your life. Let us begin our Camtra."

Sarge began slowly moving through motions with his sword as the others copied his every move. "Learn to feel the sword's energy flowing through your body. Make it one with your mind, body, and spirit." He moved so slowly that each movement seemed structured and planned.

"This is kind of like my mom's Tai Chi class at the fitness center," thought Jacob.

The movements were so slow that it was very difficult to control the heavy wooden sword, and Jacob could feel every muscle in his body screaming for rest. With every turn of his shoulders and flick of his wrist, his mind was ready to give up, but Jacob kept reassuring himself with Shawn's uplifting words.

After moving through the Camtra motions for nearly an hour, one of the boys threw his sword to the ground in frustration and said, "I have been doing this crud for almost two months. How in the heck is this slow-moving Camtra going to help us in battle? By the time I've lifted my sword, my head is going to be lying on the ground by my opponent," said the boy.

"Luke Cartwright, pick up your sword *immediately*—before I pick it up for you and place it in a most inappropriate place," Sarge commanded.

Luke, though very fatigued, realized what he had just done and picked up his sword in haste. Sarge slowly approached Luke until he was within inches from his face. Luke felt his very bones begin to shake inside his body.

"I apologize, Sarge," mumbled Luke. "I don't know what came over me."

"*Weakness!* Weakness in your body, weakness in your mind, weakness in your spirit must be released for you to learn how to properly master your sword," Sarge barked. "Camtra was developed more than four thousand years ago by the great swordsman, Conrad Feister. There has not been a better swordsman than he except, maybe our rabbi today.

"Camtra builds technique, strength, and confidence that cannot be matched. Now, everyone, form a circle around me."

The five students stood around Sarge in a circle while Sarge tied a piece of his robe around his head to cover his eyes.

"Now, let's see what you have learned thus far. The one who touches his sword to any part of my body wins a day off from activity and may lead me in any physical activity that their heart so desires. But once you have fallen off your feet, you're out of the game. Well, children, don't just stand there, *attack me!*"

All of the many days of grueling physical activity and training the students had endured thus far were finally coming to fruition. A day off and getting a little payback on Sarge was a huge motivator. The four students attacked with as much ferocity as they could muster, while Jacob stood looking on.

Sarge, even though blindfolded, seemed to see and feel each swinging sword that approached him. He used the motions of the Camtra as he gracefully blocked each sword that came in his direction. He moved his sword in what seemed like slow motions, but each block and defensive move was exact and precise.

The students stopped for a moment and looked at Sarge as they tried to catch their breath.

"Is that it?" asked Sarge, sarcastically. "All of our training thus far, and this is the best you can do? It looks like I'm going to have to step up your training another notch, eh? Make things a little tougher for you."

This made the students that more adamant about striking Sarge with their swords, and they attacked him with even more fierceness than the first attempt. Jacob continued to watch as his four peers battled. To this point Sarge had only been blocking the swords, but then something clicked. It was as if the surrounding air pressure and temperature increased. One by one, the four students tumbled off their feet as Sarge went on the offensive.

"Well, that's four," he said. "Where's the fifth student? Where is Jacob Jerlow?"

"I'm here," said Jacob.

"Why have you not attacked as I have instructed?"

"I didn't see fit to attack my teacher, sir," Jacob explained.

"And you would think it to be better to ignore your teacher's command?" said Sarge.

"No, sir."

"Then come forth. Let's see what you were born with," Sarge ordered.

Jacob firmly gripped his sword and slowly walked around Sarge, looking for the right vantage point to attack. Sarge stood motionless, listening and feeling Jacob's every move as the other students looked on.

"Feel the sword," said the now-familiar voice in Jacob's head. "Not with your hands, but with your heart and soul. Let the sword do the work; just follow its path."

Jacob closed his eyes for a moment and concentrated on the sword in his hands. He could feel the sword talking to him, almost telling him what to do. He opened his eyes and without thought began an offensive attack that was difficult for a blindfolded Sarge to handle. The other students could feel the pressure and tension in the air as the two battled against each other in swordsmanship.

Sarge had a smile on his face, as he could sense the strength and power coming from Jacob. Then, with one fell swoop of his sword, Sarge cut Jacob's legs from under him, sending him to his knees. Sarge took off his blindfold and looked at Jacob in wonderment. He was astonished by the boy's strength and technique—with no training whatsoever.

"Well done, Jacob," he said, grabbing Jacob's hand to help him to his feet. "Well done indeed. Everyone, that's enough for today. Why don't you four show Jacob Jerlow here how you get back home?"

Sarge began walking toward a corridor as the four others ran over to Jacob.

"That was amazing!" said the lone girl in the group. "I've been coming here for five months, and I've never seen anyone be able to last that long against Sarge—not even a Moldan. My name is Jezebel Flores, and I'm from Mexico. This is Jacques Leroux from Canada, but everyone calls him Jack. He speaks French and a little broken English, so many times it's difficult to communicate with him. And Luke Cartwright you have already seen in action. He's from New Jersey in the USA, of course. He and his big mouth like to do things their own way."

"Zip it, Jezebel!" ordered Luke.

Luke was a short boy whom some said had a "short man's complex," and he thought he was much more handsome than reality told.

"Oh, calm down," she replied. "And the last one here is Fred Albas, who is from Germany but now lives in Iowa. I believe you two met earlier today."

"It's nice to meet all of you," said Jacob.

"So—how did you do it?" asked Luke. "How did you survive for as long as you did with the old man?"

"I'm not really sure," Jacob said. "My body just kind of took over without me having to think about anything."

"Hmm—so you don't know, eh?" snickered Luke. "I guess it was just dumb luck."

Jezebel started walking back toward a doorway, saying, "Come on, boys. Let's go show Jacob here where the Peddle Room is."

The four teenagers led Jacob through a series of corridors that led to a room closed off by a tall wooden door, which smelled of freshly cut pine.

"You have to say the password in order to get in," directed Fred. "The Peddle Room is a very important link between Heldago and your destination. It's a means by which to lead you home."

Jezebel placed her hand on the door and said, "Amora."

The door made a series of loud unlocking sounds and opened on its own to reveal the secret room. Each station was dimly lit by a candle with a mat on which to sit on the floor.

"Each one of these positions is a link between the owner and his or her home," Jezebel said. "Triple E should have already made your station for you. That's his specialty, ya know—making stations for new Veritas and removing stations when one dies."

"Whoa—so each one of these stations belongs to a Veritas?" Jacob asked, walking through the beautifully adorned room. "How many Veritas are there in the world?"

"Should be 245—if my memory serves me correctly," Fred interrupted. "That's now including you, of course, and not including the—"

Jezebel quickly glared at Fred, stopping him from completing his sentence. There was an odd silence for a moment.

"Earlier Sarge said something about the greatest swordsman that has ever lived, and then mentioned a rabbi who may now be the best there is—who is this rabbi?" asked Jacob.

"Our rabbi is the leader of the Veritas," said Fred. "He lives in an unknown location and has secluded himself from Heldago for a very long time. Many Veritas have never met him. He does, however, once a year write on a scroll that gives his thoughts, advice, and prayers. This scroll is read aloud by a chosen Verita at our Christmas party here at the Heldago."

The four led Jacob over to his station and asked him to sit down on the floor. They directed him to close his eyes and concentrate on his home. Soon Jacob felt his body jump and his thoughts going black.

CHAPTER 8

MUSIC CALMS THE SAVAGE BEAST

Jacob opened his eyes to see that he had returned home and was lying in his bed. The sun was just coming up, and Jacob could hear his mom walking to his door. "Did you sleep well?" she asked, peeking her head through the doorway.

"Yes, Mom," said Jacob.

"Great—I have breakfast waiting for you on the table."

Jacob stepped out of bed and noticed that he was not wearing his pajamas but the training clothes that had been given to him by Shawn in Heldago. His arms and legs felt very sore from the physical activity and the blows that he sustained from Sarge.

"I really was there. My body was really at Heldago," Jacob thought.

Jacob changed his clothes and went down for breakfast.

"Are you all packed for your trip to Alaska in a few days?" asked Sarah.

"Not quite," he replied. "I still have some more things to pack up."

"OK—well. you better be getting that all done then. Do you want me to give you a hand?"

"No, that's OK, Mom. I can handle it."

Sarah looked at the large bruise on Jacob's forearm, saying, "Where on earth did you get a bruise like that?"

"Ahh—don't know, Mom," Jacob mumbled. "Must have fallen or something."

"Well, you need to be more careful, Jacob; that's a nasty-looking bruise."

After breakfast Jacob went over to Bina's house and told her all about his adventures in Heldago. Bina was very excited for Jacob and tried to imagine the beauty of the castle.

"Jacob, let's go to the Hokmah," Bina insisted. "There is something that I wanted to look at before we fly to Alaska in two days."

Jacob and Bina began walking toward the Hokmah. Jacob took the Oracle in one hand and Bina's in the other and said, "*Amor vincit omnia.*" They both disappeared from sight.

When safely inside the Hokmah's cave, Jacob asked, "So what's on your mind, Bina?"

"I remember seeing something on a parchment covered in musical notes that I needed to take another look at," answered Bina, looking through the Hokmah chest. "It may give us more insight into finding our next Dalet piece in Alaska."

After shuffling through a number of scrolls and documents, Bina lifted out a parchment that was reddish in color and smelled of cherries. It was rolled up tightly and held together by a ribbon that was adorned with many musical notes.

"Here it is," said Bina. "This is the one that I was after. I glanced at this parchment when we were here last time, but at that time nothing seemed very relevant. But yesterday something occurred to me..."

She opened the parchment and began to read silently.

"What language is that, Bina?" Jacob asked, looking at the unfamiliar writings.

"It is Hebrew," she snapped, trying to concentrate. "Here—here is what came to my mind yesterday; it says here that 'music is what calms the salvage beast that protects our paths.' This is written by the same Prince Hakim who wrote the scroll we found last time that talked about 'music leading to an open door' in Alaska.

"I believe that we are going to encounter some kind of beast that is protecting the Dalet corner, and it will need to be calmed by music."

"Makes sense," Jacob agreed.

Jacob and Bina invisibly walked back home.

"In two days, at eight a.m., we will pick you up so that we can go to the airport, Bina," Jacob instructed.

"OK, sounds great, Jacob. I can't wait for our next adventure! Moving here and meeting you was the best thing that we could have ever done!"

"I'm glad you're here too, Bina. I don't know what I would be doing right now if it weren't for you. I would probably be in a loony bin by now, with no direction," said Jacob.

Bina's happy face turned somewhat sour as her mood quickly changed. Jacob could tell that he had said something that bothered her. "I'm sorry, Bina," he apologized. "Did I say something wrong?"

"It is nothing. I will see you in two days. Be careful at Heldago, Jacob," she said, closing the door to her house.

"What did I say? What did I do? Bina was so happy and then all of the sudden sad," thought Jacob.

Jacob returned home, had dinner with his mom, and packed his bags for his trip to Alaska. Later that night while getting ready for bed, Jacob made sure not to wear his pajamas. He dressed himself in the training clothes that he had received from Shawn the prior night and lay down in his bed. He fell asleep much faster than the previous night, with not nearly as much anxiety infiltrating his every thought.

Soon, Jacob found himself standing in front of Heldago once again with Laborc and Raman, the castle's guards, staring directly at his every move. Jacob walked up the stone stairs until he reached the castle door. "Good day, Laborc and Raman. May I enter?" asked Jacob.

Laborc and Raman stared intently at Jacob with no regard to small talk.

"State your name," they demanded.

"All right then," Jacob mumbled. "Jacob Jerlow."

"You may proceed," said Laborc, placing his hand on the door to open it.

Jacob entered the door to see Jezebel Flores nearby. She was speaking to an older student Jacob had not yet met. Jezebel noticed Jacob and turned to greet him. "Hello, Jacob, it's good to see you again. This is Ramiro Vasquez, who is from Cuba," she said, introducing the young man she was talking to. "Ramiro is in the level of Clevan and is going to be tested soon for Moldan. He has the Verita's record for passing the level of Bethal in the shortest amount of time. He completed the level in only thirty-one days, which is extraordinary, especially when I have been here for five months and have not been able to pass Bethal. He was also fortunate to be selected as the reader of the rabbi's scroll last Christmas."

"It's nice to meet you, Ramiro," Jacob said with an outstretched hand.

Ramiro looked at Jacob's hand and then looked into his eyes. "I'm sure it is," he said pridefully. "I've heard many people talking about your battle with Sarge yesterday. Impressive, many are calling it."

"Just luck, I suppose," Jacob replied.

"You're probably right," Ramiro said, turning to Jezebel and looking ever more prideful and arrogant. "I will talk with you later, Jezebel."

Jacob tried to not become irritated, but something about Ramiro was not sitting well in his gut. Jezebel and Jacob heard the front castle door close; they looked back at the entrance to the castle and saw Jacques Leroux entering.

"Hola, Jack," yelled Jezebel.

"Bonjour, Jezebel," he said, jogging up to them.

"Hey, Jack—how's it going?" asked Jacob.

"Eh—Jacob Jerlow—how do you do?" Jack said in broken English.

"Well, we had better show Jacob here to Master Kang's room," said Jezebel, leading the way toward a new doorway.

"And what will we be learning from Master Kang?" asked Jacob, trying to catch up to Jezebel.

"He is our teacher of martial arts and body control," she explained. "You have three main Elder teachers to start with in the class of Bethal. They are Sarge, who teaches the sword; Master Kang, who teaches martial arts; and Don, who teaches power control."

Jacob laughed. "Did you just say our power teacher's name is 'Don'?" Jacob asked, still trying to control his laughter. "Oh no—watch out, here comes Don. That doesn't seem like a very powerful name, now does it?"

"I guess you're right, Jacob," Jezebel snickered. "But I'll let you be the judge of Don's power."

Jacob, Jezebel, and Jacques entered Master Kang's room and saw Fred and Luke already kneeling on the practice floor facing the front. The room resembled a dojo with a padded floor and mirrors decorating the walls. There was incense burning with a soothing and calming aroma. Master Kang had his eyes closed in meditation and was kneeling at the front of the classroom.

"Jacob Jerlow, I presume," he said, opening his eyes.

Master Kang stood up and approached Jacob and the others. When he got close to Jacob, he put his fist inside an open hand and bowed to say hello. Although not knowing what this represented, Jacob and the others did the same in greeting.

Master Kang was a Japanese man with long black hair that was twisted into a ponytail. His eyes and stare were so intense it felt as if he could look directly into your soul.

"Students, I think that it is proper that I teach you the meaning of the Kang greeting that was developed by my father many years ago," Master Kang started. "We use it in our greeting and before we spar with one another, so I feel it is prudent that you understand the meaning of that which you do. Please take a seat here."

The students sat with their legs crossed as Master Kang began teaching the day's lesson.

"The left open hand represents an open heart and is done so with the left arm, which leads to the heart. The left open hand also represents openness to freedom and goodwill. The closed right fist designates struggle and strife, which we will all undoubtedly bear in our lifetime. The two are brought together to denote personal freedom and human justice. We bow at this sign of peace—to show respect for our fellow humans."

"Master Kang, I thought the closed fist represented fighting," said Luke.

"Yes, Luke, most people believe this because of many myths and misinformation, but in truth the closed fist means more peace—through struggles—than fighting."

"You mean like daily struggles between good choices or bad choices?" asked Fred.

"In essence, yes," Master Kang answered. "The battles in your mind, heart, and spirit each day are a constant conflict between good and evil. Evil wants to take you down the path of self-pleasure, while good is pulling on you to take the straight and narrow path that leads to goodwill toward others. Good or evil can be addictive for many, but word of caution, my Bethal students: when evil thoughts and actions begin to control your life, you are more susceptible to the powers of evil.

"Maybe you have heard that evil begets more evil. When evil overpowers your thoughts and actions, you are more vulnerable to the Tenebras and their mind-control power."

"Mind-control power?" Jacob asked.

"Yes, Jacob. The Tenebras are very powerful at overtaking a person's thoughts and actions, especially when someone is living a life filled with ungodliness. You see, when God created humankind, he created a connection between himself and the people that needed to be kept intact to keep goodness and morality in the world. If someone turns from God and this connection is not met, then this void will undoubtedly be filled with a worldly evil. This evil could be drugs, alcohol, sexual impurity, gambling, laziness, or any other sin. But understand and always remember this—*forever trust in God's understanding and not the world's*, and in this, you will stay on the right path."

Master Kang paused for a moment to let the students think about what he had just taught, and then said, "So—a wise person once wrote, 'Do not be overcome by evil, but overcome evil with good.'"

Next, Master Kang led the students through a series of warm-ups and then began to teach them martial art skills for defense only. As with the sword, Jacob was a natural and showed great form and skill for his first day in training.

At the end of the class, all of the students showed Jacob the way to Don's class.

When Jacob entered the classroom and saw Don, he could not help but to giggle. Don was an obese man who looked kinder than any other person Jacob had ever met. "This Don—the one with the powerful name and powerful body—is to be the one to teach us powers? He looks like Santa Claus," thought Jacob.

Suddenly, Jacob felt himself begin to float up into the air. At the same time, most of the things that were sitting on the desks began to rise into the air and circle around Jacob in a clockwise direction.

"Ah yes—Jacob Jerlow," Don said, in his British accent, "it is nice to meet you. I would be the teacher with the scary name and impressive physique that you have been worried so much about."

Jacob's mouth fell open, as he did not know what to say.

"Yes—I can read minds, Jacob. And yours is not very impressive. I must say, we have our work cut out for us here, now don't we?" Don mumbled.

Jacob was still in shock and struggled to find the words. "I—I—I will do my best, Don."

Don slowly lowered Jacob into his seat and precisely placed each item back in its resting place on the desks. "Now then," he began, "today we are going to work on moving objects with our minds. I have placed a pencil on each of your desks, and it is our goal to have lifted the pencil up using our mind's power before we leave today. If we remember from last week's training, the word we use for moving objects is 'valoria.' When you concentrate with your mind and spirit, and say the word 'valoria,' you will be moving objects before you know it."

"Don, I know this is my first day, but why do you say a word, like 'valoria?'" Jacob asked. "I thought our powers just came from within."

"Good question, Jacob. Maybe there is hope for you yet my good boy. When you are developing your powers, it is much easier to start with words that help control what you are feeling and thinking. Later, after you have developed and matured more, the words will seem more like a stepping-stone that helped you to gain control of your power from within. In other words—no pun intended—once you have mastered your powers, you will not need to say the words that go along with the power. They will come naturally.

"Now—let's all try to move our pencil. Focus on the pencil, feel the pencil's energy, and then say, 'Valoria.'"

Don walked around the room instructing each student as they tried moving the pencil. Don approached Luke and began helping him with his practice, and Jacob noticed that Luke became rather scared and could not even look Don in the face.

"Valoria," Luke said, looking ever more frustrated at the motionless pencil.

"It's OK, Luke," Don comforted. "You need to clear your mind of those other things that are melting your thoughts down, and then come back through the process again."

Don came up to Jacob saying, "Mr. Jacob Jerlow, I see no movement of your pencil. What seems to be the problem?"

"Well, I'm concentrating on the pencil, just like you said, and nothing is happening."

"OK then—let me see you give it a go."

Jacob looked at the pencil, intensely concentrating, and said, "Valoria." The pencil did not move. By this time the other students were getting quite frustrated with their drill and decided to eavesdrop on Jacob and Don.

"No, no, Jacob, you are concentrating on the pencil...but you need to feel the pencil—not just think about it," Don instructed. "Now try once more, and this time feel the pencil's energy and communicate with it."

Jacob looked at the pencil. Out of the corner of his eye he glanced at his watching classmates. He then brought his focus back to the pencil. This time when he looked upon the pencil, he felt the pencil as if it were in his hand. He could feel the texture, the weight, and even smell the wood emanating from the pencil's core, as if it were just newly sharpened. "Valoria," he said.

The pencil began at first to wiggle slowly back and forth, and then suddenly it jumped into an upright position. All of the class stared at Jacob's accomplishment.

Then Jacob felt a great anger coming from within. It was an anger that had obviously been suppressed over his dad being murdered by the Tenebras. He could feel the resentment being transferred from him to the pencil. Suddenly, the pencil shattered into a hundred pieces, scattering clear across the room—some of which hit Fred and Luke in the face.

Don looked bewildered at Jacob and said, "Come with me, Jacob. I would like to talk in private with you."

Don led a stunned Jacob over to a corner of the room where the others could not hear. He placed his hands on Jacob's shoulders and looked him in the eyes. "Jacob, are you OK?" he asked.

Jacob nodded his head yes, still looking a bit shaken.

"What you did back there showed you have a great deal of power harnessed inside of you, but more importantly, you have a great deal of fear and anger bottled inside your heart and spirit that is struggling to be released. I know this because of the energy I felt coming from you when the pencil exploded. It was not positive or good but negative—evil—energy. It is this type of energy that you must never use, and avoid at all cost.

"This force can only lead you to a path of more evil and hatred. Instead, you must use the power that dwells inside of you that is good and of clean spirit. In this way, only positive thoughts and actions may come forth. Do you understand?"

"Yes, sir," Jacob said, beginning to regain his composure.

Don instructed all of the students to return to their seats as he continued on with the daily lesson. By the end of the class time, all of the students except Luke had gotten their pencils to move.

When leaving the classroom, Jacob was curious about the tension he'd witnessed between Luke and Don, asking, "Luke, what happened between you and Don?"

"Nothing—nothing at all!" Luke snapped. "That old fat man just bugs me." Luke, realizing what he just said, suddenly looked over his shoulder toward Don's classroom. "I hope he did not just hear that," he thought.

Jezebel walked to the side of Jacob and whispered, "Luke was thinking some pretty rude thoughts about Don and his weight problem when he first met him, and Don saw fit to send a power to Luke that made him do somersaults around the room the entire class time. Luke started throwing up about five minutes into class, and by the end of class he was drenched in his own vomit."

"Eww—no wonder he's freaked out by Don," Jacob said, glancing over at Luke, who was still looking fearfully back at Don's room.

The five students made their way out to the open meadow where Sarge was waiting patiently. "Good day, Bethals!" he exclaimed.

"Good day, Sarge," they answered.

"Everyone grab your sword and let's begin our Camtra."

With the direction of Sarge, the students began their two-hour stent of Camtra. By the end of the session, the students could not lift their arms because of fatigue.

"I don't know what's worse: getting beat up by the old man, like last time, or going through two hours of Camtra," said Luke as the students made their way back to the castle walls.

"Oh, no, no, Luke—I take the Camtra," replied Jack in broken English. "I'm still recovering from pain that Sarge gave us last time."

"Hey, guys, do any of you know when we will get a real sword?" asked Jacob.

"I do—Sarge explained it to me a while ago," said Fred. "Our swords are made by mysterious creatures from a distant land. They somehow know when we become a Verita, and they construct a sword that belongs to us on this day. Some say they come from heaven. Others say they come from another world—no one knows for sure. 'The sword and you will become one' is what Sarge said. When your sword feels you are ready, it will appear to you. So no one knows the exact time that it will be given to them."

"I'm pretty excited about that day," Jacob said. "I want to see my sword and feel it in my hands."

"Yeah, well, don't get too excited about it because it's not happening anytime soon," sniped Luke. "It's very, very rare for a Bethal to receive his or her sword."

Jacob rolled his eyes as they came to the door of the Peddle Room.

"You say it this time, Jacob," Fred said.

"All right then—amora," he said, placing his hand upon the massive door.

The door opened, and the five went to their station to return home.

After waking in his home, Jacob could barely get out of bed, his body was so sore from the Camtra he had performed with Sarge and the martial art skills he had practiced with Master Kang. Jacob changed his clothes and went downstairs for breakfast.

"Sleep good last night?" asked Sarah.

"Yes—I slept great, Mom," Jacob replied as he gingerly took his seat at the table.

"Have you been working out? You look like you're really sore or something."

"Yes, Mom. I started working out two days ago."

"Well, that's great," said Sarah. "We've got to get some more meat on those bones." She squeezed his arms to feel his muscles.

"Ouch!" he yelled.

"Boy—you really are sore. Why don't you slow it down a little?"

"It's not that easy," Jacob said.

"Hmm—so, are you ready to go tomorrow morning?" Sarah asked.

"Yes, Mom, all packed."

"And Bina knows we'll be picking her up at eight a.m.?"

"Yes, I told her." Jacob paused. "I hope she's still not mad at me though."

"What do you mean?" Sarah asked. "Why on earth would she be mad at you?"

"We were talking yesterday, and one moment she seemed happy, and the next she seemed like she was upset," Jacob answered.

"Jacob, girls are tough to figure out sometimes. I know, being one and all—don't ya know." Sarah giggled. "Sometimes we can take something said in the wrong way. If I were you, I would just sit her down and talk to her about it. I'm sure it's not as big of a deal as you think it is."

"OK. Thanks, Mom," Jacob said.

Jacob hadn't planned on going to visit Bina, but since these thoughts were weighing heavily on his mind, he wanted to talk to her. When he got close to her house, he saw Bina and her mother stepping out of their house so he jumped behind a fence.

"I wonder where she is going," Jacob thought. He held his medallion and said, "*Amor vincit omnia*" to disappear. Jacob followed Bina and her mother to a clinic that Jacob had seen many times from the street but had never entered. He knew the clinic was a place that helped people with mental problems and personal issues, but not much more than this.

Bina and her mother led Jacob up to the fourth floor, where they entered a room that was dimly lit. The room was decorated with flowers and pictures of Bina, her mother, and a man Jacob had never seen before. Jacob looked toward the window of the room and saw the man from the picture seated in a wheelchair staring outside.

"How are you today, Father?" Bina said, kissing the man on the cheek. "I have brought you some fruit, your favorite—grapes and cherries."

Jacob realized the man was Bina's father. He had never thought twice about asking Bina who or where her father was.

Bina began to place some of the grapes and cherries in her father's mouth. He would eat the fruit, but he never ceased his stare out the window. After the fruit was eaten, Bina grabbed her Bible and began reading:

"Do not fret because of evil men or be envious of those who do wrong; for like the grass they will soon wither, like green plants they will soon die away. Trust in the LORD and do good; dwell in the land and enjoy safe pasture. Delight yourself in the LORD and he will give you the desires of your heart. Commit your way to the LORD; trust in him and he will do this: He will make your righteousness shine like the dawn, the justice of your cause like the noonday sun" (Psalm 37:1–5).

After talking to the man about some of their normal, day-to-day events that most would see as inconsequential, Bina and her mother gave him a kiss and said, "I love you. We will come and visit after the trip to Alaska," as they left the room.

Just then it occurred to Jacob why Bina had gotten upset yesterday. Jacob had said that he might have gone into the "loony bin" if Bina had not been there to help him. "That's why she got upset," Jacob thought. "Bina's father is in a mental health clinic, and when I said 'loony bin' it upset her."

Jacob continued to secretly follow Bina and her mother on their walk home, and with every step they took Jacob felt more and more ashamed by what he had said to Bina. "Talk about putting your foot in your mouth," he whispered to himself.

Jacob waited awhile upon returning to their home and made himself visible again before going up to Bina's door to knock.

"Oh—hello, Jacob," Bina's mother answered the door. "Come in. Are you ready for the big trip to Alaska tomorrow?"

"Yes, Rebecca," Jacob replied, slowly entering. "I'm very much looking forward to the trip. Is Bina around?"

"Yes, certainly. She's up in her room. Why don't you go and say hi? I'm sure she would be delighted to see you," Rebecca instructed.

Jacob walked up the stairs to Bina's room and saw Bina lying on her bed, looking at a picture of her father through the cracked door. Jacob knocked on the door.

"Just a minute," Bina said, wiping tears from her cheek and placing her father's picture under her pillow. "OK—come in."

"Hey, Bina," Jacob said, entering Bina's bedroom.

"Hello, Jacob," said Bina. "I thought I wasn't going to see you until tomorrow morning. What's up? Is there something wrong?"

"I wanted to stop by and apologize again for upsetting you yesterday."

"It's OK, Jacob," she replied. "It was nothing. I am fine."

"It's not OK," said Jacob, apologetically. "I said something that was hateful and just plain—not right. I know about your father, Bina. I am so sorry."

"Wait a minute—how do you kn—" she started. "Well, it doesn't matter how you know. I really appreciate your apology, Jacob. You are a great friend."

"Do you want to talk about it at all?" Jacob asked respectfully.

"Umm—well—my father was a caring and loving man. He was the best a father and husband could be until...a few years ago he just stopped talking and communicating for no apparent reason. All he does is stare outside like he is waiting for something. Doctors don't know what it is. At first, they thought that he had suffered a stroke, but all of his test results show no trauma or damage to him physically. So to this day it is a mystery."

Bina began to cry.

"I'm so sorry, Bina," Jacob said, giving her a hug. "If there's anything that I can do to help, please let me know."

"Thank you, Jacob." Bina began to regain her composure. "Now, give me the details on your second day at Heldago."

"I know that I currently have three instructors. The first is Sarge, who is teacher of the sword. He's about as scary as you can imagine! Next, there is my martial arts instructor, Master Kang. He's much easier to talk to, much mellower than the others, I would say. Thirdly, there's Don, my powers teacher. He looks like your typical overweight American, but I think he's British."

"Wait a minute," Bina interrupted. "Did you just say your powers teacher's name is 'Don'?" Bina giggled.

Jacob and Bina laughed.

"I know, I said the same thing when I first heard his name as well," Jacob said, trying to control his laughter. "Oh no—watch out—here comes...*Don*—right?"

Jacob stopped laughing suddenly, and a serious look came over his face. "Wait a minute," Jacob said. "Don can read minds. I hope he can't read my mind from this far away, or I'm in deep trouble."

"What do you mean?" asked Bina.

"Don can read minds, and today he read my mind and decided to make me float in the air with half the room encircling me to prove a point—that it's not nice to make fun of someone else's name or their appearance. In fact, one of the other students, Luke, did the same thing the first time that he met Don, and Don used his powers to make Luke do somersaults all class until he had thrown up all over himself."

"Eww, that's disgusting," Bina said. "Well, he better not do something like that to you, or I'll march right down there and give him a piece of my mind."

"Ha-ha-ha, thanks, Bina," Jacob said. He paused for a minute. "But one thing that did scare me today was a drill we were doing in Don's class. He was having us practice our object-moving skills—or 'valoria,' it's called—and something went dreadfully wrong."

"What happened?" Bina asked with concern.

"We were to move the pencil lying on the desk before us—which I did—but then the pencil shattered into a hundred pieces all over the room. Don said it was because I was using negative thoughts and energy during the Valoria power, and that is what caused everything to go bad—*very* bad."

"What did you think about that was so negative?" Bina asked.

"For some reason thoughts of my dad's murder came into my head, and this anger was pushed toward the pencil," explained Jacob.

"So you need to think of good times with your family and your dad whenever you use your powers, and stay away from evil, negative thoughts. Right? Here, look at the hairbrush on my desk. Think of good, happy thoughts of times you have had with your dad, and try to bring that brush through the air and into my hand," Bina instructed.

Jacob hesitated. "But—but—I'm a little scared that I might hurt someone."

"You are not going to hurt anyone, Jacob," Bina said reassuringly. "Just think positive, happy thoughts instead of negative, fearful ones."

Jacob nodded his head in agreement and focused on the brush. He began to feel the brush from within, just as he had felt the pencil earlier, and said, "Valoria." The brush began to gently fly through the air toward Bina, as Jacob thought of the last archaeology find he'd taken with his father. When the brush was halfway to Bina, a thought of anger about Vladimir's comments came into Jacob's thoughts, and suddenly the brush began to violently spin in circles.

"Happy thoughts, Jacob," Bina said, placing her hand on his shoulder.

Jacob regained focus on his happy times with his dad, and the brush began to slowly move back toward Bina's hand.

"See? I knew you could do it, Jacob," Bina said, grasping the brush, which had just landed in her open hand. "Stay away from the negative thoughts, and you will be just fine."

"Thanks, Bina," Jacob said. "I needed that confidence."

Jacob and Bina said their good-byes in anticipation of their journey to Alaska the following morning.

While walking home, Jacob came across his teacher, Mr. Wolfe, walking slowly along with his old, withered cane.

"Hello, Mr. Wolfe, how is your summer going?" asked Jacob.

"Just fine, Jacob. Did you and Bina find what you were looking for after you visited my house?" asked Mr. Wolfe.

"Yes, sir, thank you for your help with that."

"You are welcome, Jacob," answered Mr. Wolfe. "And now, what will you be doing with the rest of your summer?"

"Well, Bina and I are going to visit my granddad in Alaska tomorrow, and after that I hope to take a trip to Italy before school starts again," Jacob said.

"Wow! And I thought I had a busy summer watering and weeding my garden." Mr. Wolfe chuckled.

"Mr. Wolfe, can you give me some advice on something?" asked Jacob.

"Certainly. Anytime."

"If a person has evil thoughts, fear or anger held inside their heart, how can they get rid of it?" Jacob asked cautiously.

"The answer is simple and true every time, Jacob," explained Mr. Wolfe. "The person must forgive and let go. If a person holds on to anger and hatred, it will only manifest and multiply inside of them, and one day something dreadful will happen. I have unfortunately seen this far too many times in my life.

"This is why Jesus stressed to teach us to love one another and to forgive like we wish for our Father in heaven to forgive us whenever we make mistakes. He stressed this...and to 'not fear' things of this world, because of the evil that can come forth from a person's soul that has been darkened."

"But what if the deed that was done to the person was more evil and painful than can be imagined?" asked Jacob. "Are we still to forgive?"

"Yes, Jacob, we forgive no matter what," answered Mr. Wolfe. "If not, who then on earth is to judge what offense is forgivable and what is not? Do we forgive the liar and not the thief? Certainly not. Deciding when to forgive and when not to forgive would be like a mother having to choose to save the life of only one of her two children from a burning house. No matter what choice she makes, there will be pain and heartache at the end. So then, we need to forgive in all circumstances—as our Father in heaven forgives us."

"Thank you, Mr. Wolfe," Jacob said. "You have been a great teacher and someone I feel I can talk to when needed."

Mr. Wolfe smiled. Jacob and his teacher said good-bye as Jacob left for home.

After falling asleep that night, Jacob entered Heldago and did not see any of the other Bethals. From a distance he noticed a woman he had not seen before entering a hallway. Unlike the other Elders, who wore long dark hooded robes, she wore a long white dress, and her hair was beautifully braided and adorned with flowers.

Sparked by curiosity, Jacob decided to see who she was. He followed her to a room that resembled a concert hall. It was furnished with musical instruments and beautiful wood that gave off an aroma of freshly cut evergreen. Jacob walked around a large wooden pillar and lost sight of the woman. He started looking in each direction when suddenly he was startled by her from behind.

"Hello," she said.

"Oh, hi—how are you?" Jacob said, looking for words. "I'm sorry for following you; I was just curious, as I had not met you before."

"It is all right," she said. "My name is Shir. What is yours?"

"My name is Jacob Jerlow."

"Really?" asked Shir. "I have heard your name spoken in the halls and your great quest for the Dalet. I am the teacher of fine arts at Heldago." Shir looked even closer into Jacob's eyes. "You play the trumpet, I see," she said.

"That's right. How did you kn—" Jacob started. "Never mind, I should just be accepting that Heldago's Elders just know things."

A trumpet that was hung on a nearby wall came floating through the air and into Jacob's grasp.

"I will make you a deal," said Shir. "If you play me a song on this trumpet, then I will sing you a song."

"Very well, Shir, I would be happy to play. Here is 'Embraceable You' by George Gershwin."

Jacob started playing the song, as he normally did—wonderfully. When a few measures of the song had passed, Jacob could feel something inside of him giving him guidance to put more feeling and spirit into the piece. He stopped thinking about the notes he was playing and where his fingers were on the keys, and each note seemed to flow directly from his heart; his music sounded better than ever before.

When the song was finished, Jacob asked, "Did you help me perform that song?"

"Oh, no, Jacob," Shir answered. "I merely helped you find your connection. That was marvelous. Now, as promised I will sing you a song. Please take your seat. I hope you enjoy it."

Shir started singing a song that Jacob had never heard before. The notes seemed to speak to him and dance in his head. He felt as though he were in a trance and could not move a muscle. The song was so beautifully sung that it tugged at every emotion in his body. Although he had never cried while listening to music before, he felt a tear running down his cheek.

When the song was finished, Jacob said, "That was marvelous. I have never heard such beautiful music. Thank you for sharing this with me."

"You are most welcome, Jacob," said Shir. "Remember, music is a connection."

Jacob left the room and walked to Master Kang's room, where he saw his fellow Bethals waiting. Jacob and the others went through their training with Master Kang, Don, and Sarge with no one getting too badly hurt.

When walking to the Peddle Room, Jezebel approached Jacob. "I think I'm ready to be tested for the Clevan level. What do you think?"

"Absolutely. If any of us are ready, it would be you, Jezebel," said Jacob.

"Great! Thanks—I needed a voice of confidence. I'll ask our instructors tomorrow when they will be available to test me."

"Jacob," he heard a voice call from around a pillar.

Jacob walked around the pillar to see Shawn.

"Oh, hey, Shawn—what's up?"

"I wanted to be lettin' ya know that I will be in Alaska with you and Bina, but I'm gonna lay a little low so ya can be a-gettin' to know yer granddad," Shawn explained.

"OK, sounds good," said Jacob. "I'll see you up there then."

Jacob and the others went to their stations and returned home.

CHAPTER 9

A GRANDFATHER NEVER SEEN

When Jacob awoke he got dressed and carried his luggage out to the car. "Now you're sure you've packed enough clothes?" asked Sarah.

"Yes, Mom, I have plenty of clothes, my toothbrush, and my mobile phone—so that I can call you. Don't worry. We'll be fine," Jacob whined.

"OK, OK. It's only natural for a mother to be worried about her only son's well-being."

Jacob and his mom finished packing the car and went to pick up Bina. Bina and her mother were waiting by her mailbox at eight a.m. sharp, as punctuality meant a lot in their book. After saying their good-byes, Jacob and Bina were off to the airport.

"And our next adventure begins," whispered Bina into Jacob's ear.

"I know—I can't believe today is finally here," whispered Jacob in return.

Upon arrival at the airport, Jacob's mom gave him a big hug and with tear-filled eyes kissed him good-bye.

On the flight Bina could sense Jacob becoming more and more anxious. She asked, "Are you OK, Jacob? You seem a little worried about something."

"Yeah—I'm starting to get really nervous about meeting my granddad for the first time," Jacob explained. "I have so many questions flowing through my head right now; I don't know where to begin."

"Well, that would seem to be normal. My advice for you—don't worry about the questions and answers now. Just get to know him, and the answers will start to be filled in as you go."

"You're right, Bina," Jacob said. "I've got nothing to be worried about. Besides, I bet *he* is the one who is worried about meeting *me*."

Bina rolled her eyes as she went back to reading her magazine.

When Jacob and Bina landed in Anchorage, Alaska, they went to the luggage claim and saw an older man holding an old, weathered piece of cardboard that had the words "Jacob's ride" scribbled on it with what looked like melted chocolate. The man had a long, un-groomed gray mustache, and he looked as though he had just come out of a very long tenure from the back woods. His clothes were badly worn, and even though Jacob and Bina were still ten feet from him, they could smell a foul odor radiating from his direction. The proliferating aroma was confirmed by the people who walked closely by the man snapping their heads quickly toward him as if to say, "What the heck is that?"

Jacob and Bina grabbed their luggage and walked up to the man.

"Granddad, is that you?" asked Jacob.

"Ah—Jacob, my boy," he said. "And this lovely lady with you must be yer friend that you were tellin' me about."

The stench of burning alcohol that came from Jacob's grandfather's mouth with each spoken word made Bina almost lose consciousness. She leaned on Jacob slightly to keep her balance.

"I can feel my nose hairs curling," Jacob thought.

"Yes, Granddad, this is my good friend, Bina," Jacob said.

Bina took a deep breath with her head slightly turned away so as to not faint, saying, "It is nice to meet you, sir."

"Buck Jensen is the name, but since you're friends with my grandson here, you can go ahead and call me Granddad. Well, come along then—we have a long ride ahead of us."

Granddad led Jacob and Bina out of the airport, but with the stench that was drifting behind him, Jacob and Bina found themselves coming to the sides of him as often as possible to catch a breath of fresh, clean air.

"Granddad, you live in Trapper Creek, right?" asked Jacob.

"Yes, my boy—a town of about six hundred folk. Just the way I like it," Granddad grumbled.

"When I looked up your town on the Internet it said it was only about two hours away, but you just said that we have a long ride..." Jacob said, stopping in his tracks as he saw the truck that his granddad was climbing into. It looked to be older than Granddad. The tires were so bald that the rim could be seen through the rubber fibers, and there appeared to be nothing that was holding the truck's body together except rust. The windshield had spider-web cracks throughout, and the sheer fact that it was still in one piece seemed to defy gravity.

"Well—when you got a truck that goes thirty-five miles per hour, it takes a little longer than two hours," explained Granddad. "But I don't see why everyone is in such a hurry nowadays...thirty-five miles per hour is plenty fast. Jump on in, daylight's a-burning, and I think my batteries are almost dead for my flashlight-headlights."

"Flashlight-headlights?" Bina tried to imagine what this meant.

Jacob and Bina jumped into the truck and said a quick prayer for safety as they drove north. The smell of dusty old furniture permeated the truck's interior.

The next hour seemed to drag on for days while they both frantically looked for a safety belt to fasten. The old truck shook and convulsed every one hundred feet, making the ride all the more nerve-racking. Meanwhile Granddad drove just as fast as the old truck would allow—all the while singing Christmas songs.

"You sure like Christmas songs, Granddad," said Jacob, looking at his grandfather rather peculiarly. "Even in June, huh?"

"Yep," Granddad replied. "No sense in just singing those great ol' songs in December. Those are classics that should be shared all year long. Besides, I haven't had a radio in this here truck fer nearly thirty years."

Thump! The car jolted as it obviously ran over something.

"What in the world was that?" asked Bina.

"I think that was dinner." Granddad laughed, quickly stopping the truck. He stepped out of the truck and returned a few moments later with a rabbit, which had apparently been killed on impact from the truck's tire. "Yep—just what I expected," Granddad said excitedly.

"We're having rabbit soup for dinner tonight. You two must be good luck seeing how I haven't had yummy, free road kill such as this in months."

"We're glad we could help out," Jacob said, shrinking into his seat in embarrassment.

Granddad threw the rabbit over onto Jacob's lap, saying, "Here, bud, hold this until we get home. But don't you start digging into it early on us though, you hear?" He laughed, with a low rasp.

"Yes, Granddad," Jacob replied, staring down at the rabbit that was seemingly staring right back at him with open eyes.

Some fifteen minutes passed, and Jacob's eyes were nearly shut for a quick nap when he was startled by something pulling on his shirt. Jacob cracked open one of his closed eyes and saw the injured rabbit nibbling on his shirt. The rabbit sat up on its hind legs and stared Jacob down—eye to eye. Jacob shrieked! A startled Bina jumped out of her seat, almost banging her head on the roof.

Granddad, who was nearly asleep at the wheel, lunged toward Jacob to grab the furry little animal for fear that it would jump out the window—and dinner would be most certainly lost. He missed with a loud, "Dag nab it!" The truck started uncontrollably swerving left and right, but Granddad had only one worry, and it wasn't staying on the road. He grabbed a hammer from his dashboard and began swinging it at the rabbit, which was hopping around the cab for its life. Jacob and Bina were petrified in the commotion.

The rabbit jumped onto the dash, and Granddad quickly swung the hammer onto its head, killing it instantly. The rabbit began to convulse and fiercely kick. Jacob flung his head out the still-moving truck's window and began violently throwing up. To his disgust the vomit that was being hurled from his mouth was all the more disturbed by a turbulent wind, and the chunky stomach acid was being flung up alongside his cheek and ear, which made him even all the more ill.

"Tough little buggers. But not tougher than a hammer!" Granddad laughed.

After what seemed like hours, they finally made it to the small town of Trapper Creek. Granddad pulled into a dirt-road driveway that led to a log cabin seated a stone's throw away from a creek. When the truck came to a complete stop, they heard a loud scratching noise on the driver's side door. The truck shook from side to side.

"Wilbur, you get down, you big lug," Granddad yelled. "Yer gonna put scratches on my truck."

Jacob and Bina jumped out of the truck and looked around the corner to see what Bina thought was a small horse but soon realized was a *very large* dog.

"Is that thing going to eat us?" they thought.

"Don't worry, ol' Wilbur here won't hurt a fly, but he may lick ya to death." Granddad chuckled to himself in his own amusement. "Now—let me see our dinner."

Jacob gladly handed the rabbit over.

Granddad pulled a knife from his pocket and within seconds had pulled all of the guts from the rabbit and had thrown them to Wilbur, who was busy licking Jacob's vomit off of the side of the truck. With another quick cut of his knife and a strong pull, the skin was completely off the animal, and Granddad was holding up dinner with pride.

"Not very much to that thing," thought Jacob. "More bones than meat."

"Yep—this here is a real treat," Granddad said, still holding the rabbit up for Jacob and Bina to see. "It's not every day that we get rabbit soup around here. And the vegetables that I'll throw in the broth were grown right over there—in my backyard. In other words, it looks as if we're eating my favorite dinner today—free dinner."

Granddad started laughing in a growling, high-pitched squeal as he led Jacob and Bina into his house. It was increasingly obvious that he had learned to amuse himself throughout the years. He grabbed some vegetables from a nearby cabinet and began chopping them into pieces and throwing them into a pot on the stove.

The inside of Granddad's house was decorated with every North American animal's head imaginable; from raccoon to porcupine, he seemed to have them all, and they gave feelings of discomfort to Jacob and Bina as they seemingly stared at their every step into the living room.

"I don't think I am going to be able to sleep here very well," Bina whispered.

"Me neither," Jacob replied, shaking his head from side to side.

Jacob continued to look around the room and came across a necklace on an elk antler with a small locket hanging from it. Jacob opened the locket and saw what looked like a younger Granddad and his mom as a young girl. They both had huge smiles on their faces, as Jacob's mom was holding up a large fish.

Jacob walked back into the kitchen and asked, "Granddad, do you want to do some fishing tomorrow?"

"Do I?" replied Granddad. "I fish almost every day. Yes, my boy, fish they be fearin' me. Maybe I can show you a thing or three."

When the soup was done Jacob and Bina, to be polite, took a big helping. They looked at each other in fear as they took their first bite. To their shock, they both enjoyed the flavor.

"This is really good soup," Bina said, surprised. "This is my first time eating rabbit soup, but I am sure that this has to be the finest made."

"Yep, you're probably right. I don't mean to go a tooting my own horn, but I make some mean rabbit soup," Granddad bragged.

After dinner Granddad showed Bina and Jacob to their rooms, because they were tired from a long day of travel. Jacob settled into his bed, which felt hard and lumpy, and found it difficult to fall asleep. He tried to calm himself for much needed rest, but was still having flash-backs of a rabbit staring him in the eyes.

Some time passed and Jacob found a softer edge of the bed that helped him to fall asleep. At Heldago, Jacob met Jezebel in Master Kang's room. "Are you going to ask Master Kang and the other teachers to test you for the Clevan level?" asked Jacob, quietly.

"Yes, after class I will ask each instructor if they feel that I am pre-pared," Jezebel replied somewhat nervously.

At the end of each class, Jezebel did as she said, asking her instructors if she was ready for the testing. Each instructor confirmed her question with the same answer: yes.

"So when will you be tested?" asked Jacob. "Will you know what the test entails?"

"I will be tested tomorrow, Jacob," Jezebel said, as they walked to the Peddle Room. "And no, I won't know what is on the test. The test is a combination of any number of things. It's really a trial of what the teacher feels you are weakest or most vulnerable on. If you cannot conquer these factors, then you aren't ready to proceed to the next level."

When the students were about to enter the Peddle Room, Don came up to them and said, "Bethals, you are not leaving just yet. Come with me. We are having a gathering."

Don led the five students up a series of stairs that led to the highest point of the castle. When they entered the room, Jacob thought it looked like a huge auditorium. It was decorated with beautiful stone sculptures that appeared to be thousands of years old.

"This is the Great Hall," whispered Jezebel. "This is where we have our Christmas gathering and where important delegations are brought forth. There must be something very important going on."

The Bethal students sat together at a table that was near the center of the room, and the other student levels took their respective tables as well. At the front of the Great Hall was a larger table where the Elders sat. To the center of this table and facing everyone in the room were the teachers and staff of Heldago.

Triple E stood up and spoke into a circular stone piece that resembled a microphone but had no cords or electricity to power it. When he spoke into the stone fixture, it was well apparent to Jacob, and anyone else who did not know, that it was some sort of voice amplifier. "Ladies and gentleman," said Triple E, trying to quiet the loud crowd. "This meeting has been called to order because of a scroll that has been sent to us by our rabbi. The scroll reads, 'My beloved Veritas, since the beginning of Earth's time, Heldago has been a safe haven for Veritas. But it has become known to me that there is an informant to the Tenebras in our walls of Heldago.'"

Suddenly, Triple E was interrupted by a great uproar of conversation throughout the Great Hall at this accusation with each table talking of who it might be.

"Quiet please!" Triple E shouted. "So that I may continue...'I do not know who it is as of yet, but *truth* always comes out, and it is *truth* that will always prevail. I am not telling you this, my brothers and sisters, to cause animosity or grudges, but to lift your spirits, because it is uplifted spirits that will triumph and overcome.

"'For in this very hour, I have foreseen the Tenebras readying themselves for an attack on the innocent like we have not seen in hundreds of years. So, my brothers and sisters, I say to you, be strong, steadfast, and resolute in your oath to uphold all that is good and righteous in the world. With love, Rabbi.'"

The room was silent with only the sound of a light breeze flowing through the open windows. Each person slowly got out of his or her chair and started walking down the stairway.

Jacob, being curious as always, had some questions that needed answering, so he asked Jezebel quietly, "How does the rabbi's scroll get into the hands of the Elders without anyone knowing where he is?"

"The scroll is sent through the rabbi's station in the Peddle Room, but the scroll appears magically on a lectern that sits in the middle of the room," Jezebel explained.

Now the questions started barreling through Jacob's thoughts. "Jezebel, how does the rabbi get chosen?" asked Jacob.

"The previous rabbi was killed around one thousand years ago. When he died his sword appeared to the new rabbi, who we have now. This is how a Verita knows he or she has been chosen to be the new leader. Most all here have never met our current rabbi, and the ones who have met him have not seen him in a long time. He has secluded himself from Heldago for years."

"So the new rabbi is chosen by the sword?"

"Yes, Jacob. The rabbi's sword is said to be made by God himself, and the sword finds out the new, worthy owner after the rabbi dies."

Jacob and Jezebel continued their conversation about where their rabbi may be living and theories into why he went into hiding on their way back to the peddle room.

CHAPTER 10

A KINGDOM OF DARKNESS

At this time, in a land that was darker than any black and was more lifeless than any outstretches of the galaxy, was an underground palace that those who entered called "La Muerte de Palacio"—or "Muerte Palace." Its walls were laden with bones of its conquered victims, and its very ceiling seemed to leak blood.

Felix Matthews was standing at its entrance talking to the guard in order to gain entrance to the palace. The guard was a three-headed snake named Domtar, which delighted in non-angelic human meals that were brought by willing Tenebras. Its eyes were black and lifeless, and its scales were harder than steel. When it spoke, all three heads spoke as one.

On the left and right of Domtar stood two goblins perched on stone blocks. The goblins were black like an eerie shadow; they smelled of rotting flesh, and their wings resembled those of a bat. They stood no more than four feet in height, and each hand and foot had three human-like fingers with blood-stained claws. Their food of choice was rotting human remains that were leftover from the Tenebra's meals. Goblins packed Muerte Palace by the hundreds, adhering to the Tenebra's every command. They had no powers to speak of except for their unknown strength to reflect most of the gnomes' powers, but their strength, speed, and flying ability made them great allies for the Tenebras.

"No, I didn't bring anything for you to eat today," explained Felix. "I did not find a suitable meal for your liking."

"Too bad…" hissed Domtar. "I haven't eaten yet today. You may enter just the same."

Felix met his friend Diablo Florentine, a boy Felix's age who enjoyed a human snack much more than the average Tenebra, as he entered Muerte Palace.

"I just got here as well," said Diablo. "I would have been here a lot earlier if that old lady hadn't put up such a fight. My father always taught me to not play with my food, but this lady was just too much… Have you eaten today?"

"Yeah, but not the same as you," Felix said, smiling. Many Tenebras ate as normal humans and would "treat" themselves to a blood meal occasionally.

In much the same way Veritas entered their Heldago during sleep or meditation, the Tenebras did the same in entering their Muerte

Palace. There were many similarities between the two schools and safe havens. Students learned in classroom environments with teachers who helped mold them into their cause, and their fortress was a secret to the world.

The Tenebras had many of the same classes like martial arts, powers, and swordsmanship; they also had four levels, or classes: Bethal, Clevan, Moldan, and Elder. The main difference between the two schools was that the Tenebras taught with a much deeper will to gain control and overpower the helpless. With this, they gained strength and happiness from an early age from feeding off the weak and helpless, and doing dark, evil deeds.

Felix and Diablo went to their first class, martial arts, and started their instruction. Their teacher, Master Fu, was finishing his lecture on the power of the pure blood that flowed through Verita's veins, and how it could increase power and strength in a Tenebra, when a messenger came.

The messenger was grossly disfigured, but he did not seem to be deformed from birth but rather from some sort of torture. He had one ear, his nose was bent to the side, and he had an extreme hunched back that looked as if it might have been broken at some point.

"Come with me, Felix," the messenger growled.

Felix looked over to his teacher, and Master Fu gave an affirmative head nod to give his permission to leave.

The messenger led Felix down a series of stairways. The air was becoming increasingly cold and clammy, and even Felix began to become nervous as he approached a room that he had never seen before. The messenger did not say a word but placed his forehead to the Tenebra's insignia on the door. The snakelike symbol began to turn and slide down the door as it seemed to be unlocking a series of locks. The thick steel door shuddered and screeched as it slowly began opening.

As the messenger gingerly led Felix through the doorway, Felix could see a large stone chair in which someone was seated, staring at his every move. He could not make out who the person was because the room had very little light.

"Get down!" the messenger commanded, getting down on his hands and knees. "If you value your life you will *not* get off of your hands and knees until given permission. Now, crawl forward—*slowly!*"

Felix got on his hands and knees and began crawling toward the large stone chair and the unknown man.

Out of the corner of his eye, Felix saw a very large man emerge from a hidden corner. The man smiled in pleasure at Felix's submissiveness. He had a goblin next to him that looked like a pet, and he slowly stroked its neck. The man's skin was reddish in color, and he had four arms that were marked with scars and burns from battles. He was bald, and his eyes glowed with what looked like fire.

"Arise, Felix Matthews," the man in the chair said.

Felix stood up and tried to see who the man was but could not make out his face.

"Come closer, my brother," said the man.

Felix slowly walked closer to the large throne, meanwhile peeking over his shoulder at the four-armed man who was creeping up behind him.

"Don't mind Bodach, he won't hurt you—unless necessary." The unknown man laughed. He stood up from the shadow of his throne so

Felix could see his face. The man was handsome and very well groomed. He was flawless from his hair to his black shiny shoes, and had a musky odor coming from him that Felix could not recognize.

"I am Prince Muammar," the man introduced.

"Oh—Prince Muammar, I've heard of you and your greatness. I'm sorry for not recognizing you, as I have never seen a picture of you before," explained Felix in reverence.

"It's fine," said Prince Muammar, putting his hands on Felix's shoulders. "It's not like my picture is dispersed among the public."

Bodach began laughing in a raspy growl until Prince Muammar glanced his direction.

"Bodach here is my bodyguard. He goes wherever I go. I sense that you fear him," said Prince Muammar.

"Yes, Prince Muammar, I suppose that I do," mumbled Felix, looking in Bodach's direction.

"Good. Fear brings allegiance, and allegiance brings power, and power brings strength...I summoned you here to let you know that I have my eye on you. Your distant grandfather was a close friend of mine. In fact, we fought in many battles together, he and I. Since it is his blood that flows through your veins, I know that I will see great things come from you," Prince Muammar said.

"I will do my best to bring glory to your name and to the Tenebra's cause around the world," said Felix, lifting his chin a little higher in pride.

"I know you will," said Prince Muammar. "I wish for you to do something for me. What do you know of this boy, Jacob Jerlow, in your hometown?

"Jacob—Jacob Jerlow? He's a nobody! Just some kid in my school who annoys me," said Felix, getting irritated.

"Interesting. You have felt this hatred toward him naturally, because he is a Verita."

"What? That little twerp is a Verita?" mumbled Felix. "Wait until I get my hands on him..."

"Not so fast, my brother," Prince Muammar said calmly. "We need him for now. I need you to watch him for us and report to me anything deemed worthy. You can find Sliggle at the front gate, and he can lead you to me if you have something to report." Muammar pointed over to the still-kneeling messenger who had led Felix.

Sliggle was instructed to lead Felix back to his class as Prince Muammar and Bodach began speaking. "I had tried for countless years to get someone on the inside of Heldago to be an informant, and finally I found a weak-minded Verita who could serve me," said Prince Muammar. "His mind was filled with darkness and evil and was so easily susceptible to my control. He has proven to be a good servant thus far."

"Vladimir was unsuccessful in his attempt to retrieve the Dalet corner, but I am sure Tao will not fail you, my master," said Bodach.

"I should hope not, because if he fails me he had better be dead—because if I get my hands on him, he will wish that he were!"

With the help of his informant, Prince Muammar had found out who Jacob Jerlow was and about his quest for the Dalet corners. It was also the informant who had told him of Jacob's journey to Brazil, and now to Alaska.

CHAPTER 11

THE MYSTERIOUS, WHITE-DRESSED WOMAN

At Heldago Jacob and other Bethals entered the Peddle Room, with Jacob being drawn to the lectern holding the rabbi's scroll that Jezebel had earlier described. It was one solid piece of wood, seemingly carved from one tree. It gave off a pleasant odor that smelled as if it had just been cut. The artwork that was carved into the wood seemed to tell a story of a man going through stages of life; it was nothing like Jacob had ever seen before.

"So one of these stations is the rabbi's," thought Jacob, looking around the room.

Jacob was very intrigued as to who this mystery rabbi was and where he came from. He continued to ponder who and where this rabbi was as he got situated in his station to return to his granddad's house. He definitely knew he had returned to his granddad's home, as he woke up to what smelled like warm, rotting fish blowing into his face. Jacob opened his eyes and saw Wilbur sitting and looking directly at his face—about one inch away. He had a piece of drool hanging from his lip that was nearly reaching the ground as he gave a big wet lick across Jacob's face.

"Oh my gosh!" gagged Jacob, covering his mouth as he ran to the bathroom. He started vomiting into the toilet. The sound of Jacob's uncontrollable gag reflex made Bina wake up and come to check on him.

"Are you OK, Jacob? Are you sick?" Bina asked.

"Wilbur—licked—my—face," he stuttered, trying to control his gag reflex.

"Oh, is that all?" said Bina, bending down to pet the large dog. "You're a good boy, aren't you?" Bina smelled Wilbur's breath and suddenly felt herself blacking out for a moment. "Whew—I see what you mean," she thought.

Just then, they heard the front door slamming open and Granddad saying, "Are you two up yet? You're not gonna let me catch all of the fish, are ya?"

Granddad flopped a stringer load of fish into the sink and began prepping them for breakfast. "You two wash up for breakfast!" he shouted. "Hot fried fish is coming up in a couple of minutes."

Jacob peeked his head out of the bathroom and looked at Bina as they both thought the same thing: "Fried fish for *breakfast*?"

After breakfast, Granddad drove Jacob and Bina to a secluded river deep in the mountainside. "Here's where the whoppers are!" he exclaimed.

Jacob had been fishing many times with his dad and mom, but Bina had never been fishing before. Jacob took his time showing her how to tie a hook to the line, thread the worm onto it so that it couldn't crawl off, and how to cast. Soon Jacob and Bina began catching numerous fish, but Granddad seemed to run out of luck and was not getting a bite. Jacob and Bina thought it amusing, as each time they caught another fish, Granddad would cast a little closer and closer to their fishing spot.

"This is very fun!" laughed Bina. "Thank you so much for taking us fishing!"

"Oh, you're welcome," grumbled a jealous Granddad.

As the day went on, Jacob felt more and more nervous as he thought about how he was going to talk to Granddad about his mom and the Verita's bloodline. Then he had an idea. "Granddad—I think I feel a bug crawling on my back, can you get it off for me?" asked Jacob.

"Sure—maybe a tick!" said Granddad. "Best to get them little critters off as soon as possible, cause they can go making you sick."

Jacob lifted his shirt so his granddad could get a look at his back. Jacob could not hear any noise from Granddad, who stood there motionless. He turned to look over his shoulder and saw his grandfather fall to his knees and begin to quietly cry. He had seen the birthmark of the Verita on Jacob's back.

"Are you OK, Granddad?" Jacob asked, softly.

"I—I—I just never thought—I never thought I was going to ever see my family have a Verita. We have not had a Verita in our family for so many hundreds of years...we—I—thought we were just going to be Deacons forever," Granddad explained.

"Well, it's real, Granddad," said Jacob confidently. "I've only recently found out my bloodlines. Mom, your daughter, never told me anything. I've only known that I was a Verita for about a week. "

Granddad began to act and talk a little more normally, saying, "Yes, your mother could not have told you anything because she never knew of her bloodlines. I never told her or your grandma."

Granddad sat down on a nearby fallen tree with Jacob.

"You see, I remember the days that went by when I was your age, Jacob...My father was so sure that I was going to break the family's 'curse' and be a Verita instead of a Deacon. 'To help rid the earth of all evil,' he used to say. When those days turned into months and the months into years, I saw my father fall into a great depression. I felt so much like I had disappointed him.

"I swore to myself that I would never act the same way that he had...but then your mother was born. As she began to get older and closer to fourteen years old, I found myself getting more and more caught up in 'breaking the family's curse' instead of being a husband and father."

"Why didn't you talk to Mom and tell her how you felt?" Jacob asked respectfully.

"I don't know why not. When your mother turned fifteen, I knew that she was not going to become a Verita, and I just snapped. I felt like

I had let everyone down all over again. It was too much for me to bear, so I just left and moved here to be away from everyone."

"That explains a lot, Granddad. I know this is all hitting you pretty suddenly, but thank you for sharing this with me. You know, Mom would love to meet with you and talk to you. She misses you dearly," explained Jacob.

"I feel so ashamed for what I have done. I don't know if I could stand to see her face to face. How could she ever forgive me for what I've done to her and her mother?"

Jacob put his arm around Granddad and said, "Believe me, Granddad, she already has forgiven you. She just wants you to be a part of her life. She loves you."

Granddad began to joyfully cry as he hugged Jacob.

After a long day of fishing, the three went home for a good night's rest. At Heldago Jacob was eager to see if his friend, Jezebel Flores, was going to pass her Bethal level.

Jezebel's three teachers—Don, Master Kang, and Sarge—were present for all three tests, as they would all judge.

"Good luck, Jezebel!" shouted Jacob as he approached the crowd of onlookers.

Jezebel's first test was designed by Master Kang. It tested Jezebel on a series of martial arts kicks and punches that challenged her martial arts skills and body control. While blindfolded she had to kick and punch through a narrow passage that was only wide enough to allow her foot or hand to barely pass through. The passage was lined with a black charcoal that would reveal white underneath if touched and mark Jezebel's hand or foot with black. Inside each passage was a padded dummy that she would strike. When the padded dummy was struck, it released a red dye from within, which would give recognition of a direct hit. If she hit the passage and did not pass directly through it, or if she did not hit the dummy with a direct hit, she would fail the test.

Since she was blindfolded, Jezebel would have to sense the passage's height and width in order to kick or punch accurately. She quieted herself and concentrated. Then, she kicked and punched through the passages with great accuracy, directly hitting each of the dummies and releasing the red dye. At the end of this test, all three instructors convened and reported to Jezebel that she had passed and was able to move onto the next test.

The crowd of students and staff screamed enthusiastically.

Don gave Jezebel her second test. He had designed multiple shelves, or stations, of varying heights that had bird's nests resting upon them. The shelves were supported by large wooden beams that reached high into the sun filled sky. In this test she would have to use the valoria spell in order to move eggs from a basket resting on the ground through a maze lined with sharp pins and needles and safely into a bird's nest. For each of the four varying heights of shelves, she had sixty seconds to complete the task without breaking a bird's egg.

The first three eggs she landed safely in the bird's nests without even coming close to one of the sharp objects that stood in her way. The fourth egg was to be lifted up almost thirty feet high, and the maze of pins and needles that it needed to pass safely through was just barely bigger than the egg. Jezebel concentrated for a moment then said, "Valoria." The egg began to move flawlessly through the air, and as it passed through the sharp, pointy circle, it rubbed across the pins, causing some scratches on the egg. However, the egg landed safely into the nest without being broken.

The spectators that were quietly watching began a murmur throughout the crowd. "Will she pass because the egg was scratched but not broken?" many of them asked.

The three judges huddled and discussed the test, and then Don broke away to announce the results to Jezebel and the crowd. "We have made our decision by a vote of two to one," he started. "Two in favor and one opposed. So congratulations, Jezebel, you have passed my test."

The crowd began to cheer loudly as everyone clapped for her achievement. Jacob ran over to Jezebel and gave her a big hug, saying, "I knew you could do it. Only one more test and you've done it."

For her third and final test, Sarge had made a series of sword-skill trials. Jezebel was given a steel sword for her testing. Unlike the wooden sword that she had practiced with for so many hours, the steel sword was sharp as a razor and grabbed Jezebel's attention as she rubbed her hand lightly across the blade.

In the first test she had to cut through a watermelon resting on a wooden post—without making the watermelon move. On top of the watermelon rested a feather that would be an easy determining factor as to whether the watermelon moved or not.

Jezebel closed her eyes and concentrated for a moment as the crowd became extremely quiet. Then, with one unfailing swoop, she sliced her sword through the watermelon. Everyone quietly froze and held their breath to stare at the feather. It did not move. The crowd went crazy, yelling and screaming in excitement.

For her second sword test, Jezebel was asked to find her practice sword, which was lent to her for the competition, in a huge pile of swords with no hands—just her powers. She was not given any information as to where the sword was in the heap of hundreds of swords, so she needed to "feel" the sword's energy and bring it to her with the valoria spell.

Jezebel and the crowd faced the heap of swords as Jezebel closed her eyes and concentrated on the hidden sword's energy. After a couple of minutes, Jezebel started to slowly turn away from the pile of swords. "Valoria," she said, facing the watching crowd. An unsuspecting student named Wolfgang felt his robe lift open, and the hidden sword come out from its hiding. The boy had a look of shock on his face, as he did not know the sword had been hidden on him by the judges. Everyone had suspected the sword to be hidden in the heap of swords, but it was a trick. The sword flew through the air and straight into Jezebel's hand. Again, the crowd went into an uproar, yelling Jezebel's name in encouragement.

For her third and final sword test, Jezebel was to make very accurate cuts while being attacked. A huge wooden apparatus with large padded beams attached to a swinging wheel was her attacker. She had to move through the swinging beams and make precise cuts through a small opening. If she missed a cut or got hit by the swinging beam, she would lose the test.

Jezebel slowly approached the daunting apparatus as she looked upon the openings that she would have to cut through with her sword and the large beams that would be swinging her way. The crowd was quieter than it had been through all of the other tests, because they knew if Jezebel passed this test, she would have passed the Bethal level.

Jezebel entered the device. Beams began swinging her way. She made her first cut through the opening—cutting the thin piece of paper. She quickly moved to the next gap, dodging a beam coming her way from her side; as she turned another beam came simultaneously from her rear, directly hitting her in her back. She was jolted to the ground, and the force dislodged her sword from her hand.

The crowd sighed. Their silence said it all. They felt so bad for Jezebel. Jacob ran over to Jezebel and helped her to her feet as she began to cry.

"It's OK, Jezebel," said Jacob. "You did amazing today."

Jacob's comforting words and helping hand made Jezebel feel a little better as they looked toward the judges. The three judges were quietly talking. Sarge stood up and announced, "Jezebel, you have fought a great battle today and have showed great strides in completing the level of Bethal. But—you have failed your defensive sword skills test. With this, you have failed the level challenge. All students are to return to classes in ten minutes. Thank you."

Many of the students felt awkward, like they should just leave Jezebel alone, so they left for their classes without a word to her. Jacob talked with Jezebel for a few minutes, comforting her and giving her more strength. Then they slowly walked toward their powers class with Don.

"We can practice together, Jezebel," said Jacob. "You'll get it for sure next time."

"Thanks, Jacob," Jezebel said, walking closely to him for comfort.

That morning when Jacob and Bina had woken, they went to have breakfast with Granddad.

"You guys sleep good?" asked Granddad.

"Oh yeah," they replied.

"So I kinda have the feeling that you two didn't just come up here to go fishing...so do ya wanna tell me what's really going on?" asked Granddad.

Jacob looked over at Bina and then back to Granddad, saying, "Well, we are on a quest of sorts. We are looking for a lost artifact."

"Oh yeah—and what clues do you have for this lost goodie?" Granddad asked with a raised eyebrow.

"We know that it's in Alaska and we know that music of some kind will help lead us to it, but we don't have much more to go on than this," explained Bina. "We were hoping that you could help us."

"Music, you say," said Granddad, walking slowly around the kitchen. "Hmm, I don't have anything coming to mind that may help, but I do know someone who may be able to help. Come on, I'll take ya to him."

The three got in Granddad's truck and drove up a steep, winding gravel road into the Denali Wilderness until they came across a secluded cabin. They got out of the truck and knocked on the front door. An elderly man, some years older than Granddad, answered the door. Immediately, he seemed to recognize Granddad and gave a halfway smile. "Old Buck Jensen—how the heck have you been?" said the man. "Come on in and bring yer friends, too."

The inside of the old man's house was decorated with antique music pieces and instruments. It was evident by the décor that the man had a definite love for music.

"Kids, this is my old friend Charles Whitman," Granddad said. "Charles, this here is my grandson, Jacob, and his friend is Bina. They are visiting me from North Dakota."

"North Dakota, you say!" Charles shouted. "I visited there some fifty years ago, pretty territory—nice folk, too...So what brings you all up to my neck of the woods?"

They all sat down to get comfortable.

"We are in search of a lost artifact that my dad looked for his whole life," explained Jacob. "All we know is that it rests in Alaska, and music will help lead us to its hidden place."

Charles's face turned somewhat pale as he stared into Jacob's eyes. "Hmm—interesting," he said softly, pausing to recollect. "I have lived in these woods for my entire 101 years of life. I was born just around the bend in a one-room log cabin that my dad built with his own two hands. Both my mother and father died in that house. I have seen and heard many things in this forest throughout my years—some things that I never could quite explain."

"What do you mean, sir?" asked Bina.

"When I was a little younger than you two, I was hunting fox in these woods, and I fell into a deep hole, breaking my leg. I would have died for sure in that hole if it hadn't been for..." He paused. "People, even my own parents, never believed me."

"Sir, tell us—please," begged Jacob.

"A woman, a woman dressed in a long white dress. She was...she was the most beautiful woman I had ever laid eyes upon. She floated down the hole and lifted me out—she did. Even more amazing, she seemed to have some kind of music coming from her body...like her body was playing a melody with no instrumentation. She looked at me and then was gone. I was able to find a branch and use it as a crutch so that I could hobble back to my house. She saved my life that day."

Charles got out of his chair and walked over to the window, saying, "There have been many times since that day that I've heard that same melody I heard coming from that lady. Sounds kinda like a sweet flute tune...I do love music, ya know? And when I hear that music, it brings me back to that day—the day she saved my life."

It was quiet in the house as Jacob and Bina looked at each other in excitement.

"Thank you so much for sharing this with us, sir," Jacob said. "Will you take us to this place where you fell into the hole?"

Charles gladly agreed to lead the three to the place where he had fallen so many years ago. The four found it to be quite the struggle trying to pass through the dense forest. The evergreen trees were thick, and they emitted a sweet, pleasing aroma, but Granddad continuously grumbled about the sticky sap that stuck to his clothes.

As they came upon the deep hole, Charles stopped for a moment and put his hands on Jacob and Bina's shoulders, saying, "Listen. Can you hear that?"

Jacob, Bina, and Granddad became motionless as they searched to hear the music.

"I do—I hear what sounds like a flute," Jacob whispered in amazement.

"I don't hear a thing but the birds playing around in the branches," Granddad said, shaking his head.

"I hear it too. The sound seems to be coming from that direction," said Bina, pointing around the bend.

"Granddad, would it be OK if Bina and I went on a hike?" asked Jacob.

"Sure, ol' Charles and I can go have a cup of coffee, and I can listen to him pick on the old guitar while you two go looking around," said Granddad. "You sure you can find your way back to Charles's house?"

"Yes, sir," said Jacob. "I'll leave a trail of string tied to branches that we can follow back, just to make sure."

"That's my boy," said Granddad.

Jacob and Bina began to follow the music as Charles and Granddad walked back to the house. Every one hundred feet or so, Jacob would tie a piece of white string that he had in his backpack to a branch, to leave a trail back to where they started.

"Bina, why do you suppose Granddad couldn't hear the music when you, me, and Charles could?" asked Jacob, tying another string to a branch.

"I think it has to do with a love of music," she replied. "You and I both love music, and Charles said he loves music, so I think it has something to do with that."

"And what about the scroll you found that said 'music is what calms the salvage beast that protects our paths'? It sounds like this woman in the white dress is no beast."

"I'm not sure yet..."

After walking for some time, Jacob and Bina stopped because they could no longer hear the music.

"Where did the music go?" asked Bina.

"I don't know—it just disappeared," answered Jacob.

Just then a woman's gentle voice came from the thick trees ahead. "Who are you and what do you seek?"

Jacob and Bina became extremely nervous.

"We're in search of a lost artifact," said Jacob anxiously. "I'm Jacob Jerlow and this is Bina Feldman."

Through the trees a bright white color could be seen approaching; then stepped forth a woman in a long white dress. She was just as Charles had described, very beautiful.

"You have followed my music?" she asked.

"Yes, ma' am," they said.

"I have been here for countless years awaiting the one to set me free. I was empowered by angels who wished to protect a valuable item. It has been written that 'It is one who loves music' who will find me. This is the easiest part. After finding me, it is also written, 'The person will perform music in such a manner that is so pleasing that it will release me and my treasure that I hold.'"

"So if we sing you a song you will give us what we search for?" asked Bina.

"It is written 'that the one who is to gain control of the treasure you seek will possess a great gift for music,' but be warned: if you are not found worthy of such an honor there is no other alternative but *death*," explained the woman.

"If we don't sing the song well, she is going to kill us," thought Jacob. "She doesn't look that tough. We should be able to escape if she attacks us."

"OK, you're the best singer, Bina," whispered Jacob. "You should sing the song."

"Are you sure, Jacob?" whispered Bina.

"Yes, definitely!"

"Do you wish to proceed?" asked the mysterious woman.

"Yes," said Jacob. "Bina will sing you a song to show our worthiness."

Bina thought of which song was her favorite song and which one she thought she had the most practice on so that she could bring pleasure to the mysterious woman. She began singing as she normally did—beautifully. Well into the song, the mysterious woman began to glow brightly as she started to float into the air. She began to show what looked like a smile.

"She likes it," thought Jacob. "It's working."

Then with no warning, the mysterious woman changed form into a beast that resembled a werewolf. It had a long dark nose, snarling teeth, large razor-sharp claws, and eyes orange like the sun. It growled and slowly approached the two, saying, "Now you must die."

Jacob grabbed Bina's hand as they ran as fast as they could toward their trail. They could hear the beast snarling and running behind them, and no matter how fast they ran, they could hear the beast's footsteps getting closer and closer.

Jacob looked over his shoulder, and just as the creature was leaping to sink its teeth into his neck, an object came flying through Jacob's sight, slamming into the beast and knocking it off of its feet. It yelped in pain. Jacob and Bina stopped running to see what, or who, had helped them. They saw a man standing between the beast and them, raising his hands and controlling many of the nearby branches and roots to ensnare it.

"That'll only hold her fer a minute," said Shawn, turning toward the two to show who he was. "Let's be gettin' you two outta here."

Shawn gave Jacob and Bina a friendly push on the back to help them to start running again. When they got close to Charles's house, they stopped running to catch their breath.

"Was that thing a werewolf?" asked Jacob, still trying to catch his breath.

"Nay, Jacob," said Shawn. "She be a lycan. They be much worse than any of yer storybooks be tell 'in of werewolves. She be under angelic power that transformed her into a lycan many years ago, and she be turnin' into the beast when danger is present. Angels that put the spell on her be wantin' her to be a lycan because most Tenebras be scared of 'em."

"But why did she think we were dangerous?" asked Jacob.

"If I may, Shawn," Bina interrupted, looking over to Jacob. "I believe the spell put on her will only let her release the Dalet piece to someone who can play or sing music in such a manner that is deemed worthy. My theory is that the angels that placed the spell on her foresaw that the one who would eventually take the corner would hold a great musical talent, and it is this person, and this person alone, who may have the piece. Anyone else would be seen as a threat and need to be dealt with accordingly."

"I think that be soundin' pretty good, Bina," said Shawn. "You be one of the brightest young women I have ever met."

Bina blushed and smiled.

"I will be leavin' ya now, but don't ya worry none 'cause I will be watchin' ya," said Shawn as he walked away.

Jacob and Bina went in the house and told Granddad and Charles that they had not found anything, but would like to come back soon to search again. That night Jacob and Bina discussed how they were going to please the mysterious woman with music.

"I have an idea," said Jacob. "I recently met a musician like I had never seen or heard before—at Heldago. Maybe she can help us. Do you think you would be OK coming to Heldago tonight?"

"Yes, Jacob," said Bina. "But how are you going to get me there?"

"Well, anything that is in my hand comes with me to Heldago, so if I hold your hand while I go to sleep, you should come with me."

Later that night Jacob and Bina lay down on the floor while holding hands. Both felt a little awkward lying next to each other holding hands, but they found themselves in front of the imposing castle Heldago in quick time.

"It's just as you described, Jacob," said Bina, standing in awe of the huge castle. "It's beautiful!"

Jacob led Bina up to the castle doors and asked the guards for permission to enter with his friend. They said they could not allow such a thing, but one would retrieve Triple E straightaway.

A few minutes passed and Triple E opened the gates for Jacob and Bina to enter, saying, "It is not our normal practice to allow a non-Verita into our walls, but Shawn has informed me of your great friendship and quest, so we will make an exception."

Jacob and Bina thanked Triple E and left to find the fine arts teacher, Shir. They went to her teaching room and did not find her, but saw a student sitting at a table painting.

"Where is Elder Shir?" asked Jacob.

"She is out on the balcony, I believe," said the student.

Jacob and Bina went outside the room to the balcony and saw Shir sitting in a chair with her eyes closed. She seemed to be in some sort of meditative state.

"Shir—Shir, can you hear me?" whispered Jacob, leaning toward the teacher.

"I hear you, Jacob Jerlow. Now sit and listen," she said softly.

Jacob and Bina sat on nearby chairs, closed their eyes, and began listening.

A few moments later Jacob asked, "What are we listening for?"

"The music," replied Shir.

"Shir, I'm sorry, but I don't hear any music," said Jacob.

"Of course you do, Jacob Jerlow," said Shir. "Listen to the wind. Listen to it touching the trees and leaves. Listen to it flowing through the halls and windows of the castle. Feel it touching your face and hands. Hear and feel the beautiful music."

Jacob and Bina adjusted themselves in their seat and concentrated on the wind. A few moments later, a smile came upon their faces as they began to "hear" the wind's music.

Time passed and Shir opened her eyes, asking, "Now do you hear the music?"

"Yes, I do," said Jacob triumphantly.

"I sense you are looking for answers," said Shir.

"I am. How do you play or sing music better? I mean, I know it takes practice and dedication to get better. But how do you reach into the depths of your heart to bring out your best music possible?"

"There have been people who have searched for this answer their whole lives, Jacob Jerlow," said Shir. "But my answer to you is simple. If you grow accustomed to something, do you still truly feel it or does it become unattached? If you struggle through something, do you not grow with it? Do you not become more attached? Do you not *feel* it more?"

Jacob's eyes grew larger as something sparked in his thoughts. "Thank you, Shir—oh, by the way, this is my friend, Bina."

Shir looked at Bina and said, "Ahh, Bina, a great song I see in your heart. You only need to find it, my dear."

Bina gave a confirming smile as she and Jacob walked off the balcony.

Jacob led Bina to each of his classes and introduced his fellow classmates to his friend. By the third class, the classmates could sense jealousy and sarcasm coming from Jezebel toward Bina. Other students picked up on Jezebel's attitude toward Bina but tried not to comment. Up to this point no one in the Bethal class had thought of Jacob and Jezebel's relationship as anything more than friendship, but by Jezebel's body language around Bina it was obvious that she had a little more than friendship on her mind.

Through the next few hours Bina was growing more and more curious about Jacob's idea that was sparked by their conversation with Shir, but she would wait until the next day to find out Jacob's thoughts.

CHAPTER 12

FIND THE MUSIC WITHIN

The next morning Jacob and Bina went for a walk after breakfast.

"How can I find this 'song' in my heart, Jacob?" asked Bina. "If I don't sing the right song to the lady in white, we might not make it out alive again."

"You will find the song, Bina," said Jacob. "And to help you I'm going to play my trumpet with you."

"You are? What song will we perform?"

"That's just it, Bina—I don't think we should perform a song we've played or sung one hundred times," said Jacob. "Because if we're too familiar with the song, then we're going to be too unattached from the song, and if we're unattached we won't be able to truly *feel* the song."

"So—we go into the forest with no song to sing and no song to play, and we perform from our hearts only?" Bina chuckled.

"Yes, Bina," Jacob said. "I know it sounds crazy, but this is what I feel...The music will come to us when we truly search for it in our hearts."

After lunch Jacob asked Granddad if he would drive them back to Charles's house so that they could search the trees again. Without hesitation, Granddad was happy to go.

Through sputtering and smoke, the old truck struggled to make it up the steep mountain roads again, and in record time, because of a strong tail wind, they pulled into the Charles's dirt driveway.

"I'll be visiting with ol' Charles here," said Granddad. "You two be careful."

Jacob and Bina walked back into the forest following the white strings that Jacob had tied to the branches the day before. After walking for some time, Jacob stopped and said, "Bina, instead of searching out the lady in white, why don't we let her find us?"

Jacob pulled his trumpet from his backpack, closed his eyes, and began to play. He did not play any song he had practiced before; instead he played a song from his heart and soul. The music was his—he was attached to the music like it was a part of him.

Bina closed her eyes and listened to the trumpet's music. Without thought, she began to sing a song. She did not think about the words and where they were coming from, but she let the song come from within.

The music from Jacob's trumpet and the song from Bina's mouth flowed together as one—like they were made for each other. After a few minutes, they could sense that someone was standing behind them, listening. They continued their song, and within a short time they finished just as they had begun—beautifully.

They slowly turned around and saw the woman in white with a tear coming down her cheek, saying, "My time here is done. Thank you"

A bright light came shining forth from inside the woman's heart toward Jacob, and a loud song released from her, making her throw her arms outward. Suddenly, the woman burst into a great ball of light, releasing the Dalet corner from her chest. The Dalet slowly fell to the ground at Jacob's feet. Jacob bent down and picked up the corner, noticing a brilliantly white dove flying into the sky from where the lady had stood.

"You did it, Jacob," said Bina joyfully.

"No, Bina," he said, placing the corner in his backpack. "*We* did it."

Jacob and Bina started their way back to the house. When coming over a small dip in the hill, they looked ahead to see an Asian man with pale skin staring at them. He was a Tenebra by the name of Tao, and Prince Muammar had sent him.

"Give me the corner now, and I will kill you quickly with no suffering, but if you struggle, you will most certainly die a slow death," Tao shouted in an Asian accent.

"Take my backpack and run back to the house, Bina," whispered Jacob. "I'll hold him off and meet you there."

Bina grabbed the backpack and ran away as fast as she could.

"Go after her," Tao commanded, pointing at Bina. "I will take care of this filthy little Verita."

A man who was hiding behind a close-by tree jumped into the air, changing into a wolf, and began running after Bina.

"You dare to challenge me," said Tao sarcastically. "You're just a kid."

Jacob became very nervous as a hundred thoughts began flowing through his mind on how he could defeat a Tenebra with his elementary skills. Just then, the voice that Jacob had heard before came into his mind: "Concentrate. Feel your sword and where it may be...and it will come to you."

Jacob grew ever more nervous as Tao began to slowly approach. He gathered his thoughts and began to search for this "sword" that the voice had told him about. A moment later, he felt the sword as if it were already in his hand. He could feel the energy of the sword and how it welcomed Jacob to call upon it. "Valoria," he said.

The sword came flying through the air from an unknown origin and into Jacob's hand. Tao stopped for a moment, looking puzzled at his young opponent's abilities. He pulled his sword's handle out from his belt and smiled at Jacob in pleasure at the upcoming battle. Tao's double-edged blade slowly came forth from its handle as he began approaching Jacob again. Then with quickness and power, he leaped through the air, slicing his sword toward Jacob's chest. Jacob felt his sword's blade shooting out from its handle as he blocked the blow with all of his might. The force of the blow threw him backwards onto his back.

Meanwhile, the wolf was gaining ground on Bina. She could hear the wolf's footsteps crushing the brittle leaves on the ground with each step, growing ever more closer as she ducked through the heaviest parts of the forest in hopes of slowing the canine down. But it was no use: the four-legged animal was too fast. The wolf lunged at Bina's feet, knocking her to the ground. The wolf hovered over Bina, drooling and seemingly teasing her before it would sink its teeth into her.

"Hey—furball!" shouted a man's voice. "Get away from her! You don't need to be pickin' on a young girl—unless you be a coward?"

Bina and the wolf snapped their heads toward the man. It was Shawn.

The wolf snapped at Bina as if to say, "I'll be back for you later," and it leaped into the air simultaneously changing into its human shape again.

"I'll show you who the coward is, heaven boy," said the Tenebra. "Do you know who I am?"

"Err—might you be Snoopy?" asked Shawn. "Or maybe, Scooby Doo? No wait, you be Ol' Yeller."

"NO!" he yelled, becoming red in the face with anger. "My name is Turfer; the mighty shape shifter."

"Ok, Turd-fur," said Shawn, jokingly. "Why don't ya make like a tree—and—leave? Ya have no business here."

"Ok—funny man," said Turfer. He made a great wind erupt, and all of the leaves from the trees and ground encircled Shawn.

Shawn struggled to make a counter-curse to get out of the whirlwind of leaves, but it was too strong. Turfer made his fingernails grow into long, razor-sharp claws as he planned his deadly point of attack. Shawn jabbed his sword with all of his might through the strong winds at the Tenebra's chest. Turfer trapped the sword with his hands and claws and ripped it from Shawn's hands, making it fly high in the air.

Turfer dropped the wind and took a swipe at Shawn's head with his claws. Shawn threw his hand back, directly hitting the unsuspecting Tenebra in the nose. His eyes began watering so badly he could no longer see Shawn's position. Shawn's sword, still falling through the air, fell into his hand and he cut through the air with pin point accuracy—beheading Turfer before he could gain his bearings.

Shawn knelt down by Turfer's body, made the sign of the cross, and said a quick prayer. He then grabbed Bina's hand helping her to her feet saying, "Grab yer back pack and let's be check 'in on Jacob."

By this time Jacob was struggling to keep up with the stronger Tao, who was having more than enough entertainment 'toying' with his competition. Jacob had tried everything that he had been taught to disarm Tao, but he was just too strong.

Then, Jacob had an idea. "OK, you're too powerful," he said, lowering his sword to Tao. "If you promise to not harm my friend Bina, I'll take you to the Dalet corner and hand it over to you."

"Wise decision," said Tao. "I don't make promises, but I tell you what...I will consider not harming her. Now—lead the way."

Jacob began leading Tao back to Charles's house.

After they had walked for some time, Jacob bent over to remove a branch from his path, obviously annoying Tao. "Get moving," Tao said.

Jacob saw his chance to escape, so he began running as fast as he could. Where would he go? How could he escape? Then it came to him. He changed directions and headed toward Charles' house. A furious Tao chased.

Slightly out of Tao's view, Jacob jumped over the hole that had trapped Charles so many years ago before Tao could see what he had done. With Tao running close behind and his eyes focused on Jacob—and the anger that raged inside of him—he did not see the deep hole in his path. He stepped directly into the hole and had no time to react to his fall. Tao let out a loud screech as he hit the bottom of the pit.

Jacob cautiously walked over to the deep hole and looked down to see a crippled Tao lying at the bottom of the hole—apparently having broken both of his legs. Jacob saw his confiscated sword on the ground next to Tao and said, "Valoria," to bring it into his hands. Just then, Shawn and Bina came around the hill and into view.

"Ya OK, Jacob?" asked Shawn, trying to catch his breath from running. "Sorry I'm late."

"I'm fine," Jacob reassured him. "Thanks for helping Bina. What are we going to do about this one?" He pointed down the hole.

Shawn looked down the hole and said, "He's not gonna be goin' anywhere soon. We can just leave him; besides, I think what be waitin' fer him from his prince be much worse than anything we can be doin' to 'em."

Shawn looked down in Jacob's hand and saw his sword's handle.

"Ya found yer sword, eh?" asked Shawn. "That be a beauty."

"Yeah, a voice in my head told me to call upon it...so I did and it appeared to me," explained Jacob, showing the sword to Shawn and Bina. "The stories I've heard about our swords are true—it feels almost like it is a third arm or leg...like it's connected to me in some way."

"Aye—well, it be soundin' like this voice ya hear in yer head be a guardian angel of sorts," said Shawn.

"Yeah, Shawn—it's kinda weird, but this voice that comes in my head sometimes gives me guidance and helps calm me."

Shawn said good-bye for now as Jacob and Bina went back to Charles's house. On the drive home, Jacob showed Granddad the Dalet corner. Granddad swelled with pride.

Over the next few days, Jacob and Bina had a very enjoyable time fishing and talking with Granddad. Leaving him was much more difficult for Jacob than he'd first imagined.

CHAPTER 13

CONTROL YOUR FEAR BEFORE IT CONTROLS YOU

Upon returning home Jacob had an emotional and long conversation with his mom as he explained Granddad's remorse in abandoning her and her mother. However, Jacob left out the information about their Verita's bloodline, waiting for the correct time to share this with his mother.

That first night back, Jacob held Bina's hand as they used the medallion to hide their walk to the Hokmah. There they hid the third Dalet corner.

"OK, Jacob," said Bina, "three down and one more to go. Let's take a look at your father's journal and see if he has any other notes about where the last piece may be in Italy."

They read through the journal again and saw the notes that Jacob's dad had made about the signs he had found that pointed to Italy, but he had come into a lot of frustration in not finding any other leads.

"This journey is going to be a little different than the other two we've taken," said Bina. "We are going to have to start with square one here."

Jacob and Bina found themselves reading and searching through scrolls for most of the night, but nothing was standing out as a good clue to help in Italy.

"Do you have any ideas as to how we can get to Italy before school starts, Jacob?" asked Bina. "I mean, we've already taken two trips this summer. How can we take another one?"

"I've been thinking about this since our last few days in Alaska, and I talked about it with Granddad," said Jacob. "On our last day there, he gave me an envelope full of cash and called it 'old birthday money' and told me to take everyone to Italy. So I'm gonna talk to my mom about a family vacation before school starts. Do you think you can talk your mom into the same thing?"

"I will find a way," said Bina. "My mother loves Italy, so I don't think I will have to twist her arm too much, especially when the trip is paid for."

The next morning Jacob asked his mom about going on a trip to Italy. He described the trip as a great family trip and a time for them to spend time together. He also added the educational and spiritual incentives of being able to view the history of the Roman ruins and the Vatican. His mom was very much leaning toward going but was worried about the finances of such a venture since she was not currently working and they were living on their savings. This was when Jacob explained the money that Grandad had given him and how it was a birthday gift for both of them to go on a family vacation.

Sarah agreed to the vacation and was very excited about spending this valuable family time together. Almost at the same time, Bina was having the vacation discussion with her mother. Unfortunately, her mother was not agreeing about taking the money for the trip from Jacob. She felt this was not right.

When Jacob found out about the money concern that Bina's mom was having, he had his mom call Bina's mother to talk her into the vacation. After all, Bina's mom had been nice enough to take him on the Brazil trip earlier that summer. After some discussion, Bina's mother agreed to the vacation, and they made plans as to the dates and times before school would start in the fall.

"It's settled then—Jacob, Rebecca, and I have just booked our flights over the Internet," said Sarah. "We were able to get a package deal with air fare, car rental, and hotel. We will be staying at the Hotel Dei Consoli in Rome near St. Peter's Square. I am really excited, Jacob. This was a fantastic idea!"

"Wait a minute, Mom," said Jacob with a raised eye brow. "What did you just say? We are staying at a hotel near where?"

"At the Hotel Dei Consoli near St. Peter's Square. Why? Is there something the matter?"

"No, no, not at all," said Jacob, giving his mom a big kiss before rushing out the door.

Jacob ran as fast as he could to Bina's house.

"What's going on?" asked Bina, answering the door.

Jacob was in such a hurry he had no time to answer. He grabbed his medallion and Bina's hand saying, *"Amor vincit omnia,"* and he began running to the Hokmah.

At the Hokmah Bina tried to catch her breath as Jacob started rustling through the Hokmah chest.

"OK, now will you tell me what this is all about?" asked Bina, breathing heavily.

"I know I saw it in here," said Jacob, pillaging through scrolls.

Bina sat down and watched Jacob, as he was far too busy to have conversation.

After some time had passed, Jacob grew more and more frustrated, and a great anxiety and fear began to overrun his mind. He felt as if the whole world were crashing in around him. It was like every worry in the world had just been put upon his shoulders and every breath he took could be his last. "What if I fail? What if the world is doomed because of me? Dad would be so disappointed in me," he thought. Once he began to think about all the worries in his life, those worries manifested themselves into more worries, and they snowballed into a mental breakdown.

For this moment in time he felt like he had no one. He felt as if he could never measure up to anything good or worthy. A whistling and screaming sound began to infiltrate his mind. Jacob felt he was going insane as he stared at the wall and fell to his knees.

"Jacob—Jacob Jerlow, I see you," said an unfamiliar voice inside Jacob's head. "Come to me and I will make you more powerful than you could ever imagine. I can take away every fear that you have. I could even help bring back your father."

Bina, sensing something was definitely wrong with Jacob, stood up and grabbed his hand, saying, "Jacob, are you OK? Jacob, it's me—Bina."

Jacob did not move or break his stare as his mind became more and more weary. The unfamiliar man's voice was overpowering his thoughts. Bina began to quietly cry as she, for a moment, saw Jacob like her father. She tried to regain her composure. She thought for a moment about where to take Jacob, and then it came to her; she would take him to Mr. Wolfe. He was a very gentle and wise man. He would know what to do.

Bina led Jacob to Mr. Wolfe's house.

"Well, hello, you two," said Mr. Wolfe, answering the door. "I hope you are having a happy and fruitful summer."

"We are, Mr. Wolfe...just not tonight," said Bina fearfully, looking over at Jacob.

Jacob was still in a state that made him not communicate. All he could think about was this voice in his head that screamed "fear."

Mr. Wolfe looked at Jacob and said, "Why don't you two come in and have some iced tea?"

They sat down in the living room as Mr. Wolfe came from the kitchen with some glasses of tea. "So, Bina—how long has Jacob been like this?" asked Mr. Wolfe.

"We were just looking for something. He was in a big rush...I mean, it's been less than an hour," Bina answered.

"I see," said Mr. Wolfe, placing his hands on Jacob's. "It's OK, Jacob. There is nothing to fear. We are here for you."

Mr. Wolfe knelt next to Jacob and began to pray in Hebrew. He was speaking very softly, but Bina could make out some of the words he was praying. He was praying for God's strength through his Son, Jesus Christ, to come upon Jacob to help him overcome his fears. Mr. Wolfe grabbed a small bottle from a nearby table that looked like olive oil and began rubbing it into the temples of Jacob's head.

After a few minutes, Jacob could feel some of the pressure that was weighing so heavily on his chest, and the screaming noise in his head, start to drift away. He could now hear Mr. Wolfe's voice, and he began to recognize that he was in Mr. Wolfe's house.

"What happened?" asked Jacob in a daze. "How did I get here, Mr. Wolfe?"

"Praise God!" said Mr. Wolfe softly. "Your friend Bina has brought you here, Jacob. What do you last remember?"

"Uhh...I—I remember running to get Bina and taking her to our favorite spot to hang out, but from there it's all fuzzy."

"Do you remember *why* you were going to get Bina? Was there something on your mind?" asked Mr. Wolfe.

Jacob struggled to recall what had happened, but it was like his mind was making him forget the events so that it could heal. "I—I was bringing Bina to find something...Wait a minute," he said, looking over to Bina. "I had thought of something—a clue that was going to help us find an artifact that we are searching for."

"Very good, Jacob," said Mr. Wolfe. "It is good to have you back again."

Mr. Wolfe walked over to Bina and said to her quietly, "I think it may be a good idea for you to head home so that Jacob and I can talk about some things man to man. He can catch up with you later."

Bina gave Jacob a hug and said that she was going to go visit her dad and that she would catch up with Jacob later.

"Jacob, come with me. I want to show you something," instructed Mr. Wolfe.

Mr. Wolfe led Jacob into his basement, where he had a giant collection of historical paintings, pictures, and books.

"This is an amazing collection of history," said Jacob, looking closely at the pictures hanging on the walls.

"Thank you. I thought you might enjoy them," replied Mr. Wolfe. "Jacob, the last time I saw you, you were asking me about forgiveness. What was weighing so heavily on your mind that you were wondering about forgiveness?"

"Well, honestly," Jacob said, looking for the right words, "I have a great amount of proof that my dad's death was no accident. In fact, he was murdered. I even know who was responsible."

"I see...and how does this make you feel?"

"Angry—like no anger I have ever felt before," Jacob described. "I have tried to forgive, but I can't find it in me. I can only find revenge in my thoughts."

"Jacob, you must listen to me," said Mr. Wolfe, placing his hands on Jacob's shoulders and looking him in the eyes. "Anger must be let go of, for it is anger that leads to worry, and worry leads to fear, and fear leads to destruction. Evil thoughts and actions only create more evil. This has been clearly seen since the beginning of humankind.

"This is why Jesus taught us to '*love* our enemies and to do *good* to those that hurt us,' because he knew that evil only produces more evil. It is quite evident that your anger has led to your fear and anxiety. It is also apparent that all of these issues have compiled, and they hit you today, causing your mind to shut down."

"Today I felt more fear than can be imagined," said Jacob, looking downward and feeling guilty. "It was like every little thing in my life was consuming me from the inside out. It's hard to put into words."

"I understand, Jacob," said Mr. Wolfe, lifting Jacob's chin with his hand. "But you are not to be ashamed. Fear has conquered the greatest of rulers in history—many of which put themselves above their kingdom and people. Fear is the root of all evil, and it is fear that rules the hearts of many and leaves a void to be filled. This empty space in a man's heart and soul is an easy means by which Satan and his demons can enter into your life. It is his evil that will cause you to doubt goodness, love, kindness, and charity and replace them with selfishness, greed, and unbelief.

"Fear is such a major enemy for us that needs to be dealt with that the Bible tells us not to fear more than three hundred times throughout its Scriptures. God knows how much fear can destroy a person and hurt the ones that he or she is close to."

"I understand that fear and anger are bad and I need to get them out of my life, but the problem is, how? How do I get them out of my life?" Jacob pleaded.

"Ah yes, Jacob," said Mr. Wolfe with a smile. "That is the question. It is obvious that your mind has tried to rid yourself of anger and fear, but it is your heart and soul that hold onto them. Unbeknownst to many in today's society, there is no amount of reading books or clinical psychiatrists that frees you of these things. The only way to rid yourself of fear and anger is faith. It is by your faith and relationship with God and his Son, Jesus Christ, that the void in your heart, filled with evil, will be replaced with goodness and love.

"For it is written in the Bible by King David in Psalms chapter thirty-four verse four, 'I sought the LORD, and he heard me, and delivered me from all my fears.' So, Jacob, knowing this, on a scale of one to ten, how would you rate your faith and relationship with God?"

"I have always held something against religion, especially after my dad died. So my relationship is pretty much a zero with God," replied Jacob.

"God, who is the one entity in this universe that can truly take away all of your fears and anxieties, and you're telling me that your relationship with Him is virtually nonexistent?" asked Mr. Wolfe, grabbing a Bible from a nearby table. "We can go to church every Sunday, read the Bible every day, and act as religious as humanly possible, but if we don't have a personal relationship with God and his Son, Jesus Christ, none of these things mean a thing."

Mr. Wolfe began reading Scriptures to Jacob that talked about salvation and building a relationship with God. They knelt down by a wooden cross that hung on the wall and began to pray together. With the guidance of Mr. Wolfe, Jacob made an affirming commitment to God and his Son, Jesus Christ, to live the rest of his life—to the best of his ability—in harmony and loyalty to God and his Kingdom through prayer, reverence, and keeping God's word true.

Jacob felt such a good feeling come through his body it was more than he could ever have imagined. He hugged Mr. Wolfe and began to joyfully cry over his new pledge to God.

Mr. Wolfe instructed Jacob, "Never relinquish your relationship to God, and never back down or compromise your beliefs when confronted by evil, because the world and its evils *will* challenge you and your faith. Anger is not always evil, especially when your anger is directed toward doing what is good and just over what is wicked. Even Jesus, who was the only one who has ever been sinless, became angry in the face of immorality. So we know it is good to fight what is evil and stand up for God's Word.

"Jacob, know this and never forget: most people of the world are blinded by pride and self-gain, and they are on a path of wanting to be 'politically correct' instead of being 'morally correct.' People search for answers through science and what they call 'logical thinking' while completely abandoning what their soul tells them. People and their belief systems may change, but God's Word is forever and unchanging. No matter how much a government or a godless society tries to tell you what is right and just and what is their definition of equality, you must trust in what your spirit tells your mind, which is directed by the holy Word of God. It is through God's love and his unchanging laws that humanity has hope. So always find comfort and wisdom in reading the Bible and praying to God for his guidance through our Lord Jesus Christ."

Jacob felt as if a very heavy load and burden had just been lifted off of his shoulders, and he could not wait to tell his mom all about it. He thanked Mr. Wolfe again and ran home. There he told his mom all about what had happened and his new commitment to God. This was a very joyous moment between Jacob and his mom, because this newly found Spirit also entered Jacob's mom's heart and soul upon hearing Jacob's news. They hugged and wept joyfully in their commitment to God's salvation.

CHAPTER 14

THE TRYOUTS

That night at Heldago, Jacob entered his sword skills class with Sarge to find many students gathered together talking about something with much passion. Jacob approached Jezebel, asking, "What is everyone talking about?"

"They've just announced that they're going to be holding tryouts for class level teams," Jezebel said excitedly.

"'Class level teams?'" replied Jacob. "Teams for what?"

"Oh, no one has ever told you about Certatim?" said Jezebel, surprised. "It's the oldest and most popular game, or competition, among the angelic people. It features our Heldago's classes against the Tenebra's Muerte Palace. Come with me; I'll show you the Hall of Shadows."

Jezebel grabbed Jacob's hand and pulled him down a corridor that he was not familiar with. At the end of the corridor there was a great red curtain that Jezebel moved so they could enter. Upon enter-ing, Jacob was in awe of the masterfully sculpted trophies and the beautifully painted winning teams upon them. The trophies were in chronological order lining the walls and shelves. Every so often there would be an empty space where there was no trophy.

"Jezebel, why are there open spaces with no trophy?" asked Jacob.

"Well—our school has a team for each grade level, and each of our four teams competes against the Tenebra's teams..." Jezebel started.

"Wait a minute—hold on," Jacob interrupted. "I didn't quite catch that the first time. Our school competes against the Tenebras in this competition?"

"Yes, it's the one day of the year that there's a treaty among our families where no fighting, except in the game, may occur," said Jeze-bel. "This treaty is so strict that anyone caught violating it is subjected to the death penalty. Now—where was I? Oh yeah...Each grade level determines a champion, and then those four champions compete to determine an overall champion. These pictures and trophies you see are the overall champions throughout the years. Where there's an open space is when the Tenebras have won, and they hold that trophy in their school."

"So what's the game?" asked Jacob as they started their way back to class.

"The Certatim is a competition of skill, wisdom, and power. Each team gets three players. Each team should have a skilled person in the powers area, sword skills, and martial arts. These are the three areas where there will be tryouts." Jezebel handed a leaflet that described the competition and its rules to Jacob saying, "Here, read this. It will tell you more about the rules. I'm going to try out for the martial arts spot. You should try out for the sword."

"Do you think so?" asked Jacob, placing the leaflet into his pocket. "I guess I'm pretty good. Ya know what? I'm gonna give it a try. It sounds like fun."

"Great! Let's sign up then. The tryouts are being held tomorrow."

There was a great multitude of students, young and old, gathered at the sign-up table. The noise and excitement was thick in the air. Jacob and Jezebel fought their way through the students to get to the table. When they got to the front of the crowd, they saw a picture of last year's overall winner. It was the Moldan class from the Tenebra's Muerte Palace. Seeing this picture of the winners holding up the trophy made Jacob feel excited for the competition, especially since he had never been a part of a team before.

Jezebel and Jacob signed the document with a large, feathered quill pen. The piece of parchment seemed to change its character and color as they signed their names, as if the names became one with the document.

"I was hoping you two were going to sign up," barked Sarge after they'd signed their names.

It was becoming more and more apparent with each passing day that Jacob had special talents that made him powerful. His classmates and the teachers recognized his gifts, but they were also somewhat hesitant because of Jacob's anger issues that would surface during training exercises.

After his classes Jacob was walking back to the Peddle Room when he noticed Shawn talking to Father Santiago. Jacob waited a few moments until they were done with their conversation and approached Shawn. "Hey, Shawn," he said. "I just signed up for Certatim."

"Good fer you," said Shawn with a hug. "I was never able to make it on the team. It would be a great honor fer ya if you be makin' Heldago's Bethal team."

"I'll do my best," said Jacob. "Say, Shawn, I was wondering…Yesterday I had a big mental breakdown—an anxiety attack if you will—and I heard a voice that I've never heard before in my head, and I was hoping you could help me with who, or what, it was. It said, 'Come to me and I will make you more powerful than you could ever imagine,' and something about how it could help bring my dad back to life.'"

"Did ya now…" Shawn paused. "Jacob, when you be at your weakest, evil be at its strongest, and when you be livin' a life apart from God and his plans where evil and sin be overrunnin' yer life, evil has a way of controllin' yer life. One thing leads to another, and one 'innocent' sin starts a-becomin' more and more. I would be guessin' the issues you've been a havin' with anger be the major culprit.

"But…Tenebras be havin' a talent in which they can enter yer thoughts and sometimes even control yer actions. It be especially important fer Veritas to be stayin' away from evil and sin, and keepin' on God's path, because of the risk of the Tenebras gainin' control of our thoughts and actions. If the Tenebras, especially their leader, Prince Muammar, gain control of a Verita, it could be devastatin' to our family and to the world."

"I've heard this Prince Muammar's name mentioned before," said Jacob. "He's the leader of the Tenebras, right? What's his story?"

"Aye, Jacob," replied Shawn. "He be their leader. Legend has it that he be a direct descendant of Satan himself. He has corrupted more minds and had his finger in more atrocities than ya could ever be imaginin'. I have read in our library of some of his actions. For instance, do ya remember learnin' about the Crusades in yer schoolin'?"

"Yeah, we learned about the Holy Wars. They mainly occurred between 1099 and 1291 AD. We learned that many innocent people were robbed and killed by the Muslims and the Christians," said Jacob.

"What ya probably learned isn't all of the truth," Shawn started. "You see, when the Christian Crusaders started fightin' the Muslims, their intentions be good, because the Muslims were tryin' to overtake their land and kill Christians...but what ended up happenin' is a young Prince Muammar was able to get into the minds of some of the Crusaders' leaders and make them do terrible things.

"From robbin' and killin' the innocent to all other evil acts, Prince Muammar had many of the Crusaders under his control. These terrible acts have been seen and heard of fer centuries, but no one could be explainin' why so many of the Crusaders went bad. If it not be the acts of a wise and courageous Verita most of the Christians in the world would be gone, and most of the world would be Muslim today."

"What of this Verita? Do you know who he was?" asked Jacob, as inquisitive as ever.

"Nay—no one be knowin' exactly who the Verita was that be helpin' the Crusaders turn from their evil paths, but rumor has it that it may be our rabbi today. We do know that there was a great battle between this Verita man and Prince Muammar, and the prince was defeated but not killed. The Verita be showin' him mercy and lettin' him go."

"Great story!" said Jacob, excitedly. "That kind of evil is unimaginable. Do you have another one?"

"Unfortunately, there be far too many," he replied. "Prince Muammar gained worldwide notoriety after the Crusades, and he killed the leader of the Tenebras to rule their family—but I'll give you one more story before you be gettin' home. I'm sure you have heard of Hitler and the Jewish Holocaust."

"Oh yes, haven't we all?"

"Aye, Jacob—but what you did not be knowin' is that Hitler's evil actions and sin-filled life as a young man led him to be an easy takin' for Prince Muammar. You see, Prince Muammar had been a-searchin' for some payback to the Jewish people because of their good will toward others and because they be 'God's chosen people' and all. So when Prince Muammar found Hitler and his pursuit fer power in Germany, he was easily able to take over his thoughts and actions.

"One thing be leadin' to another, and before we know it, the Jewish people are bein' killed by the millions. Now tell me, how did Hitler brainwash all of his country into believin' the Jews be bad enough to be exterminated? Even more, how was he able to keep this Holocaust from the rest of the world? This shows you the power of evil. Evil needs not to be feared, but it be need 'in to be respected and learned from to conquer it with goodness."

In the morning Jacob took the leaflet that he had received from Jezebel from his pocket. It read:

The *Certatim Competition* is a game of skill and power control. There is a class level match-up that places school against school, and when the class level champion is determined, there is to be a competition between *Bethal* versus *Clevan* and *Moldan* versus *Elder*. When the champion of these two matches is determined, they will then face each other in the championship match to determine the OVERALL CHAMPION.

<u>*SCORING IS AS FOLLOWS*</u>:

10 points for a blow to the body of your opponent

25 points for a takedown or knocking the opponent to the ground

50 points for disarming the opponent from his or her sword

100 points for placing your opponent in submission by making him or her say "Pareo" or by knockout

<u>RULES</u>

1. A competitor in the level of Elder must be no more than twelve months beyond receiving the rank of Elder.

2. A blow to the head or any infraction to rules is an automatic ten-point deduction from the participant's score. Two blows to the head or infractions in one match is a disqualification, and one hundred points is awarded to the opponent.

3. There are to be four matches per competition. They include martial arts, sword skills, powers, and mixed techniques. In each match the competitor may only use the titled technique in order to score points; for instance, in the martial arts match, the competitor may only use martial arts—no

powers and no sword. In the mixed-technique match, martial arts, sword skills, and powers, all may be used.

4. *There are to be three rounds with each round to be timed at three minutes. A one-minute rest is given in between rounds.*

5. *The winner is declared by either reaching one hundred points earned before time expires or by having the most amount of points at the finish of the third round.*

6. *All points that are earned by the winner of the match will be applied to his or her team's total points. Note: If a winner earns more than one hundred points in their match, all of these points may be applied to their team's total. No points are awarded to the team totals for the loser of a match.*

7. *The team winner is determined by the team with the most points after all four matches have taken place.*

After reading the leaflet, Jacob started thinking about what had come across his mind yesterday when he had rushed over to Bina's house. He knelt down on his knees and began to meditate and pray to release any anxiety in his thoughts from yesterday's experience. He felt a great relief and joyful feeling come across his body, almost like a wind. Jacob gathered his belongings into his backpack and left for Bina's house.

"Jacob, how are you feeling?" asked Bina, opening her front door to greet him. "You look much better today."

"I'm doing much better today, Bina," replied Jacob. "I'm sorry if I scared you yesterday. I had a lot of built-up frustration and evil in my mind that I didn't know how to handle."

Bina invited Jacob into her house and gave him a glass of iced tea, as the day was very hot and humid. Jacob began telling her all that had taken place with Mr. Wolfe the prior day and how he'd made a new commitment to God. Bina could see there was a difference in Jacob. He was holding himself with more confidence, and he seemed to have something about him that was "grandly contagious."

Jacob and Bina became invisible with the help of the medallion and walked out to the Hokmah. By the time they got to the Hokmah, they were sweating profusely, because of the humidity in the air. Jacob took a canteen from his backpack so they could both cool off with a big drink of ice-cold water.

"Do you remember what you were going to show me yesterday?" asked Bina curiously.

"With the help of God, I have," said Jacob, smiling. "Yesterday my mom told me that we are going to be staying at the Hotel Dei Consoli near St. Peter's Square in Rome, and it occurred to me that the Dalet corner's whereabouts may be in St. Peter's burial site because of something that I had seen in the Hokmah."

Jacob began looking through a shelf full of artifacts.

"And what has led you to this conclusion?" asked Bina, trying to look over Jacob's shoulder at the artifacts.

"This," said Jacob, holding up a small figurine of St. Peter. "I remembered seeing this small statue the first time we came into the Hokmah's cavern, but what's important is not the statue itself, but what is written on the bottom of it..."

Jacob turned the statue over and read to Bina, "'And I tell you, you are Peter, and on this *rock* I will build my church.' But that's not all." Jacob grabbed Bina's hand and pulled her over to the Hokmah chest. He pulled a tiny scroll from the corner of the chest and read again, "'Peter, you are the rock and the cornerstone of the church of God, and all paths known and unknown through this world will be held in your hands.' I believe the fourth Dalet corner we are in search of was moved to St. Peter's burial site.

"I believe this unknown author was writing a clue on this statue and on this parchment as to the whereabouts of the last corner. You see here?" said Jacob, holding up the statue and the scroll side by side. "The author's sign, or insignia, is the same after each writing. On both the paper and the statue there is a symbol with a dove and a sun behind it. These symbols are the sign of this author. They both match."

"So you believe this missing corner is referred to in this writing as 'all paths known and unknown through this world,' and it will be kept with St. Peter, because he is referenced as the rock and cornerstone of God's church?" asked Bina.

"Yes, I'm most certain," said Jacob. "The Dalet is the path to places known and unknown throughout the world, and it is held in Peter's midst. It has to be right."

"Brilliant, Jacob!" Bina exclaimed. "Your reasoning is unbelievable, and I can't believe that you remembered the statue and the scroll, and even then, put both of them together. That is just fantastic!"

"Thanks, Bina," Jacob replied. "Yesterday when I thought about this possibility, it was a jumbled mess in my thought process, but today, after I meditated and prayed, it became crystal clear to me what was being said in these two clues. I have to give thanks to God through his Holy Spirit because there's no way that I could have done this on my own."

On their walk home, Jacob and Bina talked about how they were going to study all that is known about St. Peter, his burial site, and all of the surroundings in St. Peter's square that night.

When they got home, they did just what they said they would, but they even brought their mothers into the studying, saying that it would be beneficial to their learning if they had a good foundation of knowledge before arriving in Rome.

That night at Heldago, Jacob went to the sword-testing that he had signed up for the previous day. The testing was being held in the castle's inner meadow by Sarge. Unlike the hot and humid days he was getting back in Hickson, North Dakota, at Heldago it was cool and comfortable, as it was most days.

Jacob stood in line at the entrance to the trials as he watched students from Bethal, Clevan, Moldan, and Elder go through a series of tests with the sword. There were many students who had chosen not to try out for an event looking on. Some had a favorite student and would start chants and yell encouragements as their friends went through the sword trials.

As a number of students had gone through the trials and tests, Jacob could tell which ones were in which class by the difficulty levels that were given to each student. Sarge had the students go through of series of sword maneuvers that showed their strengths and weaknesses quite quickly.

Finally, it was Jacob's turn. He felt his heart start to race in his chest with nervousness. He took a deep breath, closed his eyes, and calmed himself. When he opened his eyes, he saw in the distance of the meadow a figure of a man looking on, but could not recognize who he was.

To the amazement of many onlookers, Jacob declined the practice sword that was being offered to him as he pulled his sword from his belt and made the blade appear. Most Bethals went through all of their training without their real sword that was made for them, so to see Jacob with his sword was quite shocking to many, because it usually took an angelic born months or years of practice before he or she could call upon their sword.

Sarge gave his instructions as to the test guidelines before Jacob began. Jacob swung his sword with great determination. With each maneuver he gained more confidence, as he felt as if there were someone next to him giving him assurance and guidance. He did not miss a cut or a stab, nor did any oncoming threat touch him. As he neared the end of the test, he could tell that he was being given more difficult trials than any other Bethal student had been given, but he relished the challenge. Then—he was finished. Not one miss! Not one point deducted! Sarge looked over toward Jacob and gave him an affirmative head nod, as if to say, "That's the way it should be done."

Jacob glanced in curiosity at the meadow's horizon and saw the man that he had seen a few moments ago still looking on at Jacob. He placed his sword in his belt, under his robe, and began slowly walking toward the stranger. As he neared him, Jacob thought, "I've seen this man somewhere before." Then suddenly, it came to him as he drew closer; it was the man he had seen by the trees at his dad's funeral in the cemetery.

"Hello, sir," said Jacob. "I've seen you before, at my dad's funeral. Do I know you?"

"You do, and you do not," said the man. "I enjoyed watching your sword trials. You have progressed very well, especially as of late. And you carry your sword on your belt like it has been there for years."

"Oh, I'm sorry," said Jacob. "I didn't know you were a teacher here at Heldago. I'm still getting to know some of the teachers and students, and I guess I haven't met you yet."

"No, I am not a teacher—not in Heldago anyway," the man said. "I see a glow in your spirit."

"Oh yeah. I made a new commitment to God recently—with some help from a good friend—and it has really changed my outlook on life. Some of my friends and even my mom have been changed positively by it."

"There is no greater gift given by God than friendship and love. Good friends are like stars—you don't always see them, but you know they are always there."

"Thank you, sir," said Jacob. "May I ask your name?"

"Most of my friends call me Michael," said the man, looking toward an approaching figure. "Here comes your friend Jezebel."

Jacob turned to look toward the crowd and saw Jezebel approaching. When he looked back to the man, he was nowhere to be seen. "Where did he go?" asked Jacob.

"Where did who go?" asked Jezebel. "I saw you standing out here all by yourself so I wanted to come and ask you how your sword trial went."

"I think it went very well..." replied Jacob, looking around the area for Michael. "Uhh—How did your martial arts trial go?"

"It went amazing! I think I really have a shot at making the team!"

"You really didn't see me talking to a man a few moments ago?" asked Jacob in disbelief.

"Ah no—I think I would remember seeing a man talking to you," Jezebel said. "Why? What's going on?"

Jacob explained to Jezebel how he had seen Michael at his dad's funeral, then again watching his trial, and finally how he'd disappeared without being seen. Jezebel was hesitant regarding Jacob's recollection and dismissed it as stress in relation to the trials. They left for their classes talking about the other Bethal students from classes earlier in the day whom they had seen in action.

The next morning Jacob went to the grocery store with Bina to grab some groceries for his mom and when leaving the store saw Felix Matthews behind the store. Felix was holding up a younger student named Joseph Michelson from their school and making threats, saying, "If you don't pay me the money you owe me, something awful might happen to your family."

"Felix, let the kid go!" yelled Jacob.

Felix looked slowly over at Jacob and said, "Why don't you come over here and make me, or maybe you can send your little girlfriend home to tell your mommy."

Jacob felt anger building up inside him that grew like a forest fire as his fists clenched. He then remembered the words that Mr. Wolfe and Shawn had spoken to him about releasing anger and not letting Tenebra's evil change honorable actions. He felt more at ease and took a deep breath in and out as he walked slowly toward Felix. As he approached him, Jacob noticed that Felix's eyes looked more lifeless, and his skin more pale, since the last time he had seen him.

"You don't need to do this," whispered Bina.

"It's OK," Jacob said reassuringly. "We need to stand up to the face of evil in the world."

Felix set little Joseph Michelson down and turned to Jacob. Joseph looked at both of them, thought for a moment, and then ran away as fast as he could. Felix walked to Jacob and met him face to face. Felix was still taller than Jacob and felt even more confident than he had displayed so many times in school, looking downward into Jacob's eyes.

"I know what you are..." Felix mumbled.

"Don't you mean you know *who* I am?" asked Jacob.

"No, I know *what* you are—you filthy Verita.

"Well, I guess we know what we are and where we both came from then," said Jacob sarcastically. "Now what?"

"I would love to rip your head off and feed it to your little girl-friend right now, but I'm under oath to not hurt you—*yet!*" said Felix, looking down at Jacob's sword handle, which was connected to his belt.

"Aren't I the lucky one?" Jacob laughed. "Maybe, if you're good enough, you will be on your school's Certatim team, and you can meet me on the field."

"I'm already on the team. The question is, are you? Were you good enough to make the team?" Felix taunted.

"I don't know yet," said Jacob. "I'll find out tomorrow. What are you competing in?"

"I could have competed in any of the events because I'm the best, but I chose powers and the mixed technique to compete in," said Felix. "I will hope, and let you pray, that you've made the team, because when I meet you in the ring I'm gonna beat you down."

"We'll see," said Jacob as he grabbed Bina's hand and walked away.

"What was that all about?" whispered Bina.

Jacob explained the Certatim competition to Bina as they walked back to his house. He had even more of a competitive spirit growing inside of him with every word he used to describe the competition and its rules, now that he had seen his competition face-to-face.

That day Jacob and Bina grew more excited about their last adventure of the summer as they talked about all that they had learned from their studies of Rome and St. Peter's Square.

"I read that Peter is buried directly under the Basilica of St. Peter," Jacob started. "Even more precisely, he's buried directly below the baldachin—or canopy—and altar in the Basilica. And the Chair of St. Peter, or cathedra near the altar, is the ancient chair that was said to be used by Peter himself. Also, even more cool is this altar is where the Pope blesses the bread and wine for Mass and where he sits during special occasions and has done so for centuries."

"I read that as well, Jacob," Bina said. "One thing you might not have seen is that the name Peter is 'Petros' in Greek, coming from 'petra,' which means 'stone' or 'rock' in Greek. Just another finger pointing to Peter as being the 'rock' on which the church would be built."

Jacob and Bina sat in Jacob's living room with a cold glass of iced tea continuing their conversation.

"That is really amazing!" said Jacob. "I didn't read that. Did you read about how Peter was crucified head down because he said that he was not worthy to die in the same manner as Jesus Christ? Also, did you see that the ancient Egyptian obelisk that sat in the Circus of Nero was placed in the center of St. Peter's Square because it is the last 'witness' to Peter's crucifixion?"

"I did read that," replied Bina, getting more and more excited about facts and history. "You know, that Circus of Nero was Emperor Nero's killing site of not only Peter but countless Christians. But it was Emperor Constantine around 326 AD who ordered the Old St. Peter's Basilica to be built over the site of the Circus of Nero to show Christians overcoming their bloodshed and persecution. Furthermore, that ancient obelisk has a bronze cross at the top that contains a real fragment of the cross that held Jesus Christ.

"After the old St. Peter's Basilica became very dilapidated, it was torn down, and the new St. Peter's Basilica—which still stands today—was constructed from 1506 to 1626. But I did see that the builders made sure that the new altar was built again over St. Peter's grave, just like what had been done with the first Basilica."

"I also read those facts, Bina," said Jacob. "One thing is for certain, I would consider it to be a miracle in itself if the Dalet corner is still located near Peter's tomb because of all the building and destruction that has occurred throughout the years around his burial site."

"So we need to figure out how we're going to get down under the Basilica to see Peter's tomb," said Bina.

"Already done," said Jacob proudly. "My mother and I booked a tour to see the tomb last night over the Internet. Which I'm glad we did because they're usually booked solid well in advance. The tour is referred to as a Scavi Tour, and it will take us directly under the Basilica to see Peter's tomb."

Jacob and Bina continued talking the day away with Jacob's mom peeking her head in the living room occasionally to see if they were still talking about the trip.

That night at Heldago, Jacob entered the castle with one thing on his mind: "Did I make the team?" Jezebel met him when he entered the castle, saying, "I waited for you to see if we made the team. Come on, let's go to the wall and see the results together."

Jezebel and Jacob walked nervously to the wall that held the large ceremonial scroll. The scroll was seven feet tall and seven feet wide and was made from dried animal skins, just as it had been made for centuries. There were a great number of students and staff surrounding the scroll and talking about the teams as Jacob and Jezebel squeezed through to catch a glimpse at the names. There the teams were, easily readable due to how large the writing was. The scroll read:

BETHAL TEAM
Martial Arts: Jezebel Flores—15 years old (Mexico)
Powers: Miguel Cruz—15 years old (Spain)
Sword: Jacob Jerlow—14 years old (United States of America)
Mixed: TBA

CLEVAN TEAM
Martial Arts: Ronald Rasmussen—17 years old (Norway)
Powers: Ramiro Vasquez—16 years old (Cuba)
Sword: Tabitha Fulks—17 years old (Australia)
Mixed: TBA

MOLDAN TEAM

Martial Arts: Hiroshi Sato—17 years old (Japan)

Powers: Malik Johansson—18 years old (Greenland)

Sword: Tidarat Ban—18 years old (Thailand)

Mixed: TBA

ELDER TEAM

Martial Arts: Sachin Kumar—20 years old (India)

Powers: Ada Milano—20 years old (Italy)

Sword: Yuri Eltsin—20 years old (Russia)

Mixed: TBA

Jacob and Jezebel gave each other a big congratulatory hug as some onlookers clapped when they noticed the two had made the team. They asked each other who Miguel Cruz was, and if either of them had met him before, but neither had so they began to look around to find their Bethal teammate. After fighting through the crowd and asking many students who Miguel Cruz was, they did not have any leads.

"Congratulations, Jacob and Jezebel," said a small voice from the crowd.

Jacob and Jezebel looked at each other and said, "Who was that?"

Jacob looked down and saw a pair of small hands fighting their way through the crowd as their owner tried to make himself visible. Jacob grabbed the little hands and pulled a gnome out of the crowd of people.

"Oh thank you, I say," said the gnome. "Yelkie is my name. Watched you practice and make the team I have. Goodness now flows in you—this I have seen."

"It's nice to meet you, Yelkie," said Jacob, politely trying to still search for his teammate. "Have you seen a boy named Miguel Cruz?"

"Seen him I have," said Yelkie, pointing to the edge of the crowd.

"Oh—thank you," said Jezebel, excitedly pulling on Jacob's hand in the direction given by Yelkie.

While walking to the back of the crowd to exit, Jacob and Jezebel nearly tripped over a boy who was hovering slightly off of the ground in a meditative state. The boy was quite small in stature and had a shaved head—all the way down to his skin. His bald head showed his Verita's birthmark, which resembled that of a bear. He had his arms folded, his legs crossed, and his eyes closed, and seemed to not have any awareness of—or just did not care about—what was going on around him.

"Excuse me, but are you Miguel Cruz?" asked Jezebel, trying to gain the attention of the floating boy.

The boy opened his eyes slowly, saying, "I am...and your names must be Jezebel Flores and Jacob Jerlow."

"Oh, you've already seen the teams, Miguel?" asked Jacob.

"No, I have not," Miguel replied. "I just saw it in my mind."

Miguel had an uncanny ability to read the thoughts and feelings of people, and it was this that made him a force to be reckoned with in a battle of powers. At this time Sarge approached the three, saying, "I guess congratulations are in order, but there isn't much time for that; you three are to report to my office in ten minutes."

The three teammates began talking about their families and where they were from. Since Miguel was from a class earlier in the day, as well as many other students from his time zone, Jacob and Jezebel had never met them before. There were many classes that occurred throughout the day that gave attention to any student from any part of the world, being that not all people throughout the world slept at the same time.

The Bethal team walked into Sarge's office and met up with the other three teams that were conversing among each other on their team strategies.

"So—here we are," barked Sarge at the front of the room. "Another set of teams comprised of Heldago's elite has been assembled for this year's World Certatim Championships. It seems like yesterday I was sitting in your shoes looking at my coach for the Certatim Championships...But that was well over five hundred years ago, and now, you are our teams.

"We expect only the best from each and every one of you," he said, slowly walking around the room looking into students' eyes. "You have all been selected because you've shown a great expertise in a certain area. So do not let me, your teachers, your fellow Heldago students, or Veritas around the world be disappointed in your preparatory or game day actions."

Sarge had a way of motivating students that made them want to reach to new heights and better themselves in every way. This could be seen by clenched fists or the occasional head nod or nervous tick like a knee shaking up and down at one hundred miles per hour.

"The Certatim will start one week from today," Sarge instructed. "Each of your teachers will be spending a little extra time, beyond your normal class time, with each and every one of you this next week. So if you have any questions or skills that need to be addressed, this will be the time to take special attention to such matters. You are all free to go, except the Bethal team."

The teams left the room.

"Since this is your first experience with the Certatim Championships, I wanted to address any concerns or questions you may have so we can minimize any anxiety you may be feeling," said Sarge. "Let's start with questions. I'm sure you have some."

"Sarge, the other older students will know so many more powers and skills than us—how will we compete?" asked Jacob.

"The next week your teachers will be giving you some advanced skills to help you in your competition," explained Sarge. "I know the situation you're in puts you at a disadvantage, but this is the best we can do. Since you don't have a mixed-technique contestant yet, it'll be necessary for all three of you to attend the advanced mixed-technique class time this week. By the end of the week, your team may decide which of you three will take this position. If there's not a clear decision about who this person should be, then might I suggest drawing straws.

"The Bethal team has never made it to the championship match in the history of the Certatim, but as I look into your eyes right now, I can honestly say that this year will be the best chance ever for a Bethal team to make it."

The students stared intently at Sarge, grabbing onto every word that he spoke like it was theirs to keep.

"Well, if there aren't any more questions at this time, I wanted to tell you all one last thing...and that is about the judges for the Certatim. There are four judges, or referees, called Fulders. The reason that I tell you about them before you see them is to prepare you, because their appearance can be a little unnerving to some. These creatures don't have a face but have two large yellow eyes that can see ten times better than you or I. They don't have legs to stand on but hover over the ground and can fly around the match to take different viewing angles of the competition. Their bodies are covered with loose-fitting robes that are white on one side and black on the other, signifying the good and evil in the world.

"They are neither living nor dead. They were made in unison thousands of years ago by angels from heaven and angels from hell for the sole purpose of judging and refereeing the Certatim. Being that they were made by both sides, they don't show favoritism toward one group over another. The Fulders have no partiality. They don't care who wins. This is what makes them a perfect official for the matches, because they cannot be persuaded to take a side. The rules they enforce and the points that they award are not contested. What they say is the final decision, in all circumstances, with the competition.

"To get to the actual location of the Certatim, we use a portal. A Fulder will arrive on the day of the competition and deliver the portal key. The portal key when touched will transport the contestants and fans to the site of the competition. The only ones who know where the competition will be held each year are the Fulders. They are the ones who decide on its location, and they are the ones who cast a spell on the portal key to deliver Veritas to the site. There is also a sister portal key that is made, and it is delivered to the Tenebras in Muerte Palace. They use the key just as we do."

After their meeting the three Bethals went to their powers class. Don was quick to congratulate the three on their appointment to the team but even quicker to warn them of the hard work that they would have to put in during the next week in order to stay safe and be competitive in the Certatim. He wasted no time in showing them an advanced technique that would be needed during the competition.

"The crudaceous power is one of the most powerful forces that an angelic born possesses," Don started. "It is by no means some carnival magic trick. When perfected, it can create untold energy and force."

Don opened his hand, and a ball of white fire started hovering over his palm. With his mouth he blew some air toward the ball, and it began slowly encircling the room—just above Jacob's, Jezebel's, and Miguel's heads.

"The crudaceous power is made of energy from within, and it can be constructed into many different powerful forms of energy," said Don, "like lightning, fire, and different forms of electricity. If someone uses this force against you, then you must be able to use that same force to meet that power head-on. For instance, if Miguel here were able to shoot a lightning bolt at me, I had better be able to create a lightning bolt that can meet his opposing force.

"Where it gets more difficult and especially challenging for you for this competition is as an angelic born ages, they learn to control this inner power more and more, thus making the crudaceous power more forceful and devastating. So you may find it very difficult when confronted by an older competitor to counteract their power."

Don began teaching the students how to find and control the crudaceous power, saying, "You must find the inner parts of your being. This is undoubtedly a place you have never been. I want you all to sit, cross your legs, close your eyes, and hold your hands out, palms toward the ceiling.

"Now calm yourself and all emotions. Listen and feel your heart-beat. Feel every contraction...Once you are in this state of relaxation, you must reach further. Relax yourself and your mind, and find the spark inside your soul; when you can feel the force, tell it to rest in your hand in the form of fire."

The students relaxed and concentrated on Don's instructions. Soon Miguel had a ball of fire in each of his hands, and to his amuse-ment he had the fire bouncing up and down in his hands like a rubber ball. Jacob and Jezebel, still with their eyes closed, searched for the power. Jacob felt the power and tried to release the energy a little at a time into his hands, but the force was too much, and flames came shoot-ing from his hands, torching the ceiling and causing a huge black burn. It startled Jacob so much that he lost focus, and the fire dissipated.

The noise was so great from the explosive fire that Jezebel lost her concentration and was staring at Jacob. Miguel was giggling as he bounced one fireball from one hand to the other in a juggling manner.

"A little too much funneled through, ehh, Jacob?" asked Don.

All of the kids and Don began laughing.

"You found that force that lies within you," said Don. "Now you just need to learn to control it."

For the next few hours Jacob, Jezebel, and Miguel got much bet-ter at their control of the crudaceous power. As with most powers, Miguel was a quick learner and found the force of the power easier to control than others. Jacob showed a great deal of power and strength, but controlling it was difficult for him.

At the end of class, Triple E entered the room and instructed, "To this point you have all entered Heldago during your sleep, but it is necessary now for you to learn the meditation method of entry because you will all need to be here at the same time to train together. This is necessary because Jacob and Jezebel are from the late class and Miguel is from the early class.

"Now—if you can place yourself in a relaxed, meditative state, like I'm sure you have all learned to do by now, then you can put yourself in touch with Heldago. All that is necessary is for you to meditate and concentrate on Heldago itself, and you will be brought here just as in your sleep."

Triple E gave times in relation to where they lived so that all three Bethals would meet at the front door of Heldago the next day using the meditation method. The three said their good-byes as they entered the Peddle Room to return home.

Throughout the next morning, Jacob found himself locked in his bedroom learning how to control his newly found crudaceous power. In his training he managed to set his curtains on fire. He grabbed the old garbage can from his bathroom, filled it with water and dumped it on the flames. The smoke infiltrated the room. He quickly opened the windows and pointed his fan outside to blow the noxious fumes away.

Jacob's mom knocked on the door. "I smell smoke coming from your room," she said. "Is everything OK in there?"

"I think someone is burning leaves in the neighborhood," Jacob stuttered, nervously. "Everything is OK in here."

Sarah shrugged it off and returned to her room to read.

At this time, in Muerte Palace, Prince Muammar had just summoned Felix Matthews to his room. "Congratulations on making the Bethal's Certatim team, Felix," he sneered. "We won the Certatim both in my Clevan and Moldan years. A matter of fact, the time we won the Certatim my Clevan year, it marked the first time in history that a Clevan team had won the Certatim."

"That's fantastic, Prince Muammar," said Felix, kissing up.

"We are still awaiting a Bethal team to rise up and win the championships for the first time," said Prince Muammar. "Do you think your team could be the first Bethal team to win?"

"I don't think, my Prince; I know," Felix said, confidently. "With me in the powers and mixed-technique matches, Diablo Florentine in the sword, and Joan Braile in the martial arts, we will crush the Verita's Bethal team and anyone else who stands in our way."

"Confidence—I like confidence," said Prince Muammar, walking over to a deep pit in the corner of the room. The walls of this large hole in the ground were supported by skeletons and dried flesh, and smelled of rotten fish. "Have you seen the list of names for the Verita's team?"

"I have," Felix answered.

"What do you think about Jacob Jerlow being in the competition? I have heard rumors that he says he will crush you, send you to your knees, and make you say 'pareo.'" Prince Muammar was, of course, telling lies to Felix in order to multiply the anger inside of him.

"I will crush that piece of trash and all that he stands for!" shouted Felix in anger. "I would rather take twenty lashes to my back in front of the whole school rather than say 'pareo' to Jacob Jerlow."

"Indeed," said Prince Muammar, looking down the well. "You see our brother Tao here at the bottom of this pit...or what is left of him.

This is the kind of fate that awaits those who disappoint me and our cause."

Felix looked down the dark hole and saw Tao barely alive, having been eaten by flesh-eating beetles. Tao's hands and feet were bound, and the bugs were slowly eating away at his body. Felix nearly threw up. He quickly bit his tongue in order to stop the involuntary response.

"Flesh-eating beetles are amazing creatures," Prince Muammar began. "They can go months without eating. As you can imagine, once they are given the opportunity to eat flesh, they tear flesh away with their jaws and become quite ravenous. Their most favorite part of the body is the brain. They will fight each other over which beetle will eat its way through the ear canal so they can divulge in the delicacy of brain matter. This can be quite painful for a person, because you are alive and conscious as the beetles slowly eat away the inside of your skull."

Felix turned away from the disgusting site and said, "You can count on me, Prince Muammar—I will never disappoint you."

"I know this, Felix Matthews—I know this," Prince Muammar said, placing his arm over Felix's shoulder and walking him to his door. "Train hard, and I look forward to seeing you compete next week. And don't forget...it is power that gives you strength."

Felix went straight away and grabbed his teammates, Joan and Diablo, and began furiously training with his teachers. Each minute of training, their anger and fire grew deeper, darker, and more committed.

At this time, in Jacob's bedroom, Jacob was recalling what Triple E had told him about returning to Heldago. "According to Triple E's instructions, I am to meditate at one p.m. to meet Miguel and Jezebel at Heldago," he thought.

Jacob sat down next to his bed and began to meditate. Once he was relaxed, he concentrated on Heldago, and soon he was standing in front of Heldago—just as if he had fallen asleep. He looked over to his right and saw Jezebel and Miguel smiling at him.

"Made it with no troubles, I expect?" asked Miguel in his heavy Spanish accent.

"No, it was quite easy, actually," replied Jacob.

The three entered Heldago and went to Master Kang for martial arts. "To this point you have all learned basic offensive and defensive moves," said Master Kang. "In these next few days, we are going to practice a series of defensive moves that lead to one devastating blow to your opponent. This blow is called the kalari. It is an ancient strike that can disorientate an opponent enough to easily place them into a pareo submission."

Master Kang brought out a human dummy and pointed out the exact location on the human body on which to make the kalari strike. "The point is directly under the sternum, or chest bone," he started. "This spot that you must strike, called your 'chi,' is the center of your body and spirit. If hit correctly, it completely disorientates your opponent, making it very easy to place them into submission. The only way to hit this small area directly is with your extended middle finger."

Master Kang demonstrated striking the dummy with his thumb, his first and second fingers extended and his third and fourth fingers bent. "The middle finger must hit directly in this spot," he said, striking the dummy quickly. "The strike zone is about the size of the tip of your finger only. If you hit the chi area with more than just the tip of your middle finger, the energy from your blow is dispersed to the surrounding area and is not effective. You must strike the exact location of the opponent's center of chi with your middle finger."

Master Kang instructed the three students how to get into a fighting stance and told them to demonstrate the proper finger placement for a strike.

"Master Kang, why do we extend the thumb and first and second fingers but not the third and fourth fingers?" asked Jezebel.

"Ah—good question. You are stabilizing the middle finger for a sound strike, and by using this finger placement you are directing more of your own body's energy into the opponent's chi," Master Kang explained. "The energy that comes from your body into the strike makes the blow to the opponent's chi much more devastating."

After having the students practice the kalari strike on the dummy for almost an hour, Master Kang said, "Now that you all have the tools with which to deliver the kalari blow, you must now know how to receive the strike personally."

The three Bethals looked at each other in hesitation.

"In order for you to better understand the blow, you must have a firsthand knowledge of what it feels like," Master Kang said. "I will only deliver the blow at half speed for your first day, as its force can be quite daunting. Now—who would like to go first?"

The three students paused for a moment, hoping another would raise his or her hand.

"I will," said Jezebel confidently. "After all, I'm representing our team in the martial arts competition, so I should step up to the plate."

Master Kang called her closer to him and delivered the strike to Jezebel's chi, making her fall to her knees. She seemed to be in an extreme daze, trying to focus in on her surroundings. She was obviously disorientated. As she regained her composure on the ground, Jacob and Miguel went through the same hit to their chi, sending them to the ground as well.

After some time passed, the three regained their composure and began discussing the kalari blow and how it felt.

"It felt like someone had ripped a piece of my soul out and was dangling it in front of me out of reach," said Miguel. "I have never felt so helpless."

"I agree—well put," said Jacob and Jezebel.

The students kept up their training for a while longer, working on ways to defend the blow if another tried to deliver the strike on them. The kalari strike definitely had slowed the students and made them tired. They were looking forward to going home to get some much-needed rest.

That night, when Jacob returned home, it was dinnertime. He had dinner with his mom and relaxed for the night. During sleep that night, Jacob went to Heldago as usual but did not do any of his advanced classes. Upon arrival, his fellow classmates were very excited to talk to him and Jezebel about their training and preparations for the Certatim.

"So, Jacob, how does it feel to be king of the world?" asked Luke sarcastically in his heavy New Jersey accent.

"King of the world belongs to God," said Jacob. "I am merely his servant."

Luke rolled his eyes.

For many years now, almost in step with the human world, Heldago had drifted away from a close relationship to God. So for its students to hear Jacob so easily speak of God and his grace felt somewhat out of place. In the past, Heldago had regular religion classes, and going to church to pray was not looked upon as an order, but as a privilege, but as human society had drifted more away from God, so had Heldago. The Verita's will to do good for the world was still strong, but their relationship to their Creator had lessened throughout the years.

"Are you two nervous about competing against more skilled opponents?" asked Fred. "It must be a little intimidating knowing that you may face an Elder."

"The teachers are teaching us some advanced techniques to better equip us for the competition, but beyond that, we just need to do our best," said Jezebel. "We may not have the same level of practice that the competition has, but we have something that they cannot equal—determination and spirit."

"I am very—how do you say—excited to see you compete," said Jack in his broken English. Jack did his best with the English language, but many times it was difficult to understand him. He was a loving and caring sort of boy who cared deeply about others' feelings.

"Thanks, Jack," said Jezebel and Jacob.

"OK, OK, enough of the mushy stuff," Luke interrupted. "The whole school is talking about the Certatim competition, but maybe even more so they're talking about your quest for the Dalet. So what about it? Have you found some of the missing Dalet corners? Is this a myth or what?"

"I haven't spoken much of this journey that I've accepted because of fear of what may or may not happen, but if I can't trust my fellow Veritas then whom can I trust?" said Jacob, looking at his Bethal friends.

"It's true. A close friend of mine, Bina Feldman, and I have partaken in many journeys in search of the hidden Dalet corners. They're most certainly real and are no myth. We currently have three of the corners and are going to Italy after the Certatim to search for the last piece."

"So are the rumors true—with all four corners of the Dalet, can someone enter the doorway and go anyplace on Earth?" asked Fred.

"From what I've learned, what you've said is true, but without the fourth corner we can't be certain," Jacob explained. "Needless to say there's not an instruction manual or anything on the Internet that can explain how to use the Dalet. My dad and his dad had been putting clues together for years on where the Dalet may be hidden. Before my dad was killed by a Tenebra, he was able to find the first corner in Australia."

Jacob continued explaining his journeys with Bina and how they had battled Tenebras and beasts to get the first three corners.

"It's just like those bloodsucking Tenebras to want to gain control of the Dalet so they can prey on the innocent!" shouted Luke. "Question is, how in the heck have they known your every move? They've met you at every place to try and steal it."

"Yeah, I've racked my brain over this as well, but the only thing that would make sense is that there is a Verita telling the information to the Tenebras," said Jacob. "Remember when Triple E read us a letter from the rabbi? It said that there's believed to be a traitor in our midst. This person must be the one who has given information over to the Tenebras."

"Well, Shawn has been with you in all of these adventures, right?" asked Jezebel.

"No, no, no, there's no possible way Shawn could be the one," Jacob said abruptly, before Jezebel could make another accusation. "He's saved my life on more than one occasion. There's just no possible way that Shawn could have anything to do with information getting into the Tenebra's hands."

"I meant no offense, Jacob," said Jezebel. "But please do keep an open mind. Shawn is the only one who's been close to you and your father, and the mind-control techniques of the Tenebras can be nearly undetectable."

The Bethals gathered their things and started walking toward their first class. As they walked, Jacob found himself beginning to think more and more about what Jezebel had said about Shawn and started leaning toward Shawn as being the betrayer. "Maybe his kindness toward me has been some sort of an act to hide his faithfulness to the Tenebras. Maybe he's waiting for me to get all four corners, and then he will turn the Dalet and me over to the Tenebras. It all makes sense. I'd better keep a close eye on him," Jacob thought.

The following afternoon Jacob placed himself in meditation to return to Heldago for some advanced training in the sword. Jezebel and Miguel had not arrived yet, so Jacob entered the castle. Upon entering, he saw Sarge in the inner meadow practicing his sword skills. Jacob was amazed by how gracefully Sarge moved with his sword using his favorite Camtra skills. Sarge stopped his training abruptly and knelt to pray and meditate.

"Come over, Jacob," said Sarge after a few moments of silence.

Jacob walked to Sarge, grasping his sword in his belt. Jacob was the only Bethal with his true sword, and he held it proudly on his belt like the Elders who walked in Heldago.

"Looks like you're working hard, Sarge," Jacob said. "Do you have something planned?"

"No, Jacob, nothing planned," Sarge said, standing to his feet and placing his sword in his belt. "Preparation is more like it."

"Preparation? Preparation for what?" asked Jacob curiously.

"Oh, you never can tell," said Sarge, almost in a manner of hiding something.

Jacob thought for a moment. "Sarge, has it been a long time since there was war between the Veritas and the Tenebras?"

Sarge paused for a moment, looking at the scars on his arms. "We've had our skirmishes, but we haven't had war in..." he began. "It's been quite a while—many years as a matter of fact. War is a horrible thing and should be avoided when all possible...but sometimes there lies a necessity to preserve goodness in the world and no form of diplomacy will matter."

"I can only imagine the wars and battles you've seen," said Jacob.

"Indeed—some are unimaginable. Throughout the ages we've done our best to hide our powers and identity from the human world, but as you can imagine, some battles have been seen by humans. I guess you could say this is where many of the Greek gods and 'magic' folklore have come from throughout the nations of the world. Humans can't really comprehend our powers or our world. It's best for us to keep our world from them. Now—let me see that sword of yours," he said to change the subject.

Jacob took his sword handle from his belt and handed it over to Sarge.

"This sword is beautifully crafted," said Sarge, making the blade appear with his power. "It is perfectly balanced and razor sharp...just as you should be—perfectly balanced and razor sharp in your skills."

"Sarge, I thought that I was the only one who could make the sword's blade appear from the handle," asked Jacob.

"No, this is not true," Sarge instructed. "Anyone with the correct power control can make your blade appear, but the owner of the sword is the one who can speak to it and make it do extraordinary things. Many of these things you will learn in time, and with practice, with your sword."

Sarge made the blade disappear and handed the sword back to Jacob. He pulled his sword from his belt and picked up a piece of scrap metal that was lying close by. Sarge tossed the piece of metal into the air and sliced his blade through the falling steel. His blade glowed red and yellow with heat as it melted through the metal like a hot knife through cold butter. Two pieces of metal fell to the ground, both releasing smoke from the melted steel.

"You see," said Sarge, "you can transfer your energy through your sword and make your blade do amazing things."

Jacob paused briefly, soaking in what he just saw. "Why do you suppose I was able to call upon my sword while no other Bethal has been able to do so—as well as many Clevans?" Jacob asked.

"I don't know for certain, Jacob, but it must be one of two things. Either you have an unheard-of connection with your sword, or there is someone who gave you a little help."

Just then, Miguel and Jezebel came running through the front gates.

"I'm sorry we're late," said Jezebel.

"It's quite all right—this time—since it was necessary for Jacob and me to discuss some technique," said Sarge. "Now—let's get you three your competition wooden swords. They're much stronger than our practice swords."

After giving the Bethals their swords, Sarge helped the three put their Certatim uniforms on for their practice. The uniforms were made of a lightweight material similar to leather that could easily block a blow from the competitor without giving too much damage to the body.

"These are your protective uniforms for the competition," said Sarge. "They were made by the Fulders themselves. As you may notice, the uniform is lightweight, easily manageable, and as strong as steel. A matter of fact, it's so strong that it can slow down the strongest of powers applied to you. I'm not saying that a direct blow from a sword or power is not going to hurt with this on, but it will definitely help.

"With this said, you will wear this protective uniform in the powers and swords matches but not in the martial-arts match. In the martial-arts match, you will wear a *gi*, or martial-arts robe. Whoever is in the mixed-technique match will have the option of wearing the protective uniform or not. Except for your martial-arts classes this week, I want you all to wear these protective uniforms in your training to get accustomed to how they feel and move with your body."

After explaining the uniforms, Sarge proceeded to teach the advanced skill for the day. "Today I will begin teaching you the most deadly sword blow that can be given toward your opponent," he said. "You will undoubtedly receive this blow, or something similar, in the competition. So you must be able to defend yourself against it and be able to apply it as well. The blow is called the kama. It uses a combination of power from within and a whiplike action causing an accelerating sword. It may be delivered from the left or right, or from an extreme jump into a frontal assault."

Sarge proceeded to demonstrate the kama with a blow on a dummy with an arched back, a jump, and a whipping motion; the sword seemed to almost fly from his hand as he cut the dummy in half with his wooden practice sword.

"The energy from within you must be transferred through your sword and into the target, making the sword's blow that much more devastating," Sarge taught. "For now, you're all using wooden swords, but you can transfer your energy through it as well. It will be just that much more of a powerful blow when you use your steel sword that is made for you someday."

The Bethals trained for hours on the kama. Sarge had a way of bringing out the very best in an individual on the field of battle. His students strove to make themselves better—they trained like their lives depended on it.

The following days passed very quickly with both the Heldago teams and the Muerte Palace teams training very intensely. The intensity of the training for both schools was very similar, demanding physically and mentally but different in outlook and procedure. The Tenebras trained with hatred and the goal of placing fear in their opponents, for evil and darkness were what made them stronger. The Veritas trained with determination and honor as their guide, for truth and light were what gave them strength.

CHAPTER 15

THE CERTATIM

The night before the Certatim, Jacob went to Bina's house to ask her if she wished to come and watch the competition. Of course, she was thrilled at the opportunity. They made plans to meet the next day at five p.m. and go to the Hokmah. There Jacob would hold Bina's hand and take her to Heldago and through the portal key.

Knowing very well of the dangers in the Certatim competition that Jacob would be confronted with and the possibility of never seeing his mom again, he wanted to have dinner and quality time with her. After dinner he went for a quiet walk with his mom. The temperature outside was cool and comfortable, and there was a slight breeze that blew on Jacob's face that carried many of the summer's scents. From freshly mowed grass to burning leaves, the scents were full of memories. These scents brought Jacob back to great times with his dad on archaeology hunts. But now, with a clear mind and a forgiving heart, Jacob did not have anger when he thought of his dad, only love and compassion.

Sarah stared at her son and cherished every step of the walk she shared with him. It seemed to be few and far between the quiet times she had been able to share with Jacob—especially since her husband's death.

Upon returning home, Jacob went to his room to meditate on his competition. He found himself praying to God for strength, courage, and determination. As each moment passed, he could feel himself being uplifted and rejuvenated.

The next day Jacob picked up Bina and they walked under their invisible protection to the Hokmah. "Are you nervous?" asked Bina.

"Believe it or not," Jacob answered, "not really. I prayed and meditated last night, and I felt any worries leave me. And besides, if anything drastic were to happen to me, I know that I am safe and secure in God's hands."

"Your newer positive outlook on life is contagious to me," said Bina. "Ever since you had that talk with Mr. Wolfe, you have become more of a positive person."

Upon arrival at Heldago, Jacob and Bina saw a great multitude of people standing in the open meadow at the base of the castle's stairway entrance. There was an eerie silence among the people as Jacob led Bina to the front of the crowd. There, moving slowly toward the crowd, was the Fulder with the portal key in hand. The Fulder was just as Sarge had described, but what he had not explained was the chill in the air given off by the creature that set everyone present a little on edge—especially those who had never seen a Fulder before.

The Fulder's eyes glowed with fire as he hovered slightly off of the ground. Without a word, he stopped before the crowd and placed the portal key on the tall meadow grass. He seemed to pause for a moment, looking at Jacob. Those standing around Jacob looked at him as if to ask, "What does the Fulder want with you?" Jacob looked at the creature in amazement and curiosity. The Fulder turned his back to the crowd and slowly disappeared out of sight.

"What was that thing, and why did it stare at you, Jacob?" whispered Bina.

"That was a Fulder, and he's the referee and judge of the Certatim competition," said Jacob. "As for what he wanted with me, I don't know."

One by one and two by two, competitors and fans began touching the portal key. Once they touched it, they were gone in a blink of the eye. The portal key was a beautifully crafted piece of bronze that resembled the Heldago castle itself. It stood about five feet tall and glowed yellow when someone touched it.

From the left—in the shadows of others—ran Yelkie the gnome, stopping by Jacob and saying, "Jacob, your first portal key travel you must do. Hold your breath you should. If not, throw up you will."

Jacob looked at Yelkie a little confused but was more than grateful, as he despised nausea. "Thanks for the tip, Yelkie," he said.

"Good luck. Watching you compete I will be," said Yelkie.

"Are you ready, Bina?" asked Jacob.

"As ready as I will ever be," said Bina.

Jacob and Bina took a deep breath in—per Yelkie's advice—and touched the portal key. Before they could even imagine what would happen, they found themselves standing in a distant land. Before them was an exact replica of the portal key they had touched. "This must be the portal key to bring us back to Heldago," thought Jacob.

Their surroundings were painted with a yellow-white color. Everything from the walls to the fences to the tent was colored the same. Jacob and Bina walked a little farther and saw that the opposite side of the arena was all the same color as well. Its color was a purple-black. At the top of its tent was a large flag that had the Tenebra's snake emblem stitched upon it. Jacob looked to the top of the tent that was near him and saw the same size flag with the dove emblem of the Verita upon it.

The large stadium that could hold hundreds and hundreds of people had seating above and around the lower level competition rings. "Kind of looks like a football stadium," thought Jacob.

The four rings were raised a few feet off of the ground with sharp drop-offs for the unsuspecting falling competitor. Each ring had a flag flying next to its entrance that denoted what the competition was. The first ring's flag had a picture of a man with outstretched hands and light emanating from his palms, depicting the powers competition. The second ring's flag had a woman with a sword in hand, depicting the sword competition. The third ring had a flag with a man bowing, depicting the martial-arts competition. The fourth and final ring's flag had a man sitting cross-legged in a meditative pose, depicting the mixed-technique competition.

Next to each ring was a scoreboard that seemed to float in the air; they almost looked like dark clouds with fire emanating from within. There were four similar scoreboards above the Tenebra's and Verita's tent that were titled "Bethal," "Clevan," "Moldan," and "Elder." With a wave of their hands, the Fulders could change the scoreboards' flame directions to reflect the scores.

Many of the Tenebra's fans had already begun taking their seats, and their competitors were in the rings practicing techniques. Since the portal key had just arrived at Heldago, not many fans and competitors had arrived yet. Jacob and Bina were some of the first groups to arrive for the Veritas.

"It looks like this side of the stadium is Veritas," said Bina jokingly, looking toward the side that was a lighter, less sinister color.

Jacob and Bina, curious as ever, walked to the highest point of the stadium and looked at the surroundings. The stadium seemed to be carved directly out of the mountain. The mountain was mainly rock with nearly no vegetation to speak of. They looked into the lower grounds beneath the mountain and saw a great vast landscape—again with very little vegetation—and no sign of life anywhere. There was a burned-ash smell in the air that was similar to that of a volcano. "What kind of tundra area of the world is this? Where are we?" thought Jacob and Bina.

As the two made their way back to the Verita's tent, they came upon Felix's dad, mom, and aunt Bamilda. "Good luck today, Jacob," said Mr. Matthews sarcastically.

"Oh, thank you, Mr. Matthews," said Jacob, trying to be polite.

As Jacob passed the family by, he could see and hear them talking and laughing—almost poking fun at him. "Felix would make that boy look like a helpless little infant if he were in the same ring as him," said Aunt Bamilda.

Upon arriving at the front of the Verita's tent, Jacob and Bina noticed that while they had been out looking at their surroundings that nearly both sides of the stadium were now filled with spectators. The stadium's side of Muerte Palace had its stands full of Tenebras, Slugas, and their family pets—goblins. The Heldago's stands were filled with Veritas and Deacons along with the occasional elf and fairy, who were absolutely terrified of the goblins that would wander around the stadium unexpectedly.

"I had better go warm up," said Jacob.

Jacob and Bina gave each other a hug before Bina left for a seat. Out of the corner of his eye, Jacob saw Jezebel and Miguel running up to him.

"Jacob, we've been looking everywhere for you," said Jezebel, catching her breath. "Have you forgotten something?"

"Ahh, I don't think so," said Jacob. "Why? What's up?"

"We had not yet decided on who would compete in the mixed-technique competition," said Miguel.

"Oh my gosh!" said Jacob. "We've been so busy this week that it completely slipped my mind. Do you have three sticks so that we can draw straws?"

"Not needed," said Jezebel. "Miguel and I have discussed it, and we wish for you to take that competition. We think you have the best overall chance of helping us win."

"I feel humbled by your choice," said Jacob. "I will do all that I can to help us win."

Just then an Elder Verita competitor named Ada Milano approached the Bethals, saying, "If you three would like to get some practice in the rings, now's your chance, because the competition will be starting soon."

Ada guided the Bethals to the competition area and instructed them on entrance into the rings. "Don't be afraid of these Tenebras. You have just as much of a right to practice in these rings as they do. You see these Fulders hovering over us right now? Well, they don't put up with anything outside of competition. If they see you or a Tenebra getting out of line, they will send you home before you can say, 'Certatim.'"

The three Bethals had never been around a multitude of Tenebras, and just their presence filled the air with darkness and anger. Since Miguel and Jezebel had never even been in close contact with a Tenebra, they began to become frightened and nervous. Jacob could see the fear in their eyes as they began to look nervously at their competition.

"Come here, Bethals," said Jacob.

Jacob knelt down with Miguel and Jezebel in a small circle and began to pray. "God in heaven, we know you are the beginning and the end of all things, and we will have no fear with you in us and with us. Please be with us this day that we may bring honor and glory to your kingdom."

Some of the nearby competitors stopped what they were doing in their action of practice to see the three young Bethals kneeling in prayer. "Why do they waste valuable practice time to pray?" many onlookers whispered. The Tenebras stopped only briefly and laughed at the prayers, then went about their practice. But many of the Veritas in the stands and the rings were so moved at the sight of the young ones kneeling in the ring that they began to kneel and pray as well. It had been many years since they had seen Heldago's Veritas seeking God's righteousness in such a demeanor of prayer.

Then without warning, a loud bell was struck by a Fulder that brought everyone's attention to the Fulder's head table. The head table was a convening area where the Fulders met to discuss rulings and to begin and end the competition. It had the class level trophies and the overall Certatim trophy resting upon it for all to see.

One of the Fulders began to speak; getting right to business, he called upon the first competitors to enter the rings: "Verita Miguel Cruz from Spain against Tenebra Felix Matthews from the United States of America for the Bethals in the powers ring.

"Verita Ronald Rasmussen from Norway against Tenebra Bronson Fisher from Denmark for the Clevans in the martial-arts ring.

"Verita Tidarat Ban from Thailand against Tenebra Bon Chu from China for the Moldans in the sword ring.

"And finally, in the mixed-technique ring for the Elders will be Verita Yuri Eltsin from Russia against Tenebra Rico Estrada from Nicaragua."

The four Fulders entered their respective rings and watched as each competitor followed behind them. To initiate all battles each Fulder would make a ball of fire appear in their right hand to give warning that the match was about to start. Upon confirmation from the competitors that they were ready the Fulder would drop the ball of fire to the ground to begin the round. Also, at the start of the round the Fulder for each competition ring would motion to the ring's sand hour glass making it flip over and start the three-minute countdown for the round.

The crowd was very quiet as it watched the fireball drop to the ground. Throughout the ring it was possible to hear the breath from the competitors, nervously awaiting the start. As the fire hit the ground, the people in the crowd began screaming and stomping their feet, inspiring their favorites. The competition started slow, with each competitor feeling out the other's capabilities—all the competition except the battle in the powers ring. Felix came out against Miguel with a great anger and confidence.

The Fulders hovered around the matches, taking different angles of view to better judge a score.

Miguel was so nervous and startled that he was on his back looking up at the sky before he even knew what had happened. He had been struck directly in the chest with a crudaceous power. He was extremely weakened.

The Fulder awarded twenty-five points to Felix.

Miguel did his best to regain his bearings and slowly brought himself back to his feet. Felix could smell and sense the fear coming from Miguel, and it made him even more ferocious as he threw every ounce of strength into his powers, hurling fire and bolts of energy at Miguel. Miguel tried to regain focus, but being on the defense was not his strong suit. He blocked every power that was being thrown at him but could not find an opening to strike Felix. He was much too strong.

Felix kept at Miguel, weakening him with every strike until Miguel was on his back again. Another twenty-five-point knockdown was awarded to Felix, making the score fifty points to zero. As a weakened Miguel started to get to his feet, Felix did a move that Jacob, Miguel, and Jezebel had never seen before. He spun several times, gaining speed until he hurled his hands from his side toward Miguel. Miguel felt the power strike him but had no defense, and within a second was in such agony that he said, "Pareo." The Fulder called the match over, awarding an additional hundred points to Felix for making his opponent concede.

Felix, who was quite enjoying the torture he was inflicting, did not relinquish the power that was killing Miguel until he felt himself being lifting up into the air by the Fulder. The Fulder was very angry with the non-listening contestant and gave him a firm disqualification warning for not listening to a referee's ruling.

Jacob and Jezebel ran into the ring with Sarge, helping Miguel to his feet and supporting him as he walked out of the ring.

Felix was very popular among his Tenebra's family, many of whom thought he would go undefeated. The Tenebras came to their feet, yelling and screaming in adoration of their winner as many Veritas murmured about the rule-breaking Tenebra. Felix stood with a bloated chest as the Fulder held his hand up high. The Fulder waved his hand, and 150 points was moved from the ring's scoreboard to the Bethal's total team score that was above the Tenebra's tent.

"I'm sorry—I am so sorry..."said Miguel. "I wasn't ready. I should have..."

"It's OK, Miguel," explained Jacob. "We'll recover. We'll be OK. Just learn from what happened so that it doesn't happen to you again. This will only make you stronger."

"Well, now we know what we're up against," said Sarge, "eh, Bethals? We will need to have much more focus if we wish to be competitive."

Just then an announcement was heard for Jezebel Flores and Joan Braile to enter the martial-arts ring. Before Jezebel left, Jacob spoke encouraging words to her saying, "Fear is a path to evil, and evil is what weakens us. You're stronger than any fear on this Earth. Place any fear that you hold in God's hands before you enter this match. "

Jezebel entered the ring and stared intently at her opponent, Joan Braile. Joan was somewhat intimidating to most because of her almost shaven head and eyes that seemed to be made of blue ice. Jezebel was not scared in the least; she had left all fear outside of the ring, just as Jacob had said. She felt a great peace and comfort as the match began at the drop of the fireball.

Joan attacked with a great ferocity. She did not hold anything back, trying to disable Jezebel quickly with a kalari blow. Jezebel blocked the hit. The two traded strikes to their bodies throughout the first round with the score being a tie at fifty to fifty. The second round was much the same with both girls being very evenly matched, kicking and punching into each other's protective uniforms. The second round ended with the score again tied eighty to eighty. In the third round, the two competitors were tired, but they drew onward with the support of their schools and families. Jezebel earned first points with a round-house kick to Joan's stomach. The score was ninety to eighty with that hit. One more strike to the body, and Jezebel would be the winner.

Jezebel focused her energy into a kalari blow. With her first two fingers extended, she thrust her hand toward Joan's midsection. Joan anticipated the strike and spun into the side of Jezebel, whipping her feet to the back of Jezebel's legs and causing Jezebel to fall to the ground. The Fulder awarded twenty-five points to Joan for the takedown and deemed her the winner with a score of 105 points. The 105 points was added to the team score of Bethal Tenebras, giving them a total score of 255.

A dejected Jezebel left the ring, where Jacob was waiting with arms wide and a hug.

"You fought valiantly," Jacob comforted her. "We're going to be OK. I have faith that we can come back."

"It's on your shoulders now, Jacob," she said. "All we can do now is pray for you."

"That will do, Jezebel," Jacob said, listening to his name being called to the sword ring. "That will do."

Jezebel had to step back from Jacob for a moment as an unexplainable heat began to come from him like a radiating power. Jacob went into the ring and again closed his eyes and knelt in prayer. Many in the Verita's crowd began to become nervous, saying, "What is he doing? The match is about to begin. Is he giving up?"

The ball of fire dropped from the Fulder's hand. Jacob's opponent, Diablo, laughed at Jacob, walking slowly in circles around Jacob, looking for the correct time to take out his "unworthy" opponent. Diablo looked at Felix in the nearby stands and laughed again.

Jacob continued to meditate with closed eyes.

"Enough of this," thought Diablo. "I don't even care if I'm disqualified. I'm taking this little freak out."

Diablo jumped into the air with all of his force, coming down with his sword at Jacob's face. The Fulder began to come down from his vantage above and block the deadly blow, but he was too late. The sword was inches from Jacob's head.

In the blink of an eye, Jacob drew his wooden sword from his belt and smashed Diablo's hands, making him fall to the ground and lose his sword. The Fulder came down in front of Jacob and looked at him in amazement. He waved his hand and announced the seventy-five points being awarded to Jacob. He earned twenty-five points for a knockdown and fifty points for disarming his opponent. Jacob walked over to Diablo and reached out his hand to help him to his feet.

"I don't need your help, you lucky pig!" Diablo yelled.

"Have it your way," said Jacob.

Diablo grabbed his sword and rushed Jacob. With all of his strength, he began swinging his sword at Jacob, using every move and technique he knew. Jacob used the slow, precise movement of the Camtra to block every offensive move that came his way. It seemed to most that Jacob was toying with his opponent, and this made Diablo even angrier.

A murmur began throughout the crowd about the talent Jacob showed, and even though there were three other matches taking place, most eyes were focused on Jacob. Jacob plunged and twisted his sword, making contact with Diablo's sword. He lifted with one large heave, causing the sword to fly out of Diablo's hands and into Jacob's.

The Fulder stopped the match with another fifty-point disarming score, bringing Jacob's score to a winning 125 points. The Fulder raised Jacob's hand, and the Verita's crowd went crazy, screaming and shouting for joy. The Bethal team scores were Tenebras 255 points and Veritas 125 points. Many Tenebras looked at Diablo in disgust as he exited the ring.

Master Fu, the Muerte Palace head coach, grabbed Felix by the arm and brought him to a hidden corner. "We are ahead by 130 points in your Bethal competition, so all you have to do is let Jerlow win by saying 'pareo' before any other points are earned. Give him the hundred points, and your team moves on to the next competition."

"Master Fu, you want me to just let the twerp win?" said Felix. "I can't do that! I couldn't live with the embarrassment."

"Think of your team instead of yourself!" shouted Master Fu. "Now— you go out there and do what needs to be done for your team. Do it before he scores any points on you so he only wins by one hundred points!"

Master Fu stormed away.

"That little twerp can't beat me," Felix thought. "I'm ten times better than he is."

Just then the announcement came on for Felix Matthews and Jacob Jerlow to report to the mixed-technique ring immediately. As Jacob was walking to the ring, Shawn stopped him. "Jacob me boy, good luck," said Shawn.

"Thank you," said Jacob tentatively. He was still fighting thoughts of a possibility of Shawn's betrayal.

"No matter the outcome, you be the better man," said Shawn. "You never be forgettin' that. Ya need over 130 points to win, so I'm sure Felix's coach has told him to just say 'pareo' to be a declarin' ya the winner of the match but loser of the Bethal competition. He might just not enter the ring with his sword as well, since he be afraid of losing fifty points to a disarmament."

"That's what I was thinking as well, Shawn," said Jacob, even more confused as to Shawn's allegiance. "Well, I better be getting to the ring."

Jacob entered the ring and saw Felix staring intently at his every move. To Jacob's surprise Felix had his sword. Felix walked up to Jacob, saying, "My team wanted me to throw this match, but little do they know I'm going to do no such thing. Instead, I'm going to torture you and walk away the true winner."

"Well, good luck with that," said Jacob sarcastically, walking back to his side of the ring to kneel and pray.

Jacob prayed and then looked up into the stands to see Bina waving at him. "You can do it!" he heard her yell. He turned and faced the Fulder, waiting for him to drop the fireball. Jacob felt a great rush of emotions, from revenge and anger to love and compassion. After closing his eyes and refocusing, he brought himself back into control. Then, the ball of fire fell to the ground.

The two opponents rushed each other, both throwing strong crudaceous powers at one another. They were both so strong in their contact that they were both hurled back five feet through the air and onto their backs. The Fulder awarded each competitor twenty-five points for a knockdown. Felix could hear Master Fu shouting at him, but it did not bother him. He had one thing on his mind, and it was not his team winning, but himself.

The two began fighting with their swords. They both traded blows without either earning another point through the first round. In between rounds, Felix went to his side of the ring and was met by his coach Master Fu. "What are you doing, you selfish boy?" asked Master Fu. "You have put yourself above all others."

"I compete for myself!" yelled Felix. "My team comes second."

Both Master Fu and Felix were both thrown down to their knees as a large screaming noise penetrating their every thought. They both looked up to the top of the Tenebra's stands and saw Prince Muammar staring at them. "Let the boy compete as he wishes. He has decided his destiny," said the prince in their thoughts. The two stood to their feet, and Master Fu bowed toward Prince Muammar, showing respect.

Felix turned to face the Fulder just as the ball of fire was dropped. Jacob and Felix continued their assault with the sword, with Felix scoring a punch to the lower back, earning ten points. The two tangled themselves in arms, and Felix spit into Jacob's face, saying, "You are nothing! Just like your father was!"

Jacob became furious and began ferociously attacking Felix. His attack was not organized as before, and every blow and strike that he tried to land with a power, or with his sword, landed him no points and made him feel weaker. Felix thrived on the anger. It was just what he wanted. In the action, Felix dropped his sword upon Jacob's and left just enough room for his right hand to strike through to Jacob's midsection. It was a direct kalari blow that sent Jacob directly to his knees. Jacob blacked out for a moment, trying to regain his breath.

The Fulder began to say the ten-second knockout countdown: "Ten, nine, eight, seven, six, five, four..." Just then, the hourglass emptied and the round ended. The Fulder awarded Felix with another twenty-five-point takedown and ten points for a hit that made the score seventy to twenty-five in favor of Felix.

"I'll finish you off in the next round," said Felix, strutting past Jacob and staring proudly into his crowd.

Jacob fought his way to his feet and stumbled to his side of the ring where Sarge had a chair waiting. "Deep breaths in and out, Jacob," said Sarge. "You have the power from within..." Sarge's voice was interrupted in Jacob's head by the now-familiar voice that gave encouragement and guidance to Jacob. "You have the healing power within you, Jacob Jerlow," said the voice. "But you cannot regain anything with anger or fear inside your heart. Don't let anger be your compass. Instead replace it with love, compassion, perseverance, and faith. With these as your guide, your power is infinite."

Jacob looked up into the stands and saw the man he had met at Heldago—the man who called himself Michael. "Who is this Michael?" thought Jacob. He closed his eyes and regained his focus, releasing any and all anger from his heart. He felt a great comfort and ease come over him. Sarge, who was still giving instruction, stopped what he was saying as he felt a flow of energy coming from Jacob that gave off extreme heat. Sarge looked at Jacob in curiosity, as he had never seen a student, especially a Bethal, radiate power like this before.

The fireball dropped, and Felix, who wished to bring fear into Jacob's eyes again, hurled himself through the air with all of his might. Jacob effortlessly stepped to the side and struck Felix's sword with the kama technique Sarge had taught him. The blow was so powerful that it snapped Felix's sword into three pieces, making the Tenebra's fans take in a gasp of air at the power that Jacob showed. The Fulder awarded Jacob points for disarming Felix. The score was now seventy-five to seventy in favor of Jacob, and for the first time ever Jacob saw a gleam of fear in Felix's eyes.

Felix, still disoriented, frantically began hurling powers at his opponent. Jacob calmly and slowly raised his hands and pushed each power to the side as if it were nothing at all. Jacob seemed to be in a meditative, relaxed state with everything in his control, and this made

Felix even more frightened and angry. Jacob stuck his sword into the ground, closed his eyes, and bowed to Felix as if to ask him to battle hand to hand.

Felix began throwing kicks and punches at a blind Jacob, but Jacob felt each punch and kick like it had its own presence and easily blocked them all. Jacob stepped to the side of Felix, and in one swipe of his hand he threw a strike that included the crudaceous power and the kalari blow directly into Felix's stomach. Felix was thrown through the air ten feet and directly onto his back. As the Fulder began his knock-out countdown the crowd became extremely quiet. "...Three, two, one. Jacob Jerlow is awarded ten points for a direct hit and one hundred points for a knockout," said the Fulder.

The Fulder waved his hand, and the 185 points Jacob had earned was added to his team score, giving the Heldago Bethals a score of 310 points and the Muerte Palace Bethals a score of 255. The Veritas went crazy, screaming and yelling like they had just won the whole Certatim. Jezebel and Miguel grabbed Jacob as they embraced in celebration. Felix's teammates, Joan and Diablo, lifted Felix to his feet and helped him back to his side of the ring. Just as Felix was exiting the ring, he looked up at Prince Muammar and began to vomit uncontrollably on Diablo.

Jacob and Bina looked at each other and smiled.

Jezebel, Miguel, and Jacob got something to eat in their tent and then sat next to Bina and some of the other Bethals in the stands to watch the last rounds of competition. Soon, the matches were set for the second round. The matches would be Heldago Bethal versus Heldago Clevan and Heldago Moldan versus Muerte Palace Elder.

By now, both sides of the competition courts, Veritas and Tenebras, were intently into the competition. The fans were chanting for their favorites and trying to outdo the other side just like any typical American football game. It was amazing to many onlooking Bethals how just on this one day of the year both Veritas and Tenebras could push aside their major differences and not kill one another. Besides the occasional thrown hotdog or devilish stare, both sides seemed to avoid each other when walking outside the stands getting food or a souvenir from a vendor.

"Thank you for bringing me," said Bina. "Except for the occasional goblin freaking me out and Tenebras seemingly drooling over my neck, this has been an unbelievable experience."

Jacob and Bina laughed.

"I'm glad you like it," said Jacob. "I wouldn't want anything more than to have you in the stands cheering for me."

Jezebel leaned over to hear Jacob and Bina's conversation—seemingly growing more and more jealous. "Well, we had better get down to the ringside in order to prepare for our next competition," she said hurriedly, trying to rush Jacob. Miguel, Jacob, and Jezebel got words of support from their fellow Bethals and Bina, and left for the ringside.

The Fulder began announcing, "In the powers ring will be Miguel Cruz versus Ramiro Vasquez. In the sword ring will be Jacob Jerlow versus Tabitha Fulks, and finally, in the martial arts ring will be Jezebel Flores versus Ronald Rasmussen. You have two minutes to prepare yourselves."

Jacob pulled his two teammates in together and said, "Remember, winning or losing is not the major goal today. Rather, when we go home tonight, can we honestly say to ourselves we gave it our all every second, without fear? Did we believe in God through whom all things are possible, and did we put our trust in his guidance? If we can answer yes to these two questions, we have won—no matter what the scoreboard says."

The three entered their ring and shook hands with their competitors. Ramiro Vasquez was—as usual—arrogant in the powers ring, saying, "Hey, little man, sorry I'm going to have to put you through this, but there can only be one winner, and obviously we know who that will be."

In the martial-arts ring, Ronald came across as a gentle young man who was courteous to Jezebel. "He seems like a nice guy," thought Jezebel after her introduction.

In the third ring—the swords ring—Tabitha bashfully approached Jacob and lightly shook his hand. "Hi, Jacob—go easy on me, OK?" she asked. Jacob nodded in approval, somewhat smitten by her good looks.

The six competitors watched as the ball of fire fell to the ground. Miguel and Ramiro immediately began trading powers. Within a few moments, Miguel was being pushed back by the stronger Clevan, but he fought valiantly with no fear.

In the martial-arts ring, Jezebel approached the polite Ronald with confidence, but because of how courteous he seemed, Jezebel was not prepared for the bombardment of kicks and punches to follow. Soon Ronald was up by fifty points, and Jezebel was on her back. "Did you think I wouldn't hit a girl?" he said, smirking.

Jezebel regained her composure and became even more confident in her abilities. She lifted her chin high as she brought herself to her feet. She stood looking at Ronald for a moment, waiting for him to attack. "Enough stalling," said Ronald. He jumped into the air with all of his might, his foot approaching her stomach. Jezebel kicked Ronald's leg to the ground and struck the kalari blow directly to his core. Ronald fell to his feet from his jump and with glazed eyes dropped to his knees. The Fulder began counting, "...Three, two, one. Jezebel Flores is awarded 110 points for a hit and a knockout."

Meanwhile, in the sword ring, Jacob was feeling out his opponent and "going easy on her" when all of the sudden Tabitha exploded with rage and aggression. This little, quiet, attractive girl was no longer shy. Jacob was using all of his strength to defend every blow that came at him, and before he knew it, he was backed up to the drop-off of the ring and nearly ready to fall off. The girl paused and said, "It's nothing personal. It's just a competition."

Jacob suddenly realized that he had been played by the pretty girl and came to his senses. Tabitha lunged her sword at Jacob's legs to knock him off the ring, and Jacob blocked the sword at the same time. He quickly lifted her sword to the side, throwing Tabitha off balance. She teetered on one leg for a moment and then fell off of the ring's edge. Jacob walked over to Tabitha's sword, which was lying on the ground, held out his hand, and pulled it to his grasp with the valoria power. He walked over to Tabitha, extended his hand to help her back into the ring, and said, "Sorry—it's nothing personal. It's just a competition." Tabitha struggled to smile. The score was seventy-five to zero in favor of Jacob.

Jacob battled for just a moment more and quickly threw Tabitha to the ground again, earning another twenty-five points for a takedown.

The Fulder was quick to raise Jacob's hand and award him the winning hundred points to his team score. This brought the team score to 210 points for the Bethals and zero points for the Clevans.

In the powers ring, the score was Ramiro, seventy, and Miguel, twenty, and the first round had just ended. Miguel was fighting coura-geously against an older, stronger opponent. Jacob and Jezebel went to his ringside to cheer on their teammate. For the first time, many of the Heldago students were seeing someone stand up to Ramiro; because of his strength in power most of his fellow students could not compete more than a minute against him. But now a younger, smaller Bethal was standing his ground.

Ramiro looked toward Jacob, who was giving Miguel more inspi-ration, and began to become angry and jealous. The fireball fell to the ground, and Ramiro flew through the air, sending a great amount of energy into Miguel's chest. Miguel flew backward five feet and directly onto his back. The Fulder awarded Ramiro twenty-five points, making the score ninety-five to twenty as Ramiro stood over Miguel, staring at him in pride. Miguel struggled to regain his breath as he looked over to his teammates. The Fulder's countdown was at three when Miguel came to his feet. Ramiro stood frozen for a moment in disbelief that the much smaller opponent had the strength to bring himself to his feet. He began to have fear rise in his eyes.

"Miguel, he's scared! You can do it!" shouted Jacob.

Miguel began floating in the air and closed his eyes. Ramiro, now even more frightened by the flying boy, began sending crudaceous pow-ers toward his opponent. Miguel hurled himself in a 360-degree spin, grabbed the powers, and released them directly back into Ramiro's arms. Ramiro was directly hit and fell to his knees in agony. With that knockdown and hit, the score was now Ramiro, ninety-five and Miguel, fifty-five. Halfway through the Fulder's countdown, the round ended.

Ramiro's and Miguel's teams gathered around each other, giving support and encouragement for the final round. The two opponents entered the center of the ring—this time with Ramiro being much more cordial than the first greeting—giving each other a respectful handshake.

The fireball dropped to the ground, and both Ramiro and Miguel began slowly circling the ring, waiting to unleash a barrage on each other. By this time not only were the Verita's fans hanging onto the edge of their seats, but the Tenebra's fans were enthralled in the competition as well.

Miguel was the first to attack. Pointing both index fingers with an upside-down hand at Ramiro, he unleashed a lightning bolt that encircled Ramiro. Ramiro looked to be helpless, so Miguel moved in to give a knockdown blow. Ramiro seemed to soak up the lightning bolt, and in a flash of the eye he released it from his chest, directly hitting an approaching Miguel. The strike was a huge surprise and knocked Miguel off balance. The crowd became extremely quiet as Miguel fell to the ground. Everyone could feel the tension in the air. The Fulder awarded the twenty-five points to Ramiro, giving him a winning score of 120 points. This made the team scores Bethal, 210 points, and Clevan, 120 points, going into the final mixed-technique match.

Ramiro, seemingly humbled by Miguel's effort, stretched out his hand and helped him to his feet. "That was a great fight," he said. "You fought like no other that I've competed against before."

After catching his breath from the activity, Ramiro entered the mixed-technique ring with Jacob. A seemingly more humbled Ramiro shook Jacob's hand, saying, "Good luck, Jacob. I've been waiting for this challenge for a while now."

"Good luck to you as well, Ramiro," replied Jacob, giving him a hug. "I hope I can live up to the challenge to compete at your level."

The two closed their eyes and waited for the fireball to drop. Instantly upon the fireball hitting the ground, they both opened their eyes to view each other. In the first round they battled with the sword, and toward the middle Jacob disarmed Ramiro, giving him a score of fifty to zero. Jacob stuck his sword into the ground as the two began kicking and punching, testing one another's martial-arts skills. By the end of the round one, Ramiro had delivered two hits and knocked down Jacob once, giving him a score of forty-five to Jacob's fifty.

In the rest period, Jacob took in deep breaths and slowly gazed upon the crowd, wondering to himself, "I wonder if the rabbi is watching us?" He looked up to the top of the stands where he had earlier seen the mysterious man named Michael, but he could no longer see him. He came to his feet and waited for the round to begin.

In the second round, both Ramiro and Jacob traded blows with their powers and their martial-arts skills, but neither found the other's weak spot. At the end of round two, the score was Jacob, eighty, and Ramiro, sixty-five. In between rounds Jacob looked at Ramiro and how disappointed he was with himself for getting beaten by a younger, less-experienced Bethal. This depressed and hurt him deeply. Jacob thought to himself, "This competition is not worth ruining the self-esteem of a person, especially a brother Verita."

The third and final round began, and Jacob was not putting forth the same effort as before; soon the score was Jacob, eighty, and Ramiro, eighty-five. Ramiro recognized Jacob's lessened attacks and that Jacob was giving the competition over to him so he stopped suddenly and fell to his knees. The crowd and everyone before him hushed in silence to hear what he had to say. "Maybe not on every day would Jacob Jerlow be better than me, but on this day he was. So I will not finish this round with Jacob giving the match over to me. With this, Jacob Jerlow, I concede this match and say, 'Pareo.'"

The Fulder awarded one hundred points to Jacob, making him and his team the winners of the match. He firmly grabbed Jacob's hand and raised it in victory. Jacob, moved by sportsmanship and friendship, reached over to Ramiro and raised his hand in unison. The Verita's fans all came to their feet, clapping and shouting in victory. The Tenebras had little to think about the courageous act, but much word was spread through their stands regarding how Ramiro could just throw the match away. Their dark hearts and selfish acts clouded their view, and they could not see the kindness that had just been shown.

As the winning Bethals walked to the stands, they were surrounded by congratulatory fans. "Fantastic job! Way to work as a team!" they heard. Young, adoring fans pulled at their shirts asking for autographs. They were instant celebrities.

"And here they are, the first Bethal class to ever make it to the Certatim Championship round!" said Luke Cartwright, greeting the Bethal team. "I feel as if I should be rolling out a red carpet."

"Just a handshake will do," said Jezebel in jest.

In the following rounds between the Heldago Moldan class and the Muerte Palace Elders the Bethals got a chance to rest and watch the competition. The Tenebra's Elders were very strong and, seemingly toyed with their opponents, knocking them down at will.

"It seems we have our work cut out for us, eh, team?" said Jezebel.

"Ahh, they don't seem so tough," joked Miguel.

"Like I said earlier, if we give it our all and remain steadfast in faith, we will be the victors no matter what the scoreboard says," said Jacob.

In one of the most lopsided matches of all time, the Elders beat the Moldan class 450 to 0. The Bethal team walked toward the rings and received many "good lucks" from fans, but this time most of the looks on people's faces were of concern for their well-being rather than excitement. Upon entering the ring, the Bethals noticed that the Elders had barely broke a sweat in their previous match. As they grew closer they could see how much larger they were, being that they averaged twenty years of age.

The head Fulder came to speak. "Announcing this year's Certatim Championship competition teams. The first team is from Muerte Palace and consists of their Elder team. Their team members are Li Ting from China, who will be competing in martial arts." As each member was announced, he or she broke away from the team, standing in the ring and bowing to their school. There was a great cheer from their fans after each announcement. "In the powers ring is Abimbola Kuti from Nigeria, and finally their undefeated contestant, Rico Estrada, is competing in the sword and mixed technique." As Rico was announced, the entire Tenebra's side came to its feet and screamed in adoration.

"Undefeated, huh?" said Jacob calmly.

"Yeah, I didn't want to make a big deal about it beforehand, but ever since he was a Bethal he has never been beaten in the sword or the mixed technique. He's like a rock star to the Tenebras," Jezebel explained.

"Sweet," said Jacob with a grin.

The Fulder then announced the Bethals: "And for the first time ever in the history of the Certatim Championships, we have a Bethal team..." He continued announcing the Bethal team with the Verita's fans growing louder and louder with each passing second. The tension and competition could be felt by all.

First up was Miguel versus Abimbola in the powers ring. Miguel went to the center of the ring to shake Abimbola's hand and looked up at the giant, bald African man. He was no less than six feet, ten inches in height compared to Miguel's five feet, two inches. Miguel stood on the tips of his toes to try to get a closer look at Abimbola's face, but Abimbola was not amused and squeezed down on Miguel's hand until a cracking sound was heard. Abimbola smiled showing some of his sharp canines that, no doubt, had seen too much flesh and blood.

Miguel walked back to his corner, shaking his hand and trying to get blood flow back to his fingertips. He could hear Sarge yelling from his corner, "Remember, David took down giant Goliath! So can you!" Miguel regained his focus and stared at the Fulder, who was preparing to drop the fireball.

Before the fireball hit the ground, Miguel felt a sharp burn hit his head, as Abimbola had sent a fireball into his ear before the start. The Fulder flew down from his vantage and stepped in front of the rule breaker. The crowd was silent. The Fulder seemed to glow fire red in anger, and a strong wind blew in the face of Abimbola as it said, *"You dare dishonor my ring of competition!* That is a ten-point deduction. If it happens again, I will personally grab you by the throat and drag you back to whence you came." The Fulder waved his hand at the scoreboard, making the score Abimbola, negative ten, and Miguel, zero. Abimbola's eyes became red with fury as he again awaited the fireball drop.

Upon the start, to most fans' surprise, Miguel came out firing stronger than he had ever before. He caught Abimbola off guard and put him on the defense, backing him up to his corner. The two traded powers, both being very even in scoring, with a score of thirty to thirty to finish the first round. As Miguel sat on his corner's seat, he looked over at his opponent's corner and saw his coach, Master Fu, yelling his ear, "You are being beaten by a little boy half your size and capabilities. You dishonor your school and your people!"

At the start of the second round, Abimbola came out angrier than ever. He showed powers that had not yet been seen in the competition. With energy and light coming from Abimbola's every finger, Miguel extended both palms to receive the power. Without knowing where it came from, Miguel sensed to overturn his hands and redirect the energy toward Abimbola. The energy flowed back into his opponent, knocking him completely out of the ring. The Fulder began his countdown: "Ten, nine, eight..." The Tenebra's fans stood stunned as the countdown went to zero. Abimbola's teammates rushed over to help him to his feet and out of the pit that surrounded the ring.

The Fulder raised Miguel's hand, declaring him champion of the power match while waving his hand and awarding 140 points to the Bethal team and none to the Elder team.

"Where did that come from?" asked Sarge as Miguel walked off the ring.

"I'm not sure actually," Miguel said, smiling.

"Sometimes greatness needs no teaching," said Sarge, giving Miguel a congratulatory handshake.

"Next will be Jezebel Flores versus Li Ting in the martial-arts ring," announced the Fulder.

Jezebel and Li entered the ring and stood toe to toe to greet one another. They both stood about the same height, but Li showed more maturity in her face, being six years older than Jezebel. She had long black hair that was twisted into a bun on top of her head. Her nails were a few inches long and sharpened to points. Jezebel noticed that Li had something red on the side of her mouth and said, "You know you have something on the side of your mouth?"

"Oh, yes. I just had a little snack for energy," replied Li, wiping the substance away with the back of her hand.

Jezebel realized that it was blood and turned away to go back to her corner.

The fireball dropped and Li stood awaiting her opponent. Jezebel was in no mood for games, so she attacked with a barrage of kicks and punches. Every effort she put forth was blocked with very little effort. Then in a flash Li put forth an offensive that Jezebel could not manage—ten, twenty, thirty, forty, fifty points...Li's score grew with direct punches and kicks to Jezebel. Just before the end of the round, Li faked with one hand and delivered a direct kalari blow to Jezebel's midsection with the other. The bell rang to end the first round as Jezebel's sight became blurry and her thoughts incoherent. Sarge and Jacob rushed out to Jezebel and caught her before she hit the ground, helping her to her corner's seat.

"Deep breaths, Jezebel," Sarge instructed. "Listen to my voice and stay with me—deep breaths in and out now."

Jezebel struggled to regain consciousness and tried focusing on breathing and her chest going in and out. "I'm OK," she struggled to say. "I'm OK."

To start the second round, the score was Jezebel, zero points, and Li, sixty points. Jezebel struggled to regain her balance, as her legs felt like she was trying to stand on quicksand. She looked over at Li, who had not even broken a sweat, and readied herself for battle.

The fireball dropped to the ground, and Li slowly approached Jezebel, picking her next move. In the flash of an eye, she delivered a strike to Jezebel's stomach that scored her another ten points. Jezebel tried to retaliate but could not land a blow to score. As the second round neared its end, Li gave a swift roundhouse kick with her foot into Jezebel's back, scoring ten more points. Jezebel started to lose her balance and was nearly to the ground when Li caught her and helped her to her feet. The round bell rang. The score was Li, eighty, and Jezebel, zero.

"She caught me when I was falling to the ground—why?" Jezebel asked Sarge.

"She didn't want to win yet," replied Sarge. "She's going for the knockout to score as many team points as possible."

"She's so fast and strong. What do I do?" asked Jezebel.

"You have to dig deep and find that spot in your heart that you haven't felt yet. There you will find strength," Sarge instructed.

The third round began with Li throwing every bit of energy into a knockout, scoring ten points with a kick to the stomach. Jezebel dug deep and searched for inner strength, and to Li's surprise began battling back—and then *bam!* Jezebel delivered a direct kalari blow to Li that sent her directly to her knees. Jezebel now had thirty-five points to Li's ninety. Li, though dazed, stood immediately to her feet to show that it did not faze her, but everyone could see the fear in her eyes. She was weakened, and Jezebel could see it.

Jezebel continued to attack scoring two more direct body hits, making the score fifty-five to ninety. Master Fu stood in Li's corner, shouting instructions in Chinese. Jezebel came in with a roundhouse punch to Li's side, and Li caught it with both arms. With one quick push down she had trapped Jezebel's arm, forcing her elbow to bend in the opposite direction. Jezebel was immobilized and could not move. Her arm was trapped, and she was in excruciating pain. With a tear running down her cheek, she said, "Pareo."

Li released Jezebel's arm, and the Fulder awarded one hundred points to Li, making the team score Elders, 190 points, and Bethals, 140 points. To the joy of the Tenebras, the Fulder raised Li's hand high in victory.

"You fought with honor and courage," said Sarge, giving Jezebel a hug as she walked off of the ring holding her injured arm.

Jezebel cried—not because she was in pain, but because she felt she had let her team down. Miguel and Jacob approached her to give her support. "Did you give it your all?" asked Miguel.

"I did," she replied.

"Then you are the winner!" Miguel demanded. "You just went toe to toe with a grown woman. Most anyone else would have been knocked out in the first round."

"Thanks, Miguel," she said.

"Jacob Jerlow and Rico Estrada are to report to the sword ring at this time," said the Fulder with his loud voice that penetrated the stadium.

"Wish me luck. And pray for me. He is undefeated after all," Jacob joked.

Jacob entered the ring and went to the center of the circle to shake Rico's hand, but to no avail. Rico was busy talking to fans from his corner and awaiting the start. Jacob walked over to Rico's corner and smiled at the Tenebras, who were giving him death threats with their stares. "I just wanted to wish you good luck and introduce myself," said Jacob with an outstretched hand.

Rico was a handsome Latin man who had the ladies standing in line for just a hello.

"Well, well, well, if it isn't Jacob Jerlow," said Rico in a heavy Latino accent. "Your good friend Felix Matthews has told me all about you. Will you be giving me a challenge today? I certainly hope so, because I've never found anyone to give me a test before."

"I'll do my best," said Jacob, dodging a piece of rotten fruit that was thrown at him by a child. "OK, that's my cue to go now."

Jacob walked back to his corner and knelt in prayer to calm himself and ask for God's grace. A few moments later, he sensed the fireball hit the ground to start the round. He came to his feet and drew his sword. Rico still had his back turned to Jacob and was signing an autograph for a child. Jacob walked over to Rico and said, "Can we start now?"

Rico turned around saying, "Oh, Jacob, I'm so sorry. Yes—let us begin."

The two opponents began trading sword maneuvers, and Jacob was the first to score with a blow to Rico's stomach. They continued, very evenly, throughout the first round with the round ending with Jacob at ten points and Rico at zero. Before the second round was to start, Rico met Jacob at the center of the ring and said, "You are strong. You're good enough for me to use my dominant hand—my right hand. Good luck, little one."

Jacob kept attacking Rico into the second round with both competitors scoring two direct body hits, making the score Jacob, thirty, and Rico, twenty. Rico lunged and stepped to one side, at the same time putting force into his sword. The force brought Jacob off balance and made him fall to the ground. The score was Jacob, thirty, and Rico, forty-five. Rico smiled at Jacob, as he was actually enjoying the stiff competition. Jacob went back on the offensive, and just as the round's time was to expire, he quickly flicked his wrist in contact with Rico's sword and made Rico's sword fall to the ground. The entire Tenebra's side of the stadium gasped. Rico had never been disarmed before in competition. The second round ended with a score of Jacob, eighty points, and Rico, forty-five points.

Rico picked up his sword and smiled at Jacob as if to say, "Nice move."

In the third round Jacob and Rico traded swordsmanship evenly, and then Rico got the upper hand; within a minute span, he was able to score thirty points in hits to Jacob, making the score Jacob, eighty, and Rico, seventy-five. Jacob saw an apparent limp in Rico's left leg, which must have been injured, so he went in to sweep the leg with his sword. As he went in to attack, Rico transferred all of his weight to his left leg. Jacob hit the leg without budging it, and this left a huge opening for Rico to attack with his sword. Rico hit Jacob squarely in the side, knocking him to the ground. The Fulder awarded Rico with ten points for a direct hit and twenty-five points for a takedown, making his score 110 and Jacob's score eighty.

Jacob looked at Rico and said, "I thought your leg was injured."

"Not so, my good man—not so," replied Rico. "Everything is not always as it appears."

This made the team scores Elders, 300 points, and Bethals, 140 points. Master Fu approached Rico as he exited the ring saying, "You know what you have to do in the mixed-technique match, right?"

"Yes, Master Fu—win," Rico replied.

"We are ahead by 160 points. All you have to do is say, 'Pareo,' giving them one hundred points, and the Certatim is ours," Master Fu said, forcefully.

"I am undefeated—I've never been beaten—and you don't think that I will surely win?" asked Rico confidently.

"I do think that you would win, but why risk it when the championship is in our hands?"

"I cannot do—" Rico started, but he was interrupted by a voice from behind.

"Congratulations, Rico," said the man.

Rico and Master Fu turned and saw Prince Muammar and his bodyguard, Bodach, facing them. They bowed to show respect. "Thank you, Prince," said Rico. "We were just talking about the last match."

"Ah, a dilemma you have...Either you lose your undefeated streak and win the Certatim, or you risk competing to see the outcome. What does your heart tell you to do?" asked Prince Muammar.

"Prince Muammar, my heart tells me to compete. I know that I can win," Rico reassured him.

"Indeed. Unfortunately, your heart does not have the final say—I do...and I say you will concede and take the assured championship for our people," Prince Muammar ordered.

"Yes, my prince—I will do as you command," said Rico regretfully.

After announcing the final match, Jacob and Rico entered the mixed-technique ring. Jacob did not know what to expect. A part of him thought Rico would concede, and the other thought he would fight to keep his undefeated streak. The two opponents shook hands in the center of the ring and returned to their corners. The crowd was extremely quiet, and all that could be heard was a breeze blowing through the tents. Everyone was on edge. Would Rico concede or fight for his honor?

Rico had hundreds of thoughts rolling through his head as he tightly gripped his sword in hand, waiting for the ball of fire to drop. "I can beat this boy," he thought. "What does it matter what Prince Muammar said? If I beat him, all will be well."

Prince Muammar stared at Rico intently from his seat and could sense that Rico was second-guessing his command. Rico dropped to his knees in excruciating pain. He felt like his head would burst. Prince

Muammar was sending him a wakeup call. The pain left, and Rico stood and bowed to his prince.

The fireball dropped to the ground, and Jacob approached his opponent. Rico bowed and said, "I concede this match and say, 'Pareo.'" The Fulder came between them and awarded the 100 points to Jacob, making the team scores Elders, 300, and Bethals, 240. The Muerte Palace Elders were the Certatim champions, but none of the Tenebras were cheering. They did not know what to think. Their hero and champion had just conceded to a young Verita boy and his undefeated streak was over.

Prince Muammar stood from his seat and began clapping. Others near him saw this and joined him. A few moments later the Tenebras were celebrating the victory, forgetting about the undefeated streak.

Rico approached Jacob and shook his hand, saying, "You have taken my undefeated streak today. Someday I hope to repay the favor by taking something from you." Rico gave an evil grin and returned to his celebrating teammates.

There was a great celebration in the Tenebra's stands, for their school had won the Certatim, and this carried on into the trophy presentation. Most all stayed to watch the ceremony, even the Veritas. Jacob, Jezebel, and Miguel were surrounded by young fans wanting their autographs and a picture.

After the celebration, Jacob and Bina went back to Heldago through the portal key. Upon returning to Heldago, Jacob meditated and brought himself and Bina back to the Hokmah. They felt like they had been gone for days.

CHAPTER 16

A TRIP TO ITALY

The following days seemed to go by slowly as Jacob and Bina awaited their trip to Italy. Jacob had his bags packed, but he checked and rechecked them for days in anticipation. Finally, the day arrived to drive to the airport.

"OK—that should be everything in the car, Jacob," said Sarah. "We have a long day ahead of us today. Our flight out of Fargo will take us to Minneapolis. Then our second flight will take us to New York City. I'm so glad we only have one-hour layovers in between our flights, but our flight from New York City to Rome is a nine-hour flight—so we had better have plenty of snacks. You know it's going to be seven hours ahead of our time there," she excitedly rambled onward.

"Mom, we're good. We have plenty of snacks. We have double- and triple-checked our bags. We'll adjust to the time zone in Italy. Let's go pick up Bina and her mom," said Jacob.

"You're right, Jacob, honey. I'm overthinking things. I need to just relax. Let's go," Sarah sighed.

Jacob and his mom, Sarah, picked up Bina and Rebecca and were off to the airport. At the airport security check, Bina had to giggle when the airport security took Jacob's sword from his backpack to view the metal object that had set off the security alarm. Of course, the blade was not exposed, so it merely looked like a sword's handle, but as the officer turned the handle over admiring the artwork, Bina thought it was funny that the security agent was handling such a dangerous object and not knowing it.

"OK, you're all set. Have a nice flight," the security officer instructed while zipping Jacob's backpack up.

On the flight Jacob and Bina tried to rest when possible, but nerves and excitement slowed the process. Upon their arrival in Rome, the time was nine a.m., and the sky was a bright blue with hardly any clouds. When they exited the airport, the four tourists felt the heat that was compounded by the concrete and asphalt with the temperature nearly ninety degrees already. Rebecca was quick to wave down a taxicab driver. "Hotel Dei Consoli near St. Peter's Square, please," she instructed the driver.

The driver loaded up their luggage and sped off to the hotel. The hotel was beautiful and everything that they had expected; with amazing artwork decorating every wall, it was no wonder that the hotel was nearly always sold out. The entryway to the hotel was filled with flowers that smelled like a rose garden.

They had barely gotten into their rooms when Bina and Jacob simultaneously asked, "Can we go look around?"

"Wow—over twelve hours on an airplane and you're ready to go hiking around town, huh?" asked Sarah. "I don't know about you, Rebecca, but I need to lie down for a little while. I am exhausted."

"I agree, Sarah, but if it's OK with you, it's fine with me if the kids go see St. Peter's Square while we take a little nap," Rebecca said, kicking her shoes off and getting set for some rest.

"OK, you two—stay together and be safe. Be back by noon so that we can have some lunch together," Sarah instructed.

"Deal!" they said, grabbing their backpacks and rushing out the door.

Jacob and Bina exited the hotel and could see St. Peter's Basilica's large cupola, or dome, that reached a height of 450 feet in the near distance. They began hastily walking toward St. Peter's Square, and as they approached the Vatican, the crowds of parishioners and tourists became exceedingly more difficult to maneuver through. Soon, they entered St. Peter's Square, and before them stood the enormous church known as St. Peter's Basilica and the famous Vatican Obelisk.

"It's just how I imagined it, Jacob. Isn't it beautiful?" asked Bina.

"It is. Tomorrow morning at eight a.m. we have our Scavi Tour where we get to go beneath St. Peter's Basilica and tour Peter's tomb. Pictures aren't allowed down there so I can only imagine what it'll look like," said Jacob, snapping pictures of everything in sight.

Jacob walked closer to take more pictures of the obelisk. It was centered in the middle of St. Peter's Square and was surrounded by white marble markings on the walkway that acted as a sundial by casting their shadows. The obelisk was a long, rectangular stone that had a carved pyramid shape at its top. Atop this pyramid was a beautifully adorned cross that contained an authentic piece of the cross that held Jesus Christ at his crucifixion. At the base of the obelisk were beautifully constructed bronze lions and birds. Although it was an Egyptian obelisk brought to Rome in 37 AD, it did not have any hieroglyphics carved upon it.

The obelisk was placed as a commemoration of the Circus of Emperor Nero. It was a witness to hundreds of Christians being crucified and lit on fire at the command of Emperor Nero. The obelisk was also witness to St. Peter's crucifixion, during which he requested to be crucified upside down because he did not feel worthy to die in the same manner as Jesus Christ. He was buried near this site.

The First St. Peter's Basilica was constructed next to the Circus of Nero at the command of Emperor Constantine in AD 330. The obelisk stayed in its same position until 1587 when it was moved to its current location. This was also the year the first St. Peter's Basilica was torn down and the current "new" St. Peter's Basilica was constructed.

Jacob and Bina took hundreds of photos and briefly toured the basilica and areas of the Vatican before returning to the Hotel Dei Consoli to have lunch with their mothers. The rest of the day they all enjoyed one another's company by taking part in a tour party that was to go and see ruins around Rome. The weather was very hot, but no one seemed to mind, as their time together and the sites took the place of exhaustion.

That night at Heldago, Jacob, Jezebel, and Miguel were received with a hero's welcome by most of the Veritas of the world. Jacob began meeting many people that he had never seen before, most very politely congratulating him on his performance in the Certatim Competition.

Time and time again, people would say, "I never thought a Bethal team would ever make it to the championship round, but you did it. Congratulations!"

After some time—during which they ate mostly every cake, cookie, and pastry known to man—a small pink pixie no more than six inches in height, named Maribel, flew up to Jacob and asked, "Have you ever had a pixie stick?"

"The little sticks that are filled with a flavored sugar?" asked Jacob.

"No, silly. A real pixie stick," said Maribel.

Out of the corner of Jacob's eye, he could see a short man peeking around the corner. With another glance he noticed it was a Yelkie, the gnome, who was obviously trying to get a better look at Maribel. "I have not tried a pixie stick," Jacob explained. "What's so special about it; does it taste good?"

"Oh yes," Maribel giggled in her high-pitched voice. "Here—you try." She handed a tiny stick that was more like a splinter or a toothpick over to Jacob.

Jacob popped the stick into his mouth, and immediately his eyes lit up. The stick seemed to touch every taste bud in his mouth. He tasted sweet, then a little salty, then spicy, then sour and so on, until his mouth had experienced every flavor imaginable. "It's like a roller coaster of flavors!" he exclaimed.

"Oh, but it's not done yet," said Maribel, giggling.

As the flavors began to diminish, Jacob felt a tingly-tickling sensation that started in his toes and slowly crept up his legs, waist, stomach, chest, shoulders, out to his fingertips, and then out his nose and ears in a big puff of smoke. The smoke that exited his ears and nose made a sound like a loud foghorn. Jacob was stunned for a moment and tried to comprehend what had just happened. All the people standing around him paused for a moment and then let out a big laugh. Jacob soon joined them.

Maribel flew off, trying to control her laughter. Jacob regained his composure and walked over to Yelkie, who was still hiding behind a corner to watch the pretty pixie. "So what's up, Yelkie?" he asked. "What are you doing over here?"

"Oh—oh—nothing Jacob Jerlow," said Yelkie, somewhat startled. "Enjoying the festivities I am."

"You sure you weren't checking out Maribel?" Jacob smiled.

"Oh—um—check her out I do not do." Yelkie searched for words. "Admire her beauty, maybe I do."

"Well, have you ever talked to her or introduced yourself?"

"Talked to her I have not. Seen her for many years I have, but talked to her I have not," Yelkie explained nervously.

"Why not? She's awfully nice—what's the worst that could happen?" asked Jacob. "I'm not too sure about the pixie-stick thing yet, but she is really pretty."

"Thought about talking to her I have, but too much worry I hold."

"If there's anything I've learned in the past weeks, it's that worry and fear should hold no part in our lives. I know sometimes it's easier said than done, but for what it's worth, next time, why don't you think of something else besides your own thoughts? Like maybe...your favorite childhood memory or your favorite pastime—when you are going to talk to her. Maybe taking your mind off of your fear will help you to break the ice," Jacob instructed.

Yelkie thought for a moment and smiled at Jacob before vanishing into the air. Gnomes, after all, could transport themselves great distances in the blink of an eye. A moment later, Jacob felt a tap on his shoulder; he turned around and saw Ramiro. "Hey, Ramiro, you scared me for a minute," said Jacob.

"Sorry about that, Jacob," said Ramiro. "I just wanted to thank you again for trying to give me the match at the Certatim. That showed a lot of courage and kinship to do something like that, especially for someone that you barely know."

"You would have done the same thing for me."

"No—no, I wouldn't have, Jacob, not then—but now...now I would. And that's because you helped open my heart and helped me to see how self-centered I was becoming. I've been thinking...I think that you should test for the Clevan level and break my thirty-one-day record. You are definitely ready!"

"Ramiro, I'm totally flattered by your belief in me. I'd be honored if you would give me some tips to help me prepare myself," Jacob requested.

Over the next few hours, Jacob and Ramiro practiced maneuvers and techniques that Ramiro thought Jacob would be tested on for the Clevan level. Ramiro paused at the end of the training and said, "Jacob, if you ever need a hand, I'll be there for you. That's a promise."

Jacob smiled and enjoyed the thought of his newfound friend.

The next day Jacob, Bina, and their mothers got up and had breakfast together atop the hotel. The hotel had a restaurant on top of its roof that gave a beautiful overview of nearby sites. The sun was just making its way over the horizon and the temperature was rising quickly.

"Well, today is the day for the big Scavi Tour beneath St. Peter's Basilica," said Sarah. "I'm really excited to travel back two thousand years and see the past."

They finished their breakfast and began walking toward the Vatican and St. Peter's Square. Jacob and Bina saw Shawn standing by a corner, so they told their mothers that they would catch up. "Hey, Shawn, how have you been?" asked Bina

"I be good, and I hope you two have been just the same." By now Shawn was growing ever more curious as to why Jacob was so standoffish and not his usual talkative self. "I haven't been able to talk with ya much, Jacob. Are ya doing OK?"

"Oh yeah, I've been quite busy with the Certatim and all..." said Jacob.

"Aye. Well, ya know ya have no greater ally than the man that be standin' before ya now. If ya need me...I'll be there," said Shawn confidently.

Jacob and Bina said good-bye and began catching up to their mothers. Bina, who could see the doubt in Jacob's eyes when talking to Shawn, asked, "So you have something in the back of your mind that Shawn may betray you, huh?"

"I don't know—maybe—I guess so," said Jacob, confused.

"Has he ever given you reason to think this? Has he not saved your life on more than one occasion?"

"I know, I know, Bina," said Jacob, getting more frustrated. "It's just that he's been the only one who's known of my true whereabouts for each of our trips, and with each trip the Tenebras have found us. Doesn't this strike you as odd?"

"It does...but it does not rule out other possibilities. Please—just keep an open mind and don't condemn Shawn for actions that you have no proof of," said Bina. "He deserves that much from us."

Jacob and Bina reached their mothers just as they were coming up to St. Peter's Basilica in St. Peter's Square. There were hundreds of people trying to make their way into the basilica to take video and pictures—as there were almost every day. "Make your way through the metal detectors to your right please," an officer directed. The four travelers made their way through the security check and began taking photos together in front of the massive church.

A few moments passed, and a short man with a bad hairpiece came out from a doorway, yelling, "Would the Feldman and Jerlow families please follow me? Would the Feldman and Jerlow..."

Sarah waved her hand at the gentleman, telling him that they were making their way over to him through the thick crowd. "Here we are. We're coming," she said.

"OK. You are the Feldman and Jerlow families? May I see your Scavi ticket please?" the man asked in a heavy Italian accent. Rebecca and Sarah handed the man their tickets. The man slowly placed the tickets in his pocket and turned to reenter the door saying, "Follow me please."

The four followed close behind the man.

"My name is Aldo Esposito, but you may call me Aldo. I have been a caretaker of these halls for forty years. My English is so-so, but I manage. Now—try to keep up; we have a long way to travel," he instructed.

After they had walked for some time, the air seemed to become cooler with each step, and the brick on the walls looked more weathered. "We are now entering the necropolis, or city of the dead, under St. Peter's Basilica," said Aldo. "This area is where many Christians were buried two thousand years ago after being killed by the Romans."

They walked farther and came upon a burial site that was clearly marked as "Peter's tomb." There was a place for kneeling and prayer and also a stone statue of Peter decorating the gravesite. Jacob and Bina began looking for clues to where the Dalet corner could be hidden, with Aldo and his protective eye watching their every move. Next to the burial site was a small wall of red brick that Jacob was drawn toward. He began looking closely at the bricks and noticed a small engraving toward the bottom of the wall in one of the brick's corner. He crouched down and shined his flashlight on the brick and saw the same emblem of the dove with a sun—that was the insignia of the unknown author that Jacob had found on the Hokmah's scroll and on the bottom of his statue of St. Peter. Jacob tried to not make much of a commotion to gain the attention of their guide, but calmly brought Bina over to the brick and showed her.

"Unbelievable!" Bina whispered. "Do you think the corner is behind the brick?"

"I'm not sure, but I want to check it out. I have an idea..." Jacob started. "Aldo—is there a restroom near here?"

"Yes, just down that corridor and on the left. We will wait here for you," instructed Aldo.

Jacob and Bina walked to the bathroom, and when out of sight, Jacob used his medallion to make Bina and himself invisible. They quietly walked back to the burial site. Aldo was still explaining some history of the tomb to their mothers. They carefully got closer to the red wall, which was on the other side of a security barrier, and crouched down to remove the brick. As quietly as possible, Jacob used a knife to loosen the mortar around the brick while Bina kept a steady eye on Aldo.

Jacob used the back of his fist to jar the brick loose with a thump. Aldo looked toward the noise. Bina grabbed Jacob's arm to stop him from moving. They both held their breath as Aldo stared in their direction, trying to decipher what the noise was that he had just heard. Sarah grabbed Aldo's attention again, asking, "And what year did you say that they...?"

"That was a close one," Bina whispered. "A little quieter next time."

Jacob nodded his head and lifted the freed brick. He turned the brick over and over and looked for any signs or clues, but there were none. He lay down on his stomach and shined his flashlight into the wall's hole; he couldn't see anything. He stuck his hand in the hole and felt around—there was something in there. He grabbed it and pulled it out. "Could it be the final Dalet corner?" he thought. He opened his hand as he and Bina looked nervously into his palm. It was a small wooden cross. Frustrated, Jacob placed the cross into his pocket and replaced the brick in its original location.

Bina and Jacob went back to the bathroom and returned visible to their mothers and Aldo. "You found the bathroom OK, I presume?" Aldo asked.

"Yes, sir—thank you," said Bina.

The family started their way up the stairs, following Aldo, when Bina noticed a bronze plaque that hung on the wall. The plaque had the mysterious insignia of the dove and sun with the year 1586 printed at its bottom. "Wait—Aldo, what does this emblem signify?" she asked, pointing at the plaque.

"Ahh, I think you are the first to ever ask this question, my dear," said Aldo, "and a good question indeed. For years no one knew who or what this dove and sun signified until a journal was found in the Vatican's secret library that explained such an emblem.

"Pope Sixtus V had written a letter to Domenico Fontana, asking him to help with the architecture and engineering of the new St. Peter's Basilica in 1586, and when Domenico responded to Pope Sixtus V, saying he would accept the job, he left this same emblem at the bottom next to his name. So—this emblem is that of Domenico Fontana."

Jacob and Bina looked at each other with wide opened eyes.

That afternoon, after much more sightseeing, Jacob and Bina got away from their mothers to discuss their new clue. Jacob pulled the small, hand-carved cross from his pocket that he had found at Peter's tomb and saw the dove and sun carved into its back side. "It's obvious that Domenico Fontana knew of the Dalet corner hidden in the bricks and moved it to a new location, but where?" asked Jacob.

"I am not sure, yet. OK—we know Domenico helped with the architecture and engineering of the new basilica, but do we know anything more specific?" asked Bina. "I swear I have seen or heard his name somewhere before, but I just can't place it."

Jacob knelt in prayer with Bina as they both asked for God's guidance.

CHAPTER 17

THE OBELISK

"I have an idea. You have your mom's phone—let's call Mr. Wolfe and ask him if he's ever heard of the name Domenico Fontana before," said Jacob excitedly.

Jacob called Mr. Wolfe. "Hello, Mr. Wolfe," he said.

"Jacob, my boy," said Mr. Wolfe. "How is your summer going?"

"Fantastic! Bina and I are at the Vatican in Rome right now."

"Really, it has been years since I have been there. Now what on earth are you wasting time and calling an old man like me for?" asked Mr. Wolfe.

"It's purely educational, Mr. Wolfe," said Jacob quickly. "Bina and I heard the name Domenico Fontana in relation to the building of St. Peter's Basilica, but we were wondering if you had any more specific information to this man."

"Domenico Fontana was asked by Pope Sixtus V—in I believe 1586—to help with the new St. Peter's Basilica, but he is most well-known for masterminding the move of the Egyptian obelisk from its original position in Nero's Circus to where it stands today. It took him and about nine hundred men almost six months to move the heavy stone."

Jacob was so excited by the new information that he rushed off the phone with a quick "Thank you—I will see you soon—good-bye." He told Bina the news.

"That is where I heard his name before. He is credited with the major feat of moving the obelisk," said Bina, shaking her head, not believing she couldn't recall the history.

Jacob and Bina were a great distance from the obelisk, but they could not wait to more closely inspect the stone for a clue. When they arrived at the obelisk, they noticed that the tourists were extremely thick, as a couple of tour buses had just dropped off a group. They began scouring the obelisk and its stand for any clue that they could imagine. They looked for nearly an hour and found nothing.

Frustrated, they returned to meet their mothers at the hotel. They enjoyed dinner together and sat down to look at their digital camera's photos of their trip thus far.

"The kids sure are into the history of St. Peter's Square. They can't seem to get enough of learning about it," whispered Rebecca toward Sarah.

"I know—this is the best trip ever. I'm so glad you and Bina could come with us," said Sarah.

Jacob and Bina would pull up a picture of the obelisk on the camera and study it for minutes at a time, looking for some kind of a clue.

Bina pulled up a picture of the top of the obelisk, where the cross was located, and zoomed the picture in to get a closer look at it. She became more and more intrigued by a small etching that could be seen beneath the cross, saying, "Jacob, I would like to get a closer look at this marking on the top of the obelisk."

Jacob agreed.

Sarah and Rebecca gave Jacob and Bina permission to go out and sight-see for a while, but warned "not to be too late," because they were going to bed. Jacob and Bina grabbed their backpacks and were off to the obelisk. By now it was dark outside and there were very few people in St. Peter's Square. Even with their binoculars they could not see the marking at the top of the obelisk.

"OK, I'm going to try and elevate myself up to the top with the valoria power," said Jacob nervously.

"Jacob, that is around one hundred feet in the air! This isn't a pencil or something small—this is you, your body, that you are lifting up one hundred feet into the air," exclaimed Bina. "Are you sure you want to go through with that?"

Jacob took a deep breath and said, "There's no other way. We don't have a ladder. I'm sure."

Jacob closed his eyes and concentrated for a moment. He said, "*Amor vincit omnia*," making himself disappear to any would-be onlookers; then a moment later Bina heard, "Valoria." Jacob could feel himself rising off of the ground but did not want to look down due to his fear of heights. He concentrated on good thoughts to help manage his emotions and his control over the Valoria power. Up to this point, he'd had his eyes mostly closed, so he opened his eyes and saw the obelisk in front of him. He was nearly to the top of the obelisk where the cross was.

Bina did not want to say a word to break Jacob's concentration, but she was very curious as to where he was. Jacob reached the top of the obelisk and by accident looked down at Bina; his stomach turned and he felt nauseous. "I've made it to the top," he struggled to say in fear of vomiting down on Bina.

"You can do it," he heard from Bina below.

Just then a passerby walked by looking very peculiarly at Bina. The man looked up at the cross on top of the obelisk and said, "My dear, he already has." And without another word the man calmly walked away.

Meanwhile, Jacob was looking closely at the top of the obelisk and around the cross. He saw a small etching, the one that Bina had seen at the base of the cross, and moved in closer to get a better look. He came up very close to the marking and learned that it was indeed Domenico Fontana's dove and sun insignia with many years of sun damage. He wiped away some of the dust that covered it. It looked like a thumbprint carved into the stone surrounding the insignia, so Jacob pushed on it with his thumb. Suddenly, the obelisk began to move.

Jacob was so startled that he lost focus on his valoria power. He started to fall to the ground, but caught himself just before hitting the hard asphalt. Jacob released the invisibility charm and looked at Bina with excitement. "Piece of cake, right?" he joked.

Jacob and Bina looked over to the obelisk and noticed that the huge obelisk and its stand had moved over slightly—just enough for a person to walk downward. It was an entrance with stone steps. They both cautiously entered the hole. Once they had entered the dark hole, the obelisk moved back to its original position, closing the entrance. It was pitch black.

Jacob produced a crudaceous power in his hand, making a fireball. With the light of the fire they could see a ridge that was constructed into the walls, about five feet up from the floor, on both the right and left. The ridge seemed to be filled with some type of fluid. "I think it's a lighting system filled with a combustible fuel," Bina instructed. Jacob placed his fireball onto the ridges, and the fluid caught fire. The fire spread down the ridge very quickly, lighting up the approaching tunnel.

Bina and Jacob began slowly walking down the tunnel. The air was very cool and moist, and filled with a musky, mildew odor. The tunnel was lined with red brick from the ceiling to the walls that looked very similar to the brick that was next to Peter's tomb. Every few feet there would be a tomb in the wall with a set of dusty bones that had a wooden cross on its chest.

"This must be an ancient burial site for early Christians," whispered Bina.

They continued walking for some time, stopping at any tomb that might hold a clue to the Dalet corner, until the tunnel entered a large open area. The light was very bright in this room, with many tiers of the oil-filled ridges lighting the area. There were numerous tunnels that could be seen that looked to all end at this central location. The walls that encircled the large room were filled with tombs of hundreds of Christians. In the center of the room was a stone casket that was lit up extremely brightly by surrounding flames of fire.

Jacob and Bina walked up to the casket and saw the words PAULO APOSTOLO MART inscribed on the lid. "What does that mean?" asked Jacob.

"It's Latin for the martyr Apostle Paul," said Bina. "This must be the tomb of the Apostle Paul from the Bible."

"What better place than the burial site of the most famous writer in the Bible to hide the last Dalet corner? It must be here!" said Jacob. "You don't think Domenico put it inside the casket, do you?"

"I don't think that he would have done that. Usually, back in those days, they would only put personal belongings or something that meant a great deal to the person in their tomb," explained Bina.

With intense scrutiny, Jacob and Bina searched the casket, looking for anything that might lead them to the Dalet corner. Some time had passed, and they had searched nearly every square inch of the large room when Jacob heard, "Look to God for help," in his head. For a moment Jacob thought to pray, but then he looked to the ceiling. He saw the insignia of Domenico on a red brick directly above the head of Paul's casket. "Paul is watching over this Dalet corner, I would suppose," thought Jacob.

Jacob stood up on the altar that held Paul's tomb and used his knife to carve away the masonry that held the brick in place. With a swift punch of the back of his knife, he was able to dislodge the brick and hand it down to Bina. He stuck his hand into the opening and felt something. Could it be…? He pulled his hand from the hiding place, opened it, and saw the Dalet corner. He jumped down to the floor and hugged Bina. "I've got it!" he shouted. "We did it!"

Jacob knelt to the floor, pulled the three other corners from his backpack, and placed them together. "Now—how does this thing work?" he asked, looking puzzled.

"I will figure that out!" said a voice from one of the tunnels.

Jacob and Bina turned quickly to the tunnel, wondering who it could be. They heard the footsteps come closer. Jacob rushed to put the Dalet corners into his backpack and drew his sword as the man appeared from the shadow of the tunnel. Jacob recognized him from the Certatim; it was Prince Muammar and one of his pet goblins. The goblin looked at Bina and let out a hiss.

Prince Muammar began clapping his hands. "Thanks for doing all the work for me, Jacob, my boy—I've been searching for clues to the Dalet for hundreds of years," he said. "With its power my people and I will surely be able to eradicate the hidden Veritas throughout the world. And once they are gone, there will be no one to stop us from ruling the world and preparing the way of our lord."

"You will *never* get this! I will die first!" Jacob yelled.

"Oh—that can be arranged, my boy, that can be arranged."

Jacob heard more footsteps coming from two other tunnels. He turned to see Felix Matthews, Rico Estrada, Li Ting, and several other Tenebras—Fung Su, Mohammad Akbar, Mashir Vundu, and Dihari Nabul. Jacob smelled something that reeked of decay and rotting flesh; he turned back to look at Prince Muammar and saw Bodach, the red-skinned, four-armed bodyguard, now standing next to his leader. Jacob and Bina became nervous for their lives.

"You see, Jacob, there is no denying your fate. Now hand over the Dalet before it gets real unpleasant in here," said Prince Muammar.

Jacob started to unzip his backpack when a voice from another tunnel stopped him. "Not so fast!" the voice yelled. Jacob turned to the tunnel, and there stood Shawn. "I don't think we be handin' over anything today, Jacob," he said.

"Shawn—it has been a long time since I have seen you," said Prince Muammar.

"It be not long enough, I would gather," said Shawn. "But if you set one more foot forward, you'll be startin' a war that you don't be havin' a chance of winnin'. It would be best for you and yer friends here to turn around and be headin' home."

"Ha-ha-ha, Shawn, you are still as confident as ever. I like that about you. But even with your God, you could never stand up to all us. Give up now," said Prince Muammar.

"Things be not always as they appear," said Shawn, looking over at Rico, who had said those words to Jacob when he faked his leg injury at the Certatim.

From behind Shawn came forth Ramiro, Miguel, and Jacob's Bethal classmates: Jezebel, had Maribel the Pixie on her shoulder, Fred, Jack, and Luke. They all had swords in their hands, except Maribel, and had looks on their faces that were ready for war. "I'm ready to kick some bloodsuckers' butts," whispered Luke.

Jacob began to feel terrible inside for ever doubting Shawn and where his allegiance rested.

Both sides seemed to be in a standoff, waiting to see if Prince Muammar would take that step forward. There was an eerie silence in the underground room. Prince Muammar smiled at Shawn as he calmly stepped forward toward Jacob and Bina. The Veritas, seeing this as an act of war, attacked the Tenebras with ferocity.

"Stay behind the casket, Bina!" yelled Jacob.

Shawn had given the Bethal Veritas steel swords beforehand. Metal clashing against metal could be heard as swords clashed together.

They fought in the large room for a few moments, and then the fight started to carry into the tunnels.

Rico was definitely looking to pay back Jacob for taking his undefeated streak at the Certatim, but he could not get to him because Jezebel and Jack were in his way. They forced him backward into a tunnel and put him on the defensive.

Felix was fast to attack Jacob. "After I'm done with you, I'll take care of that little girlfriend of yours, too. She'll make a good snack before my travel home," said Felix.

Jacob sliced his sword toward Felix's neck in anger. The two traded blows that took them into a tunnel that was very dimly lit. Felix threw a crudaceous power at Jacob that nearly took his head off. Jacob returned a fireball in retaliation, not knowing exactly where Felix was in the dark. Felix jumped onto Jacob's back, trying with all of his strength to take a bite out of his neck. Jacob struggled to get Felix off, but he couldn't. He was doing everything he could to keep Felix's mouth from his neck. Then Jacob heard a loud *thud*; Felix went limp and fell to the ground. Jacob turned around to see Bina standing there with the red brick that they had pulled from the ceiling above Paul's tomb in her hand. She had hit Felix in the back of the head, knocking him out.

"I have been wanting to do that for a very long time," said Bina.

"Good show, Bina," said Jacob, trying to catch his breath. "Let's go help the others."

Shawn and Bodach were in a powerful battle while Prince Muammar watched on. Their powers they threw at each other were lighting up the tunnels and main open room. The corresponding colors of their powers of yellow, red, and white made the dimly lit underground light up like a holiday festival.

They both stopped for a moment. "Shawn, you should know by now that our power is stronger than yours will ever be!" yelled Prince Muammar. "I have never been able to figure out why you protect those helpless humans. It's not like they appreciate you. What have they ever done for you to deserve your allegiance?"

"It is not that anyone should be *deservin'* help. Everyone be havin' the right to live in harmony. No matter what evil be in their heart, everyone be deservin' a chance to survive," Shawn insisted.

Bodach drew both his swords, which still left him with two open arms. His swords' handles were adorned with ominous goblins' skulls. He and Shawn struck their blades of steel and traded blows back and forth, looking for the other's weak point. Bodach's two swords covered much more area than Shawn's one sword, but Shawn was quick to put Bodach on his heels, backing him up to the wall. Shawn lunged forward with a jab at Bodach's heart while unknowingly leaving himself open for a side attack from an awaiting goblin. Bodach's goblin struck Shawn with all of his might, knocking him to the ground.

Prince Muammar enveloped Shawn in a strange, illuminated cage that squeezed so tightly that Shawn could barely breathe. "Now watch as your young Veritas fall one by one," said Prince Muammar, standing next to a helpless Shawn.

Fung Su, Mohammad, Mashir, and Dihari were all on the offensive and had pushed Miguel, Fred, and Luke back into a corner. Miguel and his friends were trapped behind a large rock and were fighting for their lives, as they had nowhere to go. Soon, they were captured and brought before Prince Muammar.

Maribel was hiding behind a stalactite that hung from the ceiling near Shawn, trying to figure out a plan to help free him. Her powers were not nearly as strong as the angelic born, but her speed and flying abilities made her a great ally.

Jezebel and Jack were battling Rico down a lone tunnel, assaulting him with every technique and power that they could muster. Jack tried to attack from Rico's rear while Jezebel was attacking from the front, and Rico spun quickly with his sword, cutting Jack's right hand completely off. His sword and hand fell to the ground as Jack yelled in pain. Jezebel, somewhat stunned by the incident, dropped her guard for a moment, and Rico struck a kalari blow to Jezebel's stomach that made her pass out.

Jacob and Bina came upon Rico just after he'd struck Jezebel. "Well, well, if it isn't the infamous Jacob Jerlow,'" Rico whined. "I can't tell you how happy I am to see you."

"Wish I could say the same," said Jacob.

Rico sent a crudaceous power at Jacob's head, and Jacob caught it just before contact, redirecting the power into the nearby wall. Rico attacked Jacob with his sword. The two fought back and forth while Bina tried to stop the bleeding on Jack's arm. Rico hit Jacob directly on the side of the head with the handle of his sword, which sent Jacob to the ground. He was nearly knocked out and obviously dazed. Just as Rico was slicing downward with his sword to remove Jacob's head, Ramiro jumped from the shadows and stuck his sword in front of Jacob, blocking the deadly blow and saving his life.

"How dare you take away my victory!" Rico demanded.

"I told you I would be there for you, Jacob," said Ramiro.

Ramiro and Rico fought while Jacob was regaining his focus. Ramiro was defeating the more powerful Rico and nearly had him on his back when Mohammad, who had come to Rico's aid, surprised Ramiro from behind with a punch to his lower back. Mohammad grabbed Ramiro's arms, trapping them behind his back, and forced him to his knees. Jacob's eyes were just becoming clear so that he could focus in on the situation when he saw Rico approaching a helpless Ramiro.

Mashir, Fung Su, and Dihari came in at this time and held their swords to the throats of Jacob, Bina, and Jack. Rico smiled toward an onlooking Jacob. "I told you I would take something from you," he said, with his canine teeth now extruding from his mouth. Rico lunged into Ramiro's neck, sinking his teeth into his flesh. A great light emanated from Ramiro's chest as he looked at Jacob and took his last breath. Rico's eyes lit up with the Verita's blood entering his mouth. Ramiro's strength and powers were now transferred to Rico.

Jacob screamed in pain. Ramiro had given his life to protect him. Jacob stared at Rico in anger, and his eyes became bloodshot with ferocity. The cool room increased in temperature, and the air pressure began crushing the chests of the Tenebras. The stored energy from within Jacob exploded from every part of his body, throwing the five Tenebras onto their backs.

Jacob was somewhat stunned at what had just happened.

Jezebel came to from unconsciousness and arose to her feet. She grabbed Jacob by the hand and yelled at the others, "Let's get out of here!" They ran as fast as they could down the tunnel, looking over their shoulders at the fast approaching Tenebras. They came to the end of the tunnel where Li Ting and a now-conscious Felix Matthews were waiting for them in ambush. Li and Felix combined their powers and sent a holding power at Jacob and his friends that encapsulated them in a tight, mesh-like cage like the one that held Shawn.

Jacob tried to release his powers through the cage but could not.

"It's no use," said Jezebel. "This is a fearable cage, and it is nearly impenetrable from the inside."

The Tenebras lifted the cage and the prisoners with their valoria power and brought it before Prince Muammar in the large room that held Paul's tomb. "You see, Shawn, I told you that you did not stand a chance. Now you will all die, and we will have the Dalet—once and for all," Prince Muammar said triumphantly.

Prince Muammar walked around the fearable cage and grinned at his conquered captives. He pulled Jacob from the cage and had Felix and Mohammad tie his hands behind his back. "I sense a great strength in your soul, Jacob Jerlow," he said. "I shall enjoy every drop of your blood."

Prince Muammar opened his mouth and leaned into bite Jacob's neck. Jacob closed his eyes. Muammar paused for a moment as though he sensed something. KABOOM! A loud explosion occurred that shook the walls and floor. Everyone looked at each other. "Was that an earthquake?" they thought. All eyes were directed toward Paul's tomb at a nearby dust cloud that had erupted from the dirt floor. Something with a great force had just landed in the middle of the room. Everyone focused on what, or who, this could be. The silence was eerie.

The dust began to settle down to the floor, and there, in the middle of the room, stood the gnome Yelkie next to a man in a long, brown, hooded robe. The man was unrecognizable with his hood covering his face as he knelt with one knee to the floor. Yelkie looked around at the dire situation that his Verita friends were in and noticed Maribel hiding still by the stalactite. "Made an entrance we have," said Yelkie.

The kneeling man made a sign of the cross upon his head, chest, and shoulders and slowly stood to his feet. His hood was still covering his face so everyone wondered who this could be. He was facing Paul's tomb as he placed his hand upon the casket, looking as if he were speaking to the entombed apostle. The man walked closer to the Tenebra group, slowly, with a limp and the aid of a cane. Jacob struggled to see who it could be. "Is it friend or foe?" he thought.

The man's long sleeves came away slightly from his cane, with Jacob just catching a glimpse. "I've seen that cane before," thought Jacob. "But where?"

Prince Muammar looked intently at the man. "And who might you be?" he asked, rather sinisterly.

The man flipped back his hood. Prince Muammar and Shawn recognized who it was right away. Jacob struggled to see around Muammar to see the man's face.

"Rabbi!" said Shawn.

"Lazarus!" said Prince Muammar.

"Rabbi? Lazarus? Who is this?" thought Jacob.

"I have not seen you since the Crusades, Lazarus. Why have you hidden for so long?" asked Prince Muammar.

"I have not hidden myself," said Lazarus. "Just like the sun rises every morning for all to see, so do I." The man looked intently at the captive Veritas. "I see there has been enough damage and bloodshed here today. Release the young ones and leave now before any more bloodshed may come here," he said.

"Ha-ha-ha-. You come here, not being heard of for centuries, and just like that you want me to hand over my captives and our sure victory? I don't think so," said Prince Muammar. "Do you think your blessed Jesus will save you again? You are the one who should leave!"

With a nod of Prince Muammar's head, Fung Su, Mohammad, Mashir, Li Ting, and Dihari surrounded Lazarus. The Tenebras looked confidently at the fragile-looking old man who stood with the aid of a cane.

Prince Muammar stepped to the side, and Jacob saw the man called Lazarus. "No—it can't be!" thought Jacob. "That is Mr. Wolfe!" Jacob remembered Mr. Wolfe's story in school of the boy Lazarus and understood why his depiction of it was so lifelike. Mr. Wolfe was Lazarus—the one Jesus had brought back from the dead some two thousand years ago. Jacob also recalled the letter L before Mr. Wolfe's last name on his magazine in his house. "Mr. Wolfe was—no, he *is* Lazarus!" thought Jacob.

Lazarus could see there was no chance of negotiations, so he dropped his robe to ready himself for battle. The five Tenebras attacked. They were not looking to take any more prisoners but to take the life of this old man. Lazarus lifted his weathered-looking cane, and the old wood transformed into a steel blade. The blade was like nothing Jacob had ever seen. It shone so brightly that it was like the sun on a clear summer day.

A slow-moving, limping Lazarus suddenly had the speed and power of ten young men. One by one his attackers came at him from different angles, and with each attempt they landed on their backs, looking up at the ceiling. "What sort of man is this?" they thought.

While they were fighting, Felix was to be watching over the prisoners, but he found himself watching the fight instead. This gave the opportunity for Maribel to fly down next to her caged friends. The tight mesh, electrical cage needed to have a counter spell. The only way to release the fearable power was from the outside; no power from within the cage had an effect upon it. Maribel had some power, but she was not strong enough to make the whole cage go away at once. She had to say the counter spell for each strand of the mesh cage. Meanwhile, Yelkie was standing in the opposite corner, keeping an eye on the goblin that was keeping an eye on him.

In the fight the Tenebras were looking tired and weary compared to a strong and steadfast Verita. Lazarus, seemingly toying with his opponent, had enough. He sent a power that flashed yellow, and four of the five flew back on the wall, writhing in pain. The fifth, Mashir, came from behind and took a cut with his blade at Lazarus's head. Lazarus spun, hitting Mashir's sword and simultaneously cutting through his neck. The cut was so fast that the onlookers did not think that Mashir was even hit...until Mashir dropped his sword and started to fall, making his head depart from his body.

"*Enough!* Enough of this!" screamed Prince Muammar. "I will deal with you myself." Muammar kicked Mashir's head out of his way and walked up to Lazarus. "Just like old times, eh, Lazarus?" he asked.

Lazarus raised an eyebrow.

Prince Muammar pulled his sword from his belt. A cold black blade that brought a certain chill to the room appeared from his handle. Lazarus dropped his rear foot a little farther back and twisted it slightly, digging into the dirt for leverage. Muammar struck his blade against Lazarus's sword, and there was a loud *clang* when both of their blades made contact. The two traded blows and strikes of their swords back and forth, circling the room.

Lazarus paused for a moment, saying, "You still have much to learn, young one. Your path of evil and sin has clouded your mind and your technique."

Prince Muammar attacked even harder, pushing Lazarus back on his heels with a crudaceous power into his sword. Lazarus jumped and spun through the air, releasing a power into Muammar's chest. Muammar was dazed. He cut through the air and shot powers at Lazarus. He was not looking to wound his opponent but to eradicate him from the world forever.

Lazarus dropped to his knees, stuck his sword in the dirt, and put his hands together in prayer. Prince Muammar sliced his sword downward at Lazarus's head. Lazarus stopped the blade with his praying hands and twisted the blade so fast that it sent Muammar flying through the air and up against the wall.

Meanwhile, Maribel had almost completely released all of the links that held her Verita friends. She only had a couple more strands to break when Bodach grabbed her from behind. The huge four-armed man squeezed the tiny pixie in his hand until she could barely take another breath. He was just about to throw Maribel into his mouth when he heard Yelkie say from behind, "Put her down you will!"

Bodach turned around to see the small gnome staring him in the eye. The small man barely reached the bottom of Bodach's knees in height. Bodach let out a hissing laugh at the gnome. "You'll be dessert," he said, raising his hand to pop the tiny pixie in his mouth.

Yelkie threw a fireball at Bodach that entered directly into his opened mouth. Bodach stumbled backward, dropping Maribel and trying to catch his breath. Smoke was exiting from his ears and nose as he tried to extinguish the flame growing inside of him.

Just then, Lazarus sent a power at Muammar's heart that threw him backward and onto his back. Yelkie released the fearable power that held the Veritas and helped them to gather their swords. The Tenebras, including their leader, Prince Muammar, got an extreme look of terror in their eyes at the huge turn of events. "Another day, Veritas!" yelled Muammar. They turned and ran out one of the tunnels as fast as their feet would take them.

Yelkie went over to Maribel and helped her to her feet. "Not hurt you are—I hope," he said gently.

"I'm OK thanks to you—my hero," said Maribel. "My name is Maribel. What's yours?"

"Yelkie my name is. Know your name I already do."

Maribel flew up to Yelkie and gave him a kiss on the cheek. "Thank you for saving my life. Thank you for saving all of our lives. You are very brave, indeed."

Yelkie blushed.

Jacob ran over to Lazarus. "Mr. Wolfe—err, I mean, Lazarus," Jacob stuttered. "I never knew…"

"It is OK, Jacob. Why don't you just call me Mr. Wolfe in school, and Lazarus outside of school—away from the students," Lazarus explained. He looked at his people with love. "You have all fought with honor in your spirits and goodness in your hearts today. I commend you all in coming to the aid of Jacob and Bina. We also shall be forever grateful to Yelkie. Without him, I would never have been able to make it here in time and give you aid. His God-given ability to travel through space was extremely vital today."

They all looked at Yelkie and gave a round of applause. Shawn lifted him up on his shoulder, saying, "Thank you, me little friend." Yelkie, being bashful and an emotional sort, began to joyfully cry.

"Now, I believe it is in order for us to meet tonight at Heldago. Yelkie and I will bring the body of Ramiro there for a proper burial. As for telling his parents, I will find the best means to do so," explained Lazarus.

Upon returning to the hotel, Jacob and Bina were happy to see their mothers asleep. Bina helped Jacob mend his wounds and used a little makeup on his face to hide a couple of bruises. They slept next to each other on the floor so Jacob could hold Bina's hand, taking her to Heldago.

At the front gate to Heldago, Jacob and Bina were met by Lazarus asking, "I trust you have a safe place to keep the Dalet?" He asked the question as if he already knew the answer.

"You don't think I should keep the Dalet here? Wouldn't Heldago be the safest place for it?" asked Jacob.

"Unfortunately not. There seems to be a leak inside Heldago that has led the Tenebras to nearly obtaining the Dalet. In the mean time, it would be better for you to keep the Dalet in a safe and secret location," said Lazarus.

Jacob nodded.

Lazarus looked at the massive Heldago castle before him and took in a deep breath. "It has been many years since I have set foot inside these walls," he said. "I have missed it and my people greatly."

Jacob looked at Lazarus with pride and said, "Our people will be grateful to have our rabbi home." Jacob paused for a moment to think. "Rabbi, I've met a man a few times that calls himself Michael. I first saw him at my dad's funeral, but he did not introduce himself until one day in Heldago."

"You saw this man in Heldago?" asked Lazarus. "Did anyone else see him?"

"No, Jezebel approached me while I was talking to him and she said that she never saw him," Jacob explained. "It kind of freaked me out."

"I see. And have you seen this Michael any other time?"

"Yes, I saw him at the Certatim," Jacob said. "He seems to be watching me."

"Jacob, let us be keeping this Michael to ourselves for now—OK?" asked Lazarus. "I'm sure that his identity will surface soon enough." Lazarus paused for moment, looking at Jacob. "Ahh, Jacob, my boy, you have grown so much this summer. You are, undoubtedly, ready to take the level test to move to Clevan. I think you will easily break Ramiro's thirty-one-day record..."

Jacob looked at Lazarus and then at Heldago castle, saying, "Ramiro saved my life. The record is his to keep. I can wait until after thirty-one days to perform the trial."

Lazarus looked at Jacob and smiled.

ABOUT THE AUTHOR

Lance Peltier is a high school teacher in his day job. He enjoys spending time with his family and enjoying God's playground—the outdoors. Lance has a bachelor's degree from the University of Nevada Las Vegas and a master's degree from North Dakota State University. *Jacob Jerlow: To the Four Corners of the Earth* is his first published manuscript, but he has had three articles published in journals and newsletters. Lance and his wife, Robin, live in North Dakota with their four children and two energetic labs.

CPSIA information can be obtained at www.ICGtesting.com
Printed in the USA
BVOW08s0448170713

326119BV00007B/214/P